THE SPACE BETWEEN GALAXIES

Alex Fear

To Hammy,

Can't wait to hear
what you think of this.

— Alex

Axolotl Books

THE SPACE BETWEEN GALAXIES

Published by Axolotl Books

First Published in UK in 2022
By Axolotl Books

ISBN 9-781838-389918

For
Chachi

Part 1

North America

The world opens up like a drunken yawn. The sand, grain by grain re-scattering itself, the sea unwrapping, and the sky blurring into focus. The damp fabric of my sleeping bag weaving itself around me. I push myself onto my palms and feel gravel and a spikey little shrub underneath me. For a moment I'm not sure where I am. The shush-shush of the waves and the deep burr of an airplane overhead. I rub my eyes and squint at the sun, rippling like tickertape on the water. In the corner of my sun-blotched field of vision I see the Golden Gate Bridge. Almost the same as a postcard that I saw in Felix's bedroom. I look across at him, scrunched up next to me, his face half covered by red sleeping bag, his curly brown hair spilling out. It seems kind of a miracle that after everything, our two bodies are still here experiencing the world together. I nudge him, and he shifts about making a little moan.

"Felix." I prod him with my feet.

"Nurgh." he wriggles.

"Felix."

He rubs his hands into his eyes and looks at me, his face puffy and his long hair a tangled mess.

"Whys it so bright?" He complains.

I gesture at the ocean and the Golden Gate Bridge.

"Oh." He blinks, pushing himself up onto his hands.

I laugh at his bemused expression. "Were you drinking last night?" I pull my sleeping bag down to my waist and try without a mirror to adjust my crispy bleached hair.

"I don't know," he says, leaving a pause between each word.

I stumble to my feet and start rolling my sleeping bag up.

"We should probably go." I click my neck. "I don't think we're supposed to be using this place as our bedroom."

But he's too busy blinking at the horizon to listen to me.

On the short walk to the car park, he takes a really long look at everything as if he's just arrived on the planet.

"Felix!" I call after him, my voice muted by the expanse of shrubland.

He follows, mute and wide-eyed, his sleeping bag dragging in the dirt.

There are only two cars in the car park. Through the window of the one next to ours, I see a man with a beard eating something out of foil wrapper. I fiddle the key in the rusted lock on our car door. I couldn't tell you what kind of car it is, just that it's big, and old, and American. Too old to respond to one of those little bleeper things. I get in and push open the passenger door, reach over, and pull Felix in by his tie-dye vest.

"Let's get some breakfast," I say, trying to make up for his weird behaviour with a show of normalcy.

"Kyle," he murmurs.

"Yes?" I wrap my hands around the steering wheel. "I'm sitting right next to you."

"I don't want to freak you out ... but I don't remember how we got here."

"Obviously we drove her," I tell him and then pat his red dungaree shorts. "Do you have an empty hip-flask in there?"

3

"No, Kyle ..." He flaps my hand away. "We're in San Francisco right?"

I nod and gesture to the view through the dusty windscreen.

"I don't remember how we got here." He grits his teeth and puts on this strained serious tone of voice. "I don't remember yesterday. I don't remember the flight. I don't remember anything."

"Well, that's worrying." I look into his far apart eyes, trying to work out what's going on inside there. "What's the last thing you remember?"

He presses his fingers into his temples and scrunches up his face as if he's engaging in a strenuous act of telekinesis.

Through the window, I see the guy with the burger look away as if he isn't watching us.

'I remember drinking too much, I remember knocking stuff over in my room, I remember arguing ...'

'And?'

'That's it.' He turns his palms up and shrugs.

'Seriously?'

'Seriously,' he murmurs, his lips parted.

'Felix, that was a year ago.'

I love the smell of peroxide. I think I was 14, almost 15, when I first bleached my hair. I had an epiphany while reading *Smash Hits* magazine, that I too could look like a boyband member. Like Nick from *The Backstreet Boys* or H from *Steps*. I went to *Superdrug* and asked them where the men's bleach was.

'Men and women can use these,' said a shop assistant.

So, I chose the box with the smiling shiny haired woman, I most wanted to resemble. Back home, I locked myself in the bathroom and piled the strange-smelling goop onto my neatly snipped mousey-brown hair. It went a sort of vomit yellow. It was a mess – but there was something I liked about it. I kissed my reflection in the mirror and went down for dinner.

'Who did that to you?' My dad asked, like it was a black eye.

'We're going to have to get a professional to sort that out.' My mum said as if it were a leaky sink.

She took me to her hairdressers to have it dyed platinum blonde. They put lots of little foil envelopes in my hair and sat me under a heat machine next to an elderly woman. When I got home, I stood in front of the mirror for hours, putting on different outfits, looking at my almost white-blonde hair. In my blazer and tie, I felt not just like a regular schoolboy, but like a schoolboy from a porn film. After that, the muttered insults in the school corridors got a bit more frequent, and I started planning my escape.

Six years on I'm washing bleach from my roots into a worn-out sink in Bethnal Green. I wrap a towel around my hair and take a couple Valiums to disperse a persistent headache. Doing makeup on Valium is a detached experience, like painting by numbers or join the dots. First, I sponge concealer across every area of my head that isn't covered by hair. The same type of concealer they use to cover birthmarks and third-degree burns. The aim is to make myself look like a flesh-tone android, a Ken doll that hasn't been through the *Mattel* face printer. Then I draw an entirely different face on top. The kind of face that says, *fuck you*, but also, *fuck me*. Tonight, I'm a Tudor-prince-meets-B-movie-astronaut. I'm talking white PVC doublet with puffed slashed sleeves. I'm talking lace tights and Japanese platforms. I'm talking Henry VIII meets Louis XIII on the Apollo space mission 2061. I brush an editorial blob of eyeshadow into the corner of my eyelids. Then I dust everything in German holographic glitter and go for a cigarette out the window. Our neighbour, Valerie, scowls up at me and scuttles back inside. She was arranging her dying pot plants on the wall below. I hear two characters on a soap opera talking in hushed tones. A dog poo bag hangs from the single tree in the middle of some parched communal grass. Beyond that are desolate-looking blocks of flats and a glowing green tower known as *The Gherkin*. I flick the butt of my *Vogue Slim* into Valerie's shrivelled effigy of an aloe vera plant.

The next part of the process is a search for lost costume items stored in multiple quasi-organised wardrobes. This is made quite a bit more difficult by the consumption of Valium. The idea of *multiple wardrobes* may be giving you a misleading picture of this shared flat in Bethnal Green. To me, a wardrobe can be anything from a large Tupperware box of tangled jewellery to a cupboard the size of a large room. I yank a doublet and breaches from a cardboard-wardrobe. Then I search through a plastic-box-wardrobe for a crown made of pearls. I have to untangle it from a glittery gold harness. I poke around in the top part of my cupboard till I find a hatbox containing an Elizabethan ruff (the only accessory to remain consistently fashionable for the last 500 years). It sticks out about half a foot from my neck and is only slightly covered in makeup and night-club-dirt. I spray my hair into a quiff, pin the crown into it, and spirit-gum some pearls to my forehead. I finish by dotting a beauty spot over the little scar I got falling out of a tree as a kid.

Tonight, I'm a DJ. Sometimes I'm a host, sometimes I'm a model, sometimes I'm a club promoter. All these are really the same job. They require two qualities: being good at wearing clothes and being good at taking drugs – I excel at both. The club is called *Burger Bar*, it's a three-floored venue in Soho decked out entirely in red velvet. They seem to have taken all the cast-offs from the backrooms of local West End theatres and nailed them to the walls, in such an arrangement that there is more space taken up by decorations than people. In fact, the business venture doesn't really seem to be about money. I couldn't hazard a guess at what it is about, though it has a vague air of tax evasion and rent-boy acquisition. The people here tend to be what I call *barrel-scrape* people. A lady with failed plastic surgery and an aura of squandered wealth, regaling a couple of young gays with slurred stories. A guy with a bowl cut and a girl with part of her head shaved sit at a table with a strange collection of plastic figures and beer glasses. In the small dance-pit, a couple of lacklustre middle-aged drag queens are having what looks like a boozy coffee morning.

DJing is a simple matter of having the right tunes on your *iPod* and knowing what order to play them in – both qualities which evade most people. The first song I put on is from Liza Minelli's collaboration with *The Pet Shop Boys*. While it's playing, I look at the dirt wedged into the joins in the DJ booth and think about how this gig is below me. I was on the cover of *ID magazine*. Me, wearing a silver *Gucci* tuxedo and a space helmet, shot out in a forest near Ipswich. One of those editorials with cute boys looking like ethereal time travellers. I tell people that's how I got my club kid name: *Cosmo*. In reality my friend gave me it because my mum is deputy editor of *Cosmopolitan*. I was one of London's bright shiny new things, it said so in *Boyz magazine*. Only occasionally do I think I'm one of London's young, but already past-it, deluded has-beens. I put the headphones half on and pretend there is sound coming out of them.

One of my friends – Bobbi, arrives with a demonic-looking woman dressed in pink lace petticoats.

'I just put a bigger gauge in,' Bobbi shouts over the second Liza Minelli and Pet Shop Boys number of the night. He points to the two-pound-coin-sized hole in his ear lobe.

I give him an unenthusiastic thumbs up. Bobbi is one of those reckless post-humans with piercings all over their face. Constantly shaving and dying his hair like some incompetent shapeshifter. He's currently sporting an undercut and neon green plaits.

The next human interaction of the night is with one of the guys that was laughing with the aging socialite. He comes up to the DJ booth and tries to shout at me over the music. He's quite insistent, so I have to actually go to the effort of taking off the headphones I'm pretending to DJ through.

'*Celebrity Skin* by *Hole*,' he shouts, his face slightly too masculine for the eyeliner and mascara smeared around his eyes.

'I don't think I've got it,' I say. I mean of course I have it, but I can't just allow people to come up and request whatever music they want. I thought the interaction was over, but he seems to want to say more. He leans in further to the DJ booth, and I can see the concealer on his nose.

'I've got some MD, if you want some.'

I raise my eyebrows and say, 'Yeah, why not.'

He starts to get a baggy out of his pocket, then and there. I have to clamp my hand down over his.

'I'm at work!' I tell him in a loud whisper. 'Toilet ... two minutes.'

The toilet is papier-mâché'd wall to door in softcore 80's homoerotica. He's waiting, leaning against the cistern with a baggie and a student library card, a bit like a gothic James Dean. He gets out a notebook and starts crushing little crystals onto it with his library card. He's a little bit taller than me and better looking than I thought, with a good jawline and a heavily lacquered black quiff.

'We've met before,' he tells me, looking up from drug preparation.

'Have we?' I can't remember half the people I know even when I'm looking at them.

'It was at *Science Fiction* – you said I should wear less makeup.'

'You should,' I agree with my past self.

'I *am* wearing less makeup!' He looks at me cross eyed.

There's something so adorable about the expression that I lean forward and kiss him. He looks very pleased with himself and begins to scrape the powder into lines.

'You've got good bones – you don't need it.' I lean on the toilet wall, the muted sound of music coming from outside.

'You too,' he replies, looking at my makeup slathered visage. His accent is Northern though I can't quite place where in the North. He tries to hand me a cut-off neon party straw.

'What's this?' I look at it, deeply disturbed.

'A snorter.' He smiles.

9

'No, no, no.' I pull a £20 note from my pocket. With a single sparkle-nailed motion, I roll it into a snorter and hoover the slightly bigger line into my left nostril. Left nostril, because you have to alternate, and I always keep track. My nose stings like I just rubbed bleach into my sinuses. I let out a camp little screech at the searing pain and pass him the rolled up £20 note. Then we're making out, my heavily lip-glossed lips pressing against his tight pout. I do that thing, where I take a moment to breathe in and breath out against his mouth, as if this moment is so erotic. His hands move, unsure around my waist. I push him against the porn covered toilet wall and bite his lip. If anyone kisses me, I generally do it so well they can't not sleep with me. When I pull away, he holds out the rolled up £20 note, red-faced, my lip-gloss smeared across his mouth. I consider touching up my lips in the partially shattered bathroom mirror, but the makeup smear looks kind of hot.

In my absence, the playlist has lapsed into Shirley Bassey. Even the drag queens have left the dance floor. I quickly flick over to a remix of *I feel love* by Donna Summer, and the disparate tribes of weirdos begin to converge under the purple lights. After about half-an-hour, I feel a synthetic happiness working its way from my intestines outwards. I stick on the song the Goth boy with the MDMA requested and join him on the dance floor.

There was a period when every club kid in London started doing performances. Club kid performance is a genre unto itself. Usually, it involves a cute boy in partial drag taking their clothes off while lip-synching to their favourite pop song. If you're lucky, they might throw some glitter in the air, or smear their makeup, or even get their dick out. I decided I was only ever going to think of one performance. It involves me lip-synching to *Nobody Does it Better* by Carly Simon, in a handheld mirror. That's how I finish the night. The cascading piano intro plays as I stumble out of the DJ booth toward a small piece of raised floor meant to represent a stage. I hold up the mirror and mouth the words with big glittery lips.

"*Nobody does it better, makes me feel sad for the rest, nobody does it half as good as you, baby you're the best ...*"

I finish the song by acting like I'm about to kiss the goth boy. Then, I hold up the mirror and give it mouth-to-mouth, smearing it with glitter.

In the short drive from the beach to the diner, I quickly re-hashed the last year of our lives: his accident, the months he was in hospital, his semi-miraculous recovery. He quickly calmed down – maybe too much. He's always had this ability to just smile despite being in the middle of some terrible disaster of his own making. I watch him through the window, calling the doctor on a payphone, pushing his long curly brown hair behind one ear. I'm sat inside a diner filled with cliché 50's Americana: a fiberglass statue of Elvis, a jukebox, the front half of a pink Chevy coming out of a wall.

'Can I take your order now sir,' says a waiter with a little red hat. He emphasizes the word *sir*, as if he's in the military.

'I need to get my friend,' I gesture with my head in Felix's direction. He's glancing back at me, winding the phone cord around his fingers. I push the swinging double doors open into hot mid-morning air. Felix shields the phone from me, as if he's having a very private conversation.

'Okay, thank you.' He clicks the phone down on the receiver.

'What did they say?'

'Let's go inside and get breakfast.' He pats me on the shoulder.

Inside he studies the menu for a long time, which is strange, because it basically only has pancakes on it. Even after we've ordered, he continues to look at the menu.

'What did they say?' I pull the menu down so I can see his face.

'That it's unusual – but not totally unusual.'

'What is?'

'Losing your memory, when you've been through ... what I've been through.' He glances at the other people in their red padded seats. The group nearest looks like a tanned version of *The Addams Family*.

'Do we need to go back home?' I ask.

'Well –' He makes a thinking expression.

I can tell his answer is going to be flakey before I even hear it.

'– He said we should wait and see what happens.'

'Wait and see what happens!?' I press my palms into the aluminium tabletop. 'You can't remember the last year of your life, and he said wait and see what happens!'

'He said, "*See if it comes back.*" It might be a momentary thing.'

The waiter brings my cappuccino over, and Felix's cup of hot water.

'Here you are *SIR*!' He plops them down.

Felix withdraws a crumpled bag of herbal tea from his pocket and dips it into his cup. *The Ronettes* or maybe *The Crystals* sing over the tinkle of cutlery.

'What if you're having a stroke?' I lean forward across the table.

'Kyle.' He continues to plop the tea bag in and out of the hot water. 'Do I look like I'm having a stroke!?'

'I don't know. Maybe.'

'Thanks.' He looks at me with sarcastic lowered eyelids.

'Maybe we could get a brain scan or something.'

'Do you know how much that costs?' He slumps forward onto the table and looks up at me wearily.

13

'It's not about the money.'

'Let's just see what happens,' he says, with a calm not usually afforded to people who've just lost a year of their life. He holds my gaze, his big brown eyes trying to stare me down.

I barely remember leaving either, it was so quick. As soon as Felix had recovered, we got all our old travel plans out of their box and set about buying plane tickets. Next thing I knew, I was packing essential items into a leopard-print backpack. Essential items like, a gold sequin onesie and 9-inch mirror covered platforms. Felix's rucksack looked like something that had been used in 'Nam. He packed items I hoped we'd never have to use, like sleeping bags and flasks. We said goodbye to my friends at *Science Fiction* and took a night bus to Heathrow. I watched him as he stared out the airplane window at the Atlantic. The ocean just visible through stretched out cotton wool clouds.

'How does it feel?' I hold my fork above my kid-size pancake pile, not eating anything. 'Does it feel like we just had that argument?'

'No.' He forks scrambled eggs into his mouth and talks while chewing them. 'I can tell that times passed.'

'You're being very calm about it.'

'What else can I do.' He makes a little dismissive shrug, then forks a whole half a tomato into his mouth. 'I'm worried ... but at least we're here.'

I stumble into semi-consciousness and try to peel my eyes open, feeling my way to the toilet. I pull my tights down in time to aim urine all over the seat, which I clean up with my housemate James's flannel. In the mirror is a blotchy mess of concealer-filled pores, smeared mascara, and glitter. I stumble back to my room, feeling like the solo survivor of a five-car pile-up; concussed and staggering from the wreckage. Pieces of my face left in the dashboard, and something burning in the background. I see clothes I don't recognize on the floor and follow the trail up to the shape of a body under my quilt. A tuft of black hair sticking out. It's the goth boy. I completely forgot about him. Now I have flashbacks of us climbing out of a taxi, singing Cher songs at the top of our voices, and drunken groping. I pull my black fur-lined dressing gown down from the door and tie the chord tight. I wind up the blind and glare at the tree outside as if it's somehow mocking me with all its branches and dog-poo bags. The sunlight hits the Goth boy, and one eyeliner smeared eye opens a few millimetres. He flexes his back, turns over, and squints at me through twists of black hair.

'Hey Cosmo,' he croaks.

I squash my fingers into my forehead and tell him, 'I feel like Bette Davis at the end of her life.'

'I actually don't feel so bad.' He smiles up at me, all dopey and half asleep.

'Lucky you – have a medal.' I pull open a drawer where I know there are some plastic medals from a drag competition I judged. I throw one at him.

He makes a forced laugh and turns it over in his hand. I start rattling open draws, looking for paracetamol. At the same time trying to work out how to get this guy out of my bed, into his clothes, and out the door.

'What're you looking for?' He asks.

'Medicines.'

'I've got some.' He picks his jeans up from next to the bed, fishes around in the pocket, and holds up a little baggie full of powder.

'Oh, Jesus no. I need painkillers.' I pull out my beauty table draw. My last few Valiums are in there, but I don't want to squander them on a hangover.

'– Do you mind if I do some?' He asks, still dangling the baggy of white powder in mid-air.

'Actually, I might need to ask you to go.' I turn to him, my back pressed against the beauty table.

'Oh.' his expression looks like I just threw a flannel covered in piss at his face.

'I'm not being rude. I'm just very busy and very hungover.' I try to look at his smudged-up face as if I'm the adult, and I'm being very honest and reasonable.

'Sure.' He starts to unfold the sheets from his naked torso.

If I didn't have this migraine cracking across the inside of my skull, I would probably get him to fuck me one more time. I slap a Valium into my mouth as he starts seeking out and grabbing up his stuff from my bedroom floor. I spot a sweaty black indie-band t-shirt, hanging from my wall lamp and pass it to him. After he's gone, I slump down on the sofa and turn on the TV. There's a woman in a neat red dress demonstrating a stainless-steel percolator. The camera zooms in to show her matt effect press on nails, gripping and un-gripping the handle. I feel like I'm going to be sick.

Around late afternoon, I manage to step out the door wearing the biggest darkest sunglasses I could untangle from the mass of necklaces and lingerie. Going out into the sunshine worsens the feeling that my brain is splitting in half. The sun also seems to be impeding the miserable day everyone else in Bethnal Green is trying to have. I pass one man outside a kebab shop whose face is so downturned and appalled with the world, I have no choice but to shoot him three times in the head. I do it with a pink spray-painted AK47 that I once posed with in a fashion shoot. Over the road, outside the supermarket, a mum is swearing at her two squabbling children. I make a direct shot to her face, spraying blood everywhere and shattering the supermarket window. There are two men having an argument by the traffic lights. I shoot one in the lungs and the other in the bit of fat hanging out of his polo shirt. Then I just start to shoot randomly at every oncoming pedestrian with their drab clothing and mournful expressions. I even shoot a Labrador.

After the bloodbath, I arrive at my housemate James' gallery, a pokey little place off Vyner Street, with a black metal door decorated with graffiti tags. I kick it a few times, and a girl with a bowl-cut and paint-smeared overalls opens it. There's a paint smell, a pile of large heavy-duty frames, and a ladder which the girl hauls herself up and starts rollering the wall. James flounces out, in a white and red polka-dot Polo neck with red braces and his usual rectangular glasses.

'Do you want some tea, hun?' He forces me into a hug, nestling his big angular chin into my head.

'Coffee?' I mumble. '– Iced with Kahlua. I feel terrible!'

'You don't look so great.' He tries to lift my sunglasses. 'Were you wearing green makeup?'

'No!' I say offended. 'I'm going!'

'Come on, I'll show you some photos.' He puts his arm around me and scoops me over to the pile of photo frames.

I try to wriggle away. It's the series he did of club kids with their dads, blown up to glossy A1. Mine is on top. My dad looking all suave and grizzled in his grey Italian suit and hairpiece. I stand at least a foot away from him in a sheer onesie patterned with pearls.

'Cute,' says James, lifting the frame.

'Thanks.'

'Not, you, your dad.'

'My dad is the guy from *American Psycho*,' I complain. 'Except he doesn't like music.'

'That's not fair,' James says in a dopey voice, swooping his quiffy mess of dark brown hair back.

I remember James being all campy and apologetic with my dad, tipping his head back and laughing a lot. Afterwards, me and my dad went out for a meal where he drank a lot of beer, and I told him I was having sex with a drag queen. The next photo is Milo and his dad. Milo looks pale and petulant, wearing a black lace dress with a big gold Egyptian ankh necklace. His dad looks goofy, in a flat cap and sports jacket, his arm around Milo. I don't know exactly why, but the photo disturbs me deeply. I lift my sunglasses up and tell James, 'They look really good.'

'I wanna show you my masterpiece.' He scoops me over in the direction of a back room. Decorating the concrete floor of the room are all his photos of night clubs inside gold charity shop frames. I crouch and push my sunglasses into my crispy bleached hair. There's a picture of me and Milo, almost naked, almost having sex on top of a bar. Then there's Tamsin, reclining with her top off, halfway between male and female, clutching a complimentary bottle of vodka. Then Kitten, lit by neons, standing outside a club in a pink PVC detective coat with a cigarette and a disdainful look. And Bobbi, smiling for the camera with real blood dripping down his neon painted face.

'I'm just going to start banging nails into the wall and hanging them up.' James surveys the room.

I pick up a photo of myself wearing a yellow pantsuit, sitting in an alcove, Boy George looking up at me.

'You're really talented,' I tell him.

'You just like it because you're in it.' He squeezes my shoulder.

'That's only the main reason I like it.'

The room stinks of spray paint and makes me feel a bit like vomiting. I stumble in the direction of the door, pushing my sunglasses back on.

'Are you sure you're okay, hun?' James asks, following me into the other room.

'I'm just having a bit of a hang-down.' I look at him, grasping my temples and trying to stay standing up.

'A hang-down?' James invades my personal space.

'I mean, come-down, hangover. Can you get me some water?'

I gulp the whole glass down and look at James' concerned expression, hands on his hips. The girl with the bowl cut scrapes the ladder across the floor.

'One night more,' I tell James. 'Then I'm going into hibernation.'

I search my mind and wardrobes for some unique new combination of clothing and accessories. I decide to go with a classic, hoping it's well enough known that it's become iconic. A 1500's-esque suit of armour covered in holographic foil, welded aluminium panels and elastic straps, custom made by a fashion student who had a crush on me. I leave it draped over a chair and pass out on the floor.

19

I wake up hours later, to Milo knocking on the door. I know it's him because he gives three vicious little knocks, followed by a pause, then three more.

'Fuck off!' I tell him as I open the door. I'd describe Milo's current style as fashion-goth. It's a combination of black mesh, fetish accoutrements, and gold jewellery, paired with a shiny black bowl cut. He kisses my cheek and tells me I look terrible.

'Thanks.'

'You're not even dressed ... I'll make myself a cocktail.'

'Knock yourself out girl,' I head back upstairs while Milo makes his way to the kitchen to scavenge for me and James' alcohol. Milo isn't his actual name, he stole it off a tub of powdered chocolate drink. He lays on my bed, kicking his feet in the air and drinking something with a lot of ice cubes in. I try to powder and glitter my face to a normal shade of human being.

'What's this?' He says retrieving something from under my bed. He holds it up between his thumb and finger, so I can see it in the mirror; a little bag of white powder.

I try to think back to the last time I bought drugs for myself. 'Oh, I had some guy back.'

'Ooo, free gift.' Milo pops it open and is about to stick his pinkie in, then asks, 'What kind of guy? It's not meth?'

'No.' I scowl. 'I'm pretty sure it's just sherbet and washing powder.'

'Amazing,' Milo smiles, the semi-crystalised substance already halfway up his nose. He soon switches from a bitchy horizontal position to voguing around my room, mouthing inane Madonna lyrics in the mirror. I begin a frantic race to strap on holographic armour and consume enough narcotics to make me into the kind of person people just can't get enough of.

'You're not wearing *that* again are you?' Milo complains about my holographic suit of armour, talking and dancing simultaneously.

20

'It's Iconic,' I insist.

'My grandma has a dress that she's been wearing for thirty years,' Milo laughs. 'That doesn't make it iconic.'

I clatter out of the cab, and Milo pulls the taxi door shut.

He winds down the window and mutters, 'Get the door open, then I'll follow you in.'

When Science Fiction is full, they lock the doors, leaving tragic queens festering outside in their glitter and party-shop wigs. Because we're late, that is the case now.

'But I'm hosting,' I hiss at Milo.

He slides the window back up to prevent any further conversation. I grit my teeth and walk up the steps, lit by an orange streetlamp. Perched on the top step there's a guy with dreadlocks and a guy who looks like he's attending a 70's party. He appears to recognise me. I make a smile so brief, that if his vision were operating in cinematic 32 frames a second, it would probably occupy half a frame. I give a swift bang on the door, my armour rattling. On the other side of the steps, there's a tubby girl whose only adornment is a pair of incredibly large iridescent blue lashes. I give the door a further few raps.

'It's one in, one out,' the girl with the eyelashes says.

'I'm hosting this night.' I inform her and start unlacing the crotch of my armour to get my phone out.

The '70s boy is now standing next to me smiling drunkenly. 'Can you get us in?' He slurs 'I'll buy you a drink.'

'I get free drinks.' I prise my phone from the codpiece and call Tamsin.

Down the phone I hear a muddle of voices and distorted music. Tamsin's voice is distant and ethereal, 'What is it babe? What you say?'

'I'm outside,' I growl.

She clicks off, inconclusively. I'm about to phone back, but the '70s boy is now leaning drunkenly into my personal space, his long curly brown hair swaying. He seems strangely familiar, but I can't place where I've met him before.

'Can you help get us in.' He attempts to flutter his far apart eyes at me, but it's more of a Mexican wave.

'I wouldn't even help most of the people I know to get in.' I look at my phone.

'... I'm a psychic,' he blurts out.

'Yeah?' I look at the door. Still no Tamsin.

'Yeah,' he slurs, as if just saying "yeah" is proof enough. He points at my face. 'That scar under your eye is from falling out of a tree.'

I wonder where he got this nugget of information from: an interview in Boyz magazine, or my past drug-addled ramblings?

'Yup.' I answer and look at my phone, wondering if I should call Tamsin again.

The 70's guy is still stood there, looking mystified at his own faux-psychic proclamation.

'Anything else?' I ask.

'You should let me get you a drink – the drinks I buy are much better than the free drinks.' He pulls a hip flask from his flares and sloshes it in my direction.

The door opens, and the full volume of music fills the street.

'Coming in love?' Tamsin holds the door ajar with her acrylic neon talons.

Before I can escape, the '70s guy tells me his name and offers his hand to shake. I let him touch my hand and tell Tamsin that Milo's in the taxi.

'What's he doing in there?' She asks, poking her head, neon crown and pastel purple extensions, around the door to look at the stationary taxi.

'I don't know – meth?'

There's a mass of people in varying degrees of drag. Cute boys in lingerie and fetish harnesses, waist length neon wigs studded with LEDs, lips drawn to the nostrils. A guy with multicoloured dreadlocks, a jockstrap and a blow-up back-pack gyrates on a pole, his face and body covered in children's glitter stickers. Lounging on worn leather couches and lazily voguing are boys dressed in black almost-gothic attire, a sprinkling of makeup, piercings, and well-coiffured hair. Others are ironically dressed in sportswear, basketball vests and American football shirts swamping their lank bodies. Some of them one-time models, some of them aspiring models, some retired models turned drug addicts, sporting gaunt pasty complexions having gone from 18 to 80 in the space of about 2 years. A guy I saw in a Uniqlo campaign lurches past me with coloured lights flashing over his gurning face. Then there are women, either too butch, too burlesque, or too bawdy for their own kind – doomed forever to hang out with gay men. This category includes my friend Kitten, who looks like a miniature Naomi Campbell, with flawless dark brown skin and close-cropped pink hair, and a face that usually rests somewhere between annoyed and non-plussed. She's the only person I know who is actually from London. She seeks out gays wherever she can find them, working on a department store perfume counter or doing half-naked performance art at an unknown gallery on Vyner Street. She can find gays better than gays can find gays. She introduced me to my last boyfriend. As I shook hands with him, she whispered in my ear, 'He's a total asshole.'

'You look tired.' Kitten presses her lips together.

'Thanks, people keep telling me.'

We have to air hug due to her conical breasted corset and my suit of armour.

'I think I'm getting old.'

'You're like twelve. Come with me, I'm just about to –' She makes a gesture that is much less subtle than if she were to say, *snort some drugs.*

'What's the –' I try to formulate the delicate question of what it is.

'I don't know.' She grips my hand. 'Some guy gave it me – it's good.'

Her hands are small, with a tight tendinous grip and heavily lacquered nails. She pulls me across the dance floor, through multi-coloured bodies, some of which try and stop to talk with me. She won't let go, so I just say, 'hey hun,' to each of them, as if I were the queen and it were a formal greeting I bestow on my subjects.

In the toilet cubicle, Kitten starts telling me about some incident in a charity shop, involving her and Bobbi trying to buy a mink coat. All I'm able to do is stare at the pink powder she is scraping into two lines with her weathered travel card.

'I used to say you should never party when you're sick,' I grumble. 'But I also used to say you should work when you're sick and save your sick day for when you're well. I'm not sure which one this is, work or party.'

'It's a party. Now where are your drink tickets?' She taps the residue out of her nostril.

I undo the drawstrings on my armour and fish the tickets out of the codpiece.

'Coming?' She asks, sticking a couple of tickets into her right boob.

'I actually need to use the facilities.'

While sitting on the toilet, I hear cackles and snorts from the next cubicle.

'Well, he looks like a potato,' someone laughs. I don't recognise the voice, but I don't recognise two-thirds of the people I know, even when I'm looking at them.

24

'It's just fucking out of order,' the other says, his voice echoes off of the toilet walls. 'I told him to fuck right off.'

I'm not really paying attention, more trying to put the kinetics of my brain into motion.

'Oh my god, he's wearing it again!' One says.

'What?'

'That suit of armour, he's wearing it again!'

'I told you, that's what he wears. He's got a whole cupboard full of them.'

I grimace at having become the subject of this drug-fuelled lavatory bitch-fest.

'It's the same one. He's trying to remind people he was on the cover of a magazine.'

'What magazine?'

'Oh, nothing big.'

Nothing big! It was *ID* magazine! They go on to talk about people whose looks are much more "*current*" and much more "*fierce*" than mine. The list includes a stupider, younger clone of myself, called Ash, whose look is my hair and women's designer clothes he bought off *eBay*. Am I really washed up, a month after my 22nd birthday? I consider how to extricate myself from the toilet, without them hearing the distinctive clang of my armour as I leave. The only thing worse than hearing your fashion sense being belittled in a night club toilet, is the people belittling your fashion sense knowing you heard them. I try to wait it out, looking at the pleas for blow jobs and penises daubed on the inside of the toilet door. They start complimenting each other:

'No, I think you have such an interesting style. I don't think there's many other people who make their own garments. Where do you get PVC like that?'

I make my own garments! Not only do they sound like they're about to fuck, but I'm starting to feel whatever Kitten gave me making me want to move a lot. I stumble out of the cubicle. Their nasal voices don't even pause for breath.

On the way to the bar, Tamsin corners me and hands me a ten-pound note.

'From your friend,' she says, sticking it between two plates of my armour.

'Milo?'

'No, your friend outside – John Lennon.'

'Oh, him. I don't know him.'

'Well, you do now.' She winks at me, multiple pairs of eyelashes precariously balanced on her eyelids. 'He wrote his phone number on it.'

I unfold it and underneath the line-drawing of the queen is a mobile number written in biro.

'C'mon, I'll get us drinks,' I say, folding the note back up. 'Just let me use you as a battering ram to get to the bar.'

'Honey, nobodies using me as anything.' She flicks a bit of pastel purple hair extension away from her lips. 'You can get me a double G&T and meet me in the green room.'

The green room is actually a store cupboard, and it's actually a dirty beige. It only seems exclusive to people who aren't in there. The people who are in there are mostly the people who are getting paid to be here. There are two semi-naked performance artists in the corner, one of whom is attempting to Gaffer-tape two condoms filled with fake blood to the others' chest. Tamsin's bangle covered arm reaches out for one of the drinks I'm holding. She's hunched up in a sunken old leather chair. When she drinks the G&T, she looks like a goblin, knees at the same level as her silicone breasts. Next to her is Moth, half wrapped around a male model from an American Apparel advert, who looks strangely enamoured with Moth. I say strangely, because Moth has the aesthetic of a possessed child from a European B movie. Blue painted skin and a bleached blonde bowl-cut. He ran away from the States with half

26

his parents' savings and a plan to consume as much Ketamine as humanly possible.

'Come here, come here,' Tamsin hisses conspiratorially and pats the arm of the sofa, her bangles and neon bondage gear rattling.

I step over Moth and sit down primly, as if I want to be perched on the arm of a dirty sofa.

'Has Rocco done anything to make this night different from *Flasher Slasher*?' Tamsin asks.

Flasher Slasher was the once amazing club night that ended here last Wednesday, before this very similar night, called *Arcade 3000*, launched.

'No, of course not.'

'That's so Rocco.' She rolls her eyes and presses the straw between her big pink lips.

Ash, Bobbi, and Milo are all managing to sit in one armchair. Ash waving his legs about in fishnets, paired with an aboriginal pattern leotard and furry Hasidic headgear. I hear him telling a story about how he met Lilly Allen and Lilly Allen's brother.

'She asked me where I got my belt,' he squawks.

In my opinion, that kind of name dropping is how you go about having no class. Still, I can't stop myself from leaning over and saying, 'I fucked Lilly Allen's brother.'

'Alfie?' Ash stops waving his legs about. 'He's not gay.'

'He is now,' I laugh, and don't know if I'm telling the truth or not.

The performance artists go out to be gross all over the stage, and some kid called Prozac Efron enters in an affected manner. He's still holding onto the time when everybody had comedy names, when Kitten was Dot Kitten, and Bobbi was Bobbi Beige. He's wearing sunglasses and some monstrosity made from purple metallic PVC, with wings sprouting from the back. He makes his presence known by greeting each person in the room with a 'hey gurl' whether they like him or not. He then proceeds to push some dated copies of *Boyz* magazine off the little glass table and rack up a few lines of some disturbingly green powder.

Milo rolls his eyes at me, about this whole performance, but when Prozac has finished, he still barks out, 'Give me some,' grabbing the rolled-up ten-pound note from Prozac's PVC fingerless gloves.

'You want some?' Prozac asks me, in an attempt to win my approval.

Realising his is the voice from the toilet, and having entered some less lucid plane of existence, I just reach out and squash my palm onto the remaining powder and lift it to my nose. Moth's model friend laughs at my nonchalant approach to debauchery.

It wasn't always like this, there was a time when I had that joie de vivre, when I was that enfant terrible. Hanging from the chandelier and destroying the general decorum of any venue I entered, through a campy drug-fuelled display of how big my ego was and how much I could get away with. I've lasted longer than most people. The average life span of a club kid is a cicada like two years. They come to London to fulfil their dreams of being as gay as possible. They pout around a few night clubs wearing a bit of lipstick and a party wig. Then suddenly, they evolve into some lingerie-clad space fish, taking ecstasy every other night, hanging around with out-of-work models, and hanging off balustrades, screaming at people to get them a drink. Next thing you see them wandering around Old Street with a messy weave, a beard, and an overcoat. Either trying to score, trying to get laid, or having realised the whole universe is a simulation and trying to unplug themself. Then they're ripping the extensions out of their scalp while wearing bug-eye sunglasses, on a bus back to the Brecon Beacons. Moth's model friend leans over him to talk to me, and they both smile as I'm very candid and witty and almost lucid.

I let my body waft through the party on a wave of drugs, and *'gurls'* and *'darlings'*. I watch myself from above, on autopilot, knowing when to grind, when to smile, and when to laugh, only gurning a little bit. Watching from up here, I'm not even the puppeteer. I'm the programmer, and my body is a party roving automaton, fuelled by MDMA and calibrated to the perfect combination of bitchiness, friendliness, and quasi-extrovert behaviour.

'Cosmo, Cosmo!' Someone is clicking in front of my face, trying to call me back for an actual mind on mind conversation.

I slam my hand down on their's, trying to squint through the vapour trails and movement distortion lines, to work out who the hell is in front of me. He's wearing a red sequin tuxedo, his rounded Korean features painted with red and white polka dots.

'Rocco!' I say.

'You're fucked,' he informs me, 'I was going to ask you to come to *The Mint.*'

The Mint is a club behind an unmarked green door, that has a perpetual gaggle of rich people outside, shouting at the bouncer to let them in. They hire Rocco to snare club kids in and give it an air of avant-garde, even though Rocco is about as avant-garde as Pepsi. His actual club kid name is Rococo, but nobody calls him that because it's stupid.

'I need to get paid!' I slur at him, and he makes an expression like this is no problem.

'I'll get it out the safe.' He leads me through the VIP room, which is even more full of people than before.

We have to step on them to get past. They try to talk to us, like amicable zombies. Rocco makes a laughing face and bats away their comments with a campy hand gesture. I just murmur 'hey hun'. Then we're in Lars, the club owner's office. Rocco through some strange extension of trust, has been given the keys. He clicks open the safe and counts out twenties while I sit in the office chair. I allow my limbs to slump and splay out.

'No time for this.' He wafts £100 in twenties under my nose.

I reach out and despite the strong movement blur, I manage to grab the notes out of his hand.

Any night, especially a night you're running, you should consider leaving about half an hour before the lights come on. This isn't always achievable. If Rocco hadn't grabbed me, I probably would have stayed here glued to the wall, gurning and talking in a frenzied manner about the new *Illamasqua* makeup range. We push our way through the gurgling, swaying, semi-naked masses to the stairwell. We make it up the stairs with only a few brief interactions, then get into a cab that someone else hailed.

Rocco explains to them with a smile, 'This one's ours.' He taps the drive on the shoulder and says, 'The Barbican.' Like they do in old films.

'Why the Barbican?' I can hear the drugs in my voice.

'Pick up a friend,' Rocco says, distracted by his phone.

At the back of the Barbican, I hear the click of cameras and see flashes. Paparazzi in North Face jackets shout in gruff voices to get the attention of a celebrity. A younger version of myself might've opened the door to get in on this photo opportunity, but I just look out the windscreen, at the red brick tunnel in front of us. For a brief while in gossip magazines and tabloids, my name would appear under photos, with the word model next to it. But now I'd just be '*boy wearing armour*' which is maybe more degrading than not being in the photo. Our celebrity manages to pull herself into the taxi. The flashes briefly reflect off the side of my face and fill the interior with light.

'Your clothes are shiny,' she slurs in a cockney accent hunching up in the seat in front of me.

I recognise her from TV, she's a singer with a huge mess of tangled black hair and a lip piercing.

'Thanks,' I say. 'I was trying for 1660 meets 2060.'

'Where'd you find this one,' she jokes at Rocco, chewing a piece of gum while she talks.

'*Arcade 3000*, my new night,' he shamelessly promotes in a monotone voice.

The celebrity begins to fall back into her car seat and looks like she might drop off to sleep. Suddenly she remembers she's offended about something and turns to Rocco and says, 'I thought when you said you were coming to get me, you'd be driving.'

'I don't drive,' Rocco states innocently.

'You wanna get papped going in with me,' she says, withdrawing a baggie of some powdery substance from her bra.

I've never seen Rocco look awkward or lost for words like he does in this moment.

She pours a bump of the substance onto her knuckle, and it disappears into her nostril. Then she tells Rocco, 'Whatever, I don't care.'

I must be staring a little too hard, as she asks me if I want some.

'I am ...' I try to think of a witty way to say no, but instead stutter, '... already very high.'

'Suit yourself,' she says and begins to bicker with Rocco.

It's normally against all my principles not to accept drugs from a celebrity. What is wrong with me? Everybody's saying I look ill. What if I've done something to myself, fucked up my kidneys or given myself a blood clot. I try to attribute these low dopamine musings to whatever Kitten put up my nose.

The taxi door opens and the paparazzi waiting outside the club lunge for a photo. People behind red velvet rope stumble out of the way. Rocco gives the bouncer a nod, making a rectangular robot smile as flashes go off around him. He pulls the singer into the club, and I clatter in after them. In the circular foyer there is what looks like a missile launcher painted gold. On top of it is a girl acting like she is on a mechanical bucking bronco, waving her arm about and screaming. Models dressed in early 90s attire stand in front of green velvet curtains discussing something in whispers. Rocco and the singer head upstairs, into the tribal sounds of an art performance. I stand a few meters from the 90s girls. I consider telling them their hats are stupid or maybe telling them their hats are cool. Neither of these seem appropriate responses to their headgear. I don't trust my intuition, my social abilities have dropped to just above vegetative. I hear the music changing in decibels as people open and close the door. A guy in an Oxford shirt appears at the top of the stairs and beckons one of the models away with him. I'm left with the other two, now sullenly getting out cigarettes. I remember that I'm not the kind of person who waits around in lobbies of even the most expensive clubs. I quickly exit to a less rapturous response. I push past an angry man in a tuxedo and try to hail a taxi before I pass out in the street.

'Skipping, skipping,' says Felix in his goldfish pattern shirt, kicking up dirt and woodchip. 'Jumping, jumping ... running, running.'

'I can see what you're doing,' I tell him. 'I don't need narration.'

'I'm not saying it for you.' He trudges back, running his hand along the fence that separates us from trees that reach up to the sky like pillars in a cathedral. '– It's a meditation.'

'It's a very active meditation.' I raise an eyebrow.

'I'm a very active person.' He purposefully bangs into me.

'Hey!' I push him halfway across the path. 'You're very jolly for someone who can't remember anything.'

'I started thinking, *do I actually need to remember anything*?'

'Yes,' I tell him.

'Like what?' He flutters his eyelashes at me, beams of sunlight filtering between tree trunks.

'I'd prefer you to remember for yourself.' I stop and lean on the fence.

He gives me a dubious expression and flaps my comment away with his hand. 'I've already started remembering some stuff anyway.'

'Yeah?'

'Yeah ...' He makes an expression like he's trying to force a memory out right now. 'I remember everything being dark, then hearing you and my grandma's voices.'

'Any more?' I ask.

'The physiotherapy – I remember walking with the two bars.'

I'm about to say, *I told you about that in the car.* But he looks so impressed with himself for remembering, that I can't.

'What do you remember about it?' I ask.

'It's just like photos, snapshots.' He makes his fingers into a frame shape and positions them around the Giant Sequoia in front of us, its roots like a dinosaur's foot. 'When are we going to climb under the fence?' He looks around.

A chubby family walks past, all wearing polo shirts. When they're gone, he scrabbles under the fence and crawls commando style through the woodchip and pine needles. I relent and follow him.

We crawl right up into the roots. They're big enough that we can hide from the tourists or park rangers there. We sit cocooned, the smell of bark and resin dense in the air.

'I can't believe we're actually here.' Felix twists upside down, so his legs are on the tree, and his torso is on the ground.

'Me neither,' I admit, still uneasy about Felix's memory loss. I tilt my head back and look up. Furry red bark leads like a road into a spiral of jagged branches.

'She's been here for thousands of years,' Felix says, 'And she doesn't remember any of it.'

'She doesn't need to remember anything.' I poke him with my foot. 'She just needs to keep standing there and making pinecones.'

'Why can't I just lie here, making pinecones?' He turns his head in the dirt to look at me, his hair full of pine needles.

'It's like you've become an advocate for amnesia,' I make a dissenting expression.

'I've had some quite extreme things happen in my life.' He lifts a handful of dirt and woodchip and lets it flutter to the ground. 'Maybe it's easier not remembering.'

Here it comes, bang, bang, bang, like someone is stood over me with a sledgehammer, smacking it directly into my skull. My left-hand scratches around my bedside table. It tears two paracetamols singlehandedly from the foil and forces them down my parched throat. I know I really need water, but it's not in me to make the eight-meter journey to the bathroom. I imagine myself crawling across the carpet, like William Blake's Nebuchadnezzar. Wretched and bedraggled with splintered three-inch nails. I pull the quilt over my head to shield my eyes from the sunlight and try to relax into the feeling of having my head bludgeoned against the pillow.

Later I manage to stagger, stomach twisted and fuzzy-eyed, to the toilet. The lower half of me still in holographic armour. Instead of the stream of piss I expected a jut of translucent vomit spews from my throat. I catch a glimpse of myself in the wall mirror; red-eyed with smeared makeup. Then I hunch back over the bowl and finish emptying my digestive tract. What the hell is happening to me? I'm supposed to be a professional. Last night was a totally average night, but I've felt better after three-day drug binges. I know I'm giving off the air of a pathetic failed figure of decadence, ailing under his own excess. But I've gone weeks without narcotics. If I'm addicted to anything, I'm not sure what it is because I don't buy my own drugs. I sit on the toilet floor spitting out bits of congealed vegetable matter, my headache starting to relent. I make a pact with myself that if I still feel like this after a few days of non-partying I'm going to call my doctor whoever he is. I take another paracetamol and embark on a journey of regeneration, eating fruity snacks and watching the shopping channel. I try to ignore my irregular heartbeat and morbid thoughts about how it's time to quit the club scene and do a poorly paid internship as a pattern cutter or become a makeup artist for weddings. Instead I concentrate on the slightly septic feeling the presenter's wrinkled fingers are giving me as they caress a pair of pink wellingtons.

A few hours later, I wake up to a polyphonic ditty reverberating from my phone. A man on TV, who looks like he's never used a power tool, feigning that he in love with a *Black&Decker* jigsaw. My brain isn't working properly. I plan on hanging up, but when I get the phone in my hand I accidentally answer.

'Cosmo?' Says a gruff voice.

'Nuh!' I groan.

'Are you on your way to the shoot mate, we're starting soon.'

'Uh, yeah, I'm almost there.'

'Be quick, see you soon.'

'See you.' I don't hang up. I hear the beep of him hanging up. Then it dawns on me that I was supposed to be doing a shoot for *Boyz* magazine. I know it's only *Boyz* magazine, but I have to keep up the pretence that I'm still a model. I pull on some leggings and a giant t-shirt depicting Mickey Mouse with the top of his skull open, his brain in neon pink. I grab a bunch of makeup wipes, simultaneously swilling toothpaste round my mouth and trying to excavate my face from layers of makeup. I splodge concealer back on, which I can rub in later. On the way to the station, I realise I still smell of vomit, so I run into Superdrug and ask the assistant if I can try their *Dior Homme*. She points to the concealer blobs on my face and says, 'You've got –'

'I know,' I tell her.

She slowly gets out a little slip of card to spray the perfume on. Through some sleight of hand, I manage to yank the perfume bottle from her and spray it all over myself.

'Mmm, smells nice,' I say.

I arrive at the graffiti covered warehouse in Hackney Wick, shaken and half conscious. I knock loudly on the corrugated metal door and attempt a confident pose. A man, whom I recognise from a previous shoot as the photographer, opens the door a few inches. He has boy-band hair despite being in his 40's.

'Sorry Cosmo, you're really late, I don't think we can use you.' He says "*we,*" but it's him in control of the shoot.

In the background, I see Ash and two other pretty boys letting out high pitched squeals and wearing monochrome beachwear. A big hot spotlight melting their perfect skins. I make an expression like someone who has just seen a bit of congealed snot.

'I'm not being rude mate,' he continues, "but you don't look so good neither.'

'So, I've been told.' I try to show no emotion, which isn't hard.

'Long weekend?' He asks and doesn't wait for an answer. 'You should think about taking a rest.'

'Sure,' I say, looking over at Ash messing around with a fishing net.

The photographer gives me an amphibian smile then closes the door. I hear him draw the padlock across. I trudge off through the hipster populated wasteland of Hackney Wick. 'GAME OVER' sprayed in big white letters on the wall of an abandoned yard.

On the way back, my state of mind has become too grim to even entertain my usual sociopathic fantasies of shooting everyone. When changing trains at Kensal Green, I contemplate pushing a woman in Ugg boots under the train, maybe even taking myself with her. But thoughts like that are too much for my post-MDMA brain to handle. At Newington Crescent, some private school boys get on the tube in tuxedos with nicely combed hair. They look at me in my leggings with a mild contempt. They don't know that once, I was one of them. I wonder if there's any trace of it still on me. Walking around Surrey with friends in Oxford shirts, laughing along with their jokes. Maybe laughing too high pitched with too much limp-wristed hand waving. How can I have changed so much that, that was normal for me then and now this is my every day? My state of mind finds something melancholic in the fact that I'll never be that person again. I've come too far along another trajectory to even contemplate retracing my steps. I'm not saying I have any desire to be a yuppie. The come-down is just making me feel wistful about time's one-way street. I raise my eyebrows at them. One whispers something to the other and lets out a pompous laugh. It makes me question if I was ever really one of them. Maybe, what I am right now, is what I was always going to be.

'What do you remember?' I ask Felix, both Cross-legged on the floral quilt as if we're meditating.

We're in a trailer in the desert, grainy UFO photos in little homely frames on wooden plank walls. Shafts of late afternoon sunlight cut through the blinds. Other than the air conditioner, the only sound we can hear is the occasional car on the road outside dividing the town and the mountains.

'I'm in a wheelchair in my Grandma's house,' says Felix. 'You're there too, in the armchair.'

'Yeah?' I take a sip from my can of *Lime-a-rita* and wait for Felix to elaborate.

'That's it, I'm just getting moments.' His eyes close and his nose scrunches up as he tries to go back into the memory.

I look at the TV in its inlaid cabinet, silently playing a courtroom reality show.

'I remember the nurse asking me questions and moving my eye to answer them.'

'What did she look like?'

'It's blurry,' he says, his face straining to remember.

It seems like progress. But it could also just be regurgitation of stuff I've already told him.

'How well did I remember this anyway?' He asks.

'I think you remembered some of it.' I take his point. 'What about something more recent?'

He puts on a pretend thinking expression for a moment then reaches forward and grabs my foot.

'Why don't you tell me something?'

'Because it's you who's lost their memory,' I tell him.

'Did I do something bad that you're not telling me?'

Maybe, I say in my head. Maybe we both did. I wonder if he blanked out the last year for the same reason I'd like to.

'I just think it's better, you remember on your own.' I sip the *Lime-a-Rita.*

'Tell me one thing.' He puts his head on one side, so his brown curly hair hangs down, trying to look cute. 'One thing.'

'Ummm ...' I adjust myself against the pillows and look at him for a while. His far apart eyes waiting for news. 'Y'know the bit I always remember is you opening your eyes.'

'Yeah?' He shifts closer.

I put my palms over my own eyes so I can remember the moment better. 'I remember the smell of the flowers that your grandma left. The nurse with the curly black hair and glasses leading me into the room and ... It was happy and scary.'

'Why scary?'

'Your eyes weren't moving. It meant you were going to be okay, but the doctor told us you might never walk or talk again.'

'What did you think about that?' He asks.

'I made myself believe you'd be okay. I did that thing you told me about, where you imagine something happening so hard, it actually happens.' I turn away from him to watch the motes of dust floating, like TV static, in the light from the blinds.

Everything is in its place, there's just a 23-hour gap between me going to sleep and waking up. drag.

'Mother Mary, please forgive me for I have sinned,' one guy slurs.

'Was it the sin of thinking a plaid shirt was acceptable attire for a night club?' I reply, then give him a half-smile to act like I'm not really a bitch.

The rest tell me how great my look is and that I should be allowed to go and dance in the club. Honestly, I'd much rather lurk in this ticket booth, sipping from a glass filled with ice cubes. Suddenly James is in front of me, blue lipstick smeared all around his mouth, right up to the nostrils. He leans almost all the way into my little booth. I have to push him backwards by the face.

'Where were you at my private view?' He slurs.

'Oh crap,' I murmur in realisation of my failure as a best friend. 'I slept for like a whole day.'

'I know, I saw you on the sofa.' He's got a guy with him who I possibly remember seeing on stage, covered in fake blood in a children's bathtub lip-synching to Celine Dion. 'I sold the photos of people with their dads, all of them, £800 each.'

'Wow,' I say, quelling the flames of jealousy I feel at anyone else's success. 'Entry is ten pounds.'

James leans into the booth and takes the little rubber stamp and smears it on his and his friend's hand.

'I'll get our taxi home,' he shouts, galloping off into the club.

The bouncer gives me a look as if to say, "Do I need to go after them?"

I shake my head and flap my hand.

In the cab home, James' long legs are splayed all over me and the back seat. His voice has become very English, and his use of the word "*Honey*" has quadrupled.

"But honey –" He squints, his eyes look smaller without his glasses. "– Some people buy artist's work to store it up and make it worth more."

He's drinking out of a bottle of Vermouth he got from the corner shop.

"Give me that." I grab the Vermouth off him and taste it. "This is terrible!"

"We can go to the Eagle and get something better ... or we can go to the sauna!" He says this hazy eyed as if the sauna is a really mystical magical place.

"Honey," I repeat his catchphrase in a droll tone. "I've got a headache and I don't need to go to the sauna to get sex."

"We're going for rehabilitative purposes." He says, his normal queer intellectual drawl becoming a slur.

"Anyway, they're not going to let you in with that face."

"What face?" His blue lips mouth.

James props himself up on the counter, trying to argue with the Eastern European Sauna receptionist. I roll my eyes and pick up a copy of Boyz magazine from the counter.

"That's me," I tell him, pressing the magazine to the kiosk window. "We're gay celebrities."

So, he hands us towels. James skips in, strips off, and ends up going off with a guy who looks like a middle-aged Philosophy lecturer. I sit in the sauna sweating off the , my body feeling jittery and tired. I go for a naked swim in the little subterranean 4x2 meter pool, lots of wavering blue swimming pool light around it. A couple of older men stood nearby watch me, and I enjoy feeling like a hot twink in a French gay film.

James returns from his drunken fuck, blue lipstick smeared all over his face. I'm sitting in a sun lounger reading about myself in Boyz magazine. They've set the sun loungers up by the side of the pool as if this were a beach resort, not a scummy underground sauna in Central London.

"Marks out of ten?" I ask him.

"Very satisfactory actually." James looks down at me. "You?"

'Sometimes I can't tell if I'm high or ill.'

He looks at me with drunken concern and props himself cross legged on the other sun lounger as if he's my therapist.

'Do you think I'm getting too old for it?' I ask.

'Honey, you're like twenty-two,' James laughs. 'I think if anyone did what you do, they'd feel like shit. I support the hedonism, in principle. But ...'

'— Rocco just turned thirty,' I look at his naked torso in the flickering pool lights, white towel around his waist. 'I don't want to be hosting club nights when I'm thirty ... Maybe we should move to Berlin.'

'What would you do in Berlin?'

I get his point. '— Maybe I should do a fashion apprenticeship.'

James perks up, looking like he's just remembered something. 'Are we still going to that Vivienne Westwood show tomorrow?'

'James, look at me.' I loll over the side of the sun-lounger, affecting an extreme malaise. 'I can't go to a Vivienne Westwood show. Plus, I don't want to see Ash mincing down the runway when it should be me.'

'I'd really like to go,' he says, meaning he's my plus one and can't go without me.

I make some frail writhing motions on the edge of the sun lounger.

'Vivienne Westwood,' he says in a voice that he stole from 1930's cinema. 'Vivienne Westwood.'

I think about how I missed his show, and how we've been growing apart recently.

'Vivienne Westwood,' he keeps saying until I finally agree to go.

Felix is filling out glittery postcards that he bought in Las Vegas, while I manoeuvre around roads blown out of red cliffs, the morning sun glaring through the windscreen. I glance over at the mess Felix is making, getting all the glitter from the postcards on the dashboard.

'Morocco?' I see the address in his rounded italic scrawl.

'Yeah, it's for Leon.'

'How'd you remember the address?' I have to keep my eye on the twisting highway.

'I didn't, it was in my bag.' He stops doodling for a moment.

'How'd you remember where you put it?'

'I don't know.' He shrugs.

We both look out the dusty window at the strange red rock formations coming into view, strata of auburn and maroon. It's like the background of a Salvador Dali painting.

'Is this what memories are normally like?' He shuffles his postcards and puts them away in the glove compartment. 'You have this feeling like you can remember everything. But really you just remember bits.'

'Yeah, but not as bad as yours.'

'Because my memory feels intact.'

'I'm sure it is, somewhere in there.' I point at his head. The hot dusty air huffs at the partially open window. We pass a motel, then we're on what looks like the main street, tourists sauntering in and out of new age shops and steak restaurants.

'Do you wanna look?' I ask, seeing the words *psychic* and *vortex* somewhere and knowing Felix likes both those things.

'No, no, I'm all about the nature today.'

'Which direction is the nature?' I ask.

He extracts a map from the glove compartment and says, 'Cathedral rock ... straight ahead and first left.'

We leave the main street and enter what looks like Martian terrain, except for the occasional mansion.

'*New age superstore,*' I read off a big purple sign.

'Nature,' he repeats.

'You're very eager.'

'Look at this place.' He makes a dramatic gesture out the front window. 'And my heart feels better than it has in like forever. Wanna feel it?' He leans towards me offering his chest. A thick scar running from the hollow of his neck to where his flamingo-pattern shirt buttons.

'I'm driving!' I turn a corner onto a road with a bit of an incline.

A woman with a straw hat and sunburn walks by the side of the road.

'Is this the road?' I ask.

'Yeah, yeah,' Felix says, more interested in the red rocks. 'Oh look! A church.'

I twist my neck so I can see the trapezoid-shaped window built into a red cliff face. 'I guess that's cathedral rock?'

'No, Cathedral rock's just a rock. But let's have a look.'

I slow, then pull into a space. He whacks the door open, and I smell the hot dusty air. He grabs his hat off the back seat.

'You're not wearing that, are you?'

The hat is decorated with fur, beads, and horns. He bought it in a Las Vegas gift shop, off a woman wearing a sweatshirt with a picture of a wolf on it.

'Why not?' He raises his eyebrows to the rim of his neon tribal headgear.

'If you're wearing that, I need something too.' I kneel on the seat so I can root through the bags in the back of the car. I pull out a bandana and tie it, so the two flaps hang down at the front, like a '60s housewife. I feel in this moment like we're really back to being us. The people we were during some brief interim between both of our hospital stays.

I step from the train like someone who had returned from a prisoner of war camp, frail and wide-eyed. Wide-eyed, from consuming the dregs of my one-night-stand's MDMA, in an attempt to tide me through this last ordeal. It's turned me into a jittering zombie wearing a chrome silver shirt, hauling my corpse up the stairs leading to the sound stage. I try to wave to Boy George, but I'm unable to lift my arm above the level of my pectoral muscle. Everyone that was ever on *The Clothes Show* is here, everyone that is in pictures of charity galas at the back of *Hello* magazine. Everyone I would normally want to talk to if my throat didn't feel like it is slowly constricting. Zandra Rhodes sits in front of me, her trademark pink hair bobbing as she laughs with a couple of gays. Techno music plays and beautiful gaunt women and men parade their bodies down the runway wearing tweeds in a post-apocalyptic style.

I cling to James' arm mumbling my mantra, 'Hibernation, hibernation, hibernation.'

He tries to politely shrug me off, asking if I'm okay a few times. I reply with the sound of my eyes clicking back into my skull. Ash prances down the runway in a suit with a tweed cape. The spotlights on the rig above us highlight every perfect bone in his skull. I turn away, grimacing, holding onto the edge of my chair, like I'm out at sea in the midst of a storm, clinging onto the mast, hoping that the little strength left in me will stop the boat from capsizing. Squirming about in my seat, I know I'm drawing some attention from the factions of glitterati around me. Not least the woman behind me, whose shiny black shoes I can currently see my contorted reflection in. I hear James' voice, but the words are inaudible above the rush of waves. With my last milligram of strength, I try to turn back toward the catwalk and act like a normal person. I can't see anything above Zandra Rhodes' neon pink hair and the models' calves, just a parade of perfect tan high heels. In this moment I see myself almost in an out of body sense and know that something has been really wrong these last few days. I should've gone to the doctor, I should've called in sick to work, I shouldn't have snorted half the things I did. Now I'm just a passive observer, approaching one of those a pivotal moment when a switch flips and you can never go back. Like a car accident playing in slow motion, but you're already halfway off the road. Like a sinking ship, where they're already handing out the life jackets, lights flashing and flares going off.

I vomit on the floor, just missing Zandra Rhodes' head. I'm in the second row of a Vivienne Westwood show, and I just vomited on the floor. This is not cool, this is not fabulous. It came up so quickly that I couldn't even turn my head or think to grab James' bag. I stumble to my feet, people bending to the side and ducking out the way as I plunge forward. I try to stop up my mouth with my hand but the vomit squirts through my fingers. I make for the double doors, the venue staff unable to stop me. I rush past them looking for the toilet and cling onto it, spitting out stomach acid.

It's one of those strange silent late-night taxi rides. Our backs pressed into the black leather seat, bhangra playing at low volume from the radio. I'm wearing my gold sequin onesie with a leather jacket over the top. Felix is wearing his horned hat and tie-dye vest. We both look out opposite windows at lights proclaiming: "*Hollywood #1 Souvenir Shop,*" "*Hollywood Vintage Superstore,*" and "*Hollywood Hotdog*". I pay the driver and almost forget to tip him. Then I tip him too much, and he grumbles anyway. We trudge through the gravel that makes up the atrium of our cheap motel.

'Please don't be angry at me,' whines Felix.

I mount the stairs for the second tier of rooms. Everything is lit by pinks and blues from the huge neon sign facing out toward the road. Below, a few cracked-out people slur nonsense at each other.

I give Felix a drunken sigh. 'I'm only angry because I care about you.'

'I didn't get as drunk as you.' He leans on the banister, his hair lank with sweat.

'You've got a heart problem. You shouldn't be drinking at all.'

'I had a passion fruit margarita.' He sulks behind me.

'And shots!' I hear my own voice, slurred and camp and pedantic. I'm angry at him for making me act like this. 'I just worry you'll hurt yourself again. Maybe it was drinking that made your memory go.'

'I don't think so,' he mumbles.

I push the key card into the metal pocket on the door and pull the handle down. The room is mostly filled by a bed with musky pink sheets and a big old TV. In the light from the sign, I can already tell something's wrong. Our suitcases are open, and our stuff is all over the floor. Felix reaches past me and switches on the light.

'Did we do this?' He asks.

'No, someone broke in!'

'But –' Felix half slurs, half stammers, '– we're on the second floor.'

'Fuck! Our passports!' I get on the floor and start throwing clothes onto the bed, looking for the little Ziploc bag with our passports and bank cards in. 'Did you leave the window open?'

'I don't think so.' He surveys the mess.

'Here they are!' I pull the wallet out of the secret pocket in my bag. Kneeling in my sequin jumpsuit, I flick through the contents, 'It's all still there. What have they taken?' I look up at Felix who is staring at the bed. I follow his eyes to something black between the pillows. 'What is it?'

He walks over, picks it up and passes it to me. It's a figurine with wings. Not very heavy, a bit shorter than my forearm. It's burnt all over, ash coming off in my hands.

'Is it yours?' I ask.

'No, someone must've put it there,' he whispers.

I pass it back to him and wipe the ash off my hands onto the duvet.

'You think this is some kind of homophobic attack?' I'm suddenly filled with a discomforting thought that the person could still be in the room. My eyes dart to the space under the bed and the dark of the bathroom. I rush to the bathroom and slam on the light. But its empty. 'We should tell reception. Tell them to phone the police.'

The reception is housed in a static caravan and seems to be looked after by the same chain-smoking woman 24/7. Her lipstick bleeding into her wrinkles, her beehive hairdo sagging. She locks the office and follows us, trudging through the gravel in her slippers. She surveys the damage from our doormat taking derisive little drags on her cigarette.

'Are you sure you didn't do this?' She croaks and gesticulates at us with her cigarette to remind us of our costumes.

'Yes! Someone broke in!' I cross my arms over my gold sequined onesie.

She takes another long look at us, then scans the room for clues, a reluctant late-night detective. She sucks hard on her cigarette as if this is very stressful for her.

'You left the window open.' She points, accidentally flicking ash on the floor.

'But we're on the second floor,' I tell her.

She seems unphased by this information.

'There's some desperate people around here. What did they take?'

'That's the strange thing. I don't think anything's missing.'

'That is strange,' she says, turning to go.

'They left this!' I grab the burnt angel figurine from where Felix left it, on the side of the bed.

She holds it briefly by the wing, with the tip of her thumb and finger. Her nails are painted the same maroon as the motel doors. She drops it into the white plastic bin by the TV and says,

'Problem solved.'

'I've called a taxi to the hospital,' I tell an upside-down James, who is standing in my doorway. Upside down, due to the way I am hanging off the edge of my bed. Everything has a grainy twilight quality.

'You call an ambulance to the hospital, not a taxi,' says James' silhouette.

'Is it here?' I ask him.

'Yeah.'

'Can you help me down? I haven't got much power left.' I feel the bile in my throat and five sledgehammers all pounding my head.

'I think you should've called an ambulance.' He heaves my arm around his shoulder.

'I shouldn't have gone to Vivienne Westwood's show and been sick on the floor,' I gurgle, unable to keep my head up.

James helps me stagger down the stairs. The blurry view of our house interior seems more like a memory than something that is happening in the here and now. I hear Valerie's voice from outside complaining.

'There is taxi driver ring my doorbell.' When she sees me drooling and barely conscious, supported by James, she says, 'Oh what is happened now! It is drugs, I know!'

I make a weak guttural noise, that expresses everything I want to say to her. My mind is unable to decipher the sounds reverberating in my ears. The shuffle of our feet and the click of the taxi door. I'm pushed into the back like a large piece of luggage. The engine burrs into motion and the Taxi driver grunts,

'Look mate, I'm not running a hospital delivery service for junkies. What's he taken?'

I mentally urge James to stand up for me.

'I don't think he's taken anything," James says. "Have you taken any drugs?'

'Blurgh!' I make a noise, half-way between a gurgle and a growl.

'Well as long as he doesn't throw up in my cab,' the driver grunts.

But I can already feel it, surging up my oesophagus. The lolling of my head synchronised with the bumps in the road. An acrid sting of stomach acid fills my throat and James holds something to my mouth.

'It's going to be okay,' he tells me.

The patch of light on the taxi floor gets further and further away, until there's just a pinpoint of light and then darkness.

Part 2

Latin America

At first, through bleary eyes, I think I've woken up in an office, eggshell-yellow walls and white hardboard tiles for the ceiling. Then my mind starts to come into focus, I see the suspended curtain rails and the beds. There's something on my face and something stuck to my arm. I try to move but I feel sluggish and distant, not in control of my own limbs. Before I can remember how I got here or pull the oxygen mask from my face a person appears in the room. She's wearing blue, she touches my arm and says my name in a Scottish accent,

'Kylian, hello? Can you hear me?'

'Nuh.' I try to remove the mask, so I can talk to her.

'Don't panic. You're in the Royal Hospital in Whitechapel.'

My eyes dash to the tubes coming out of my arm. I follow them up to one of those things that looks like a metal coat stand, a packet of blood hanging from it.

'You're having a blood transfusion. It's okay. You've just been out for a few hours.'

I look at her, shortish auburn hair, face slightly puffy with age.

'I'm going to go get the doctor for you.' She leaves the room before I can answer.

58

I'm left looking at machines with wires that lead under the white sheets and attach to my body. Over the almost silent whoosh of the oxygen mask and the tiny bleeps, I try to remember what happened. My brain is foggy. Trying to use it is like trying to cut through stale bread with a blunt knife. I remember the fashion show, and I remember throwing up.

The doctor briskly enters the room in his striped shirt and white coat, with a rosy face and an almost spherical head.

'Hello, Kylian. I'm Dr Browning,' he tells me and pulls the oxygen mask off my face and over my head. 'How're you feeling?'

'Wuh-woozy,' I stutter like a drunk child.

'That will partly be the painkillers and partly the blood transfusion.' He speaks with a practiced kindliness, leaning on a machine next to my bed. His features are all squashed together in the middle of his face.

'Blood?' I mumble. 'Did I overdose?'

'No ... We've done some blood tests and your white blood count is very low.'

My stomach starts to tense up. 'Aids?'

'You don't have HIV.' He hesitates. 'There's a possibility this could be leukemia or lymphoma ... Again, it could just be a virus, a very strong one. We need to do some tests, so we can start treating it as quickly as possible.'

Leukemia, lymphoma! The words echo in my brain alongside images of children with pale skin and bald heads from adverts for cancer charities. I'm not able to listen anymore. It's like when you're at a club, drugged to the nines, and some random person is jabbering at you. You're looking directly at them and nodding, but not hearing a word they're saying. He says something about a CT scan and a bone marrow biopsy. I don't know what those things are, but they sound serious.

'Have you got any family members you'd like us to contact?'

'Where's James?' I ask.

'The friend you came in with?'

I don't remember coming in.

'I think so.' My voice is shaky and unfamiliar.

'He left his number with reception.'

'Tell him to come.' I gulp.

The doctor says he will, and I'm left staring up at the holes in the white hardboard ceiling.

Later, two nurses take me in a wheelchair down a series of hallways painted in tasteless pastel shades. They talk to me with an annoying camaraderie,

'I really like your hair,' says the one with freckles on her arms.

'Thanks,' I say, unused to interacting with normal people. I feel like I've suddenly been thrust into someone else's life, and I haven't been informed of the lines or the motivation for the part. Cosmo doesn't sit in a wheelchair in an elevator while nurses make small talk about how fashionable he is.

I'm wheeled into the haematology ward, where I'm left with a woman with streaky grey hair and an Indian lady in a beige cardigan, who says, 'We're going to give you a painkiller called *Midazolam.*'

I mentally remark on what a good name for a drug *Midazolam* is. 'I've never heard of it before, is it good?'

'It'll help you forget the procedure.'

Next thing I'm lying on a bed having fluid injected into my arm. Then a huge comedy size syringe is stuck into my hip bone. I feel this stinging pressure and make a *gnrghhh* sound and feel a tear run across my face. She sucks out a few syringe-fulls of this dark red stuff and smears it onto little glass slides. Then while everything swims quite pleasantly around me, I'm taken in a wheelchair to another room that contains a piece of alien technology. I'm placed on a bed, then the bed slides into a giant white plastic doughnut. A woman behind a little window tells me through an intercom to take deep breaths. I consider that I might have been abducted by aliens, shapeshifters who take the form of dumpy fashion-less middle-aged women. They've given me a drug that's going to make me forget the whole experience, and now they're sequencing my DNA and stealing my memories.

I'm wheeled into a new solo-suite. James is waiting for me with a canvas bag from the supermarket filled with my clothes. He looks somewhat taken aback when he sees me.

'James,' I slur in a helium tone and almost dribble on myself.

'Kyle ... how's it going?'

'Not great.' I heave myself up from the chair. 'They just stuck a needle in my spine.'

'Into your hip,' says the nurse from behind me. 'Do you want to get into bed? We're going to hook up another blood transfusion soon.'

'Do they know what's wrong?' James asks in hushed tones when the nurse is gone.

'They said it might be cancer: leukemia, or a really bad flu.' I give him a deadpan stare.

'I hope it's flu hun.' James squeezes the handles of the bag together.

'Yeah. But I'm getting the feeling it's not.' Before he can offer false hopes or sympathies, I continue, 'They gave me something called Midazolam. It's really good.'

'Have you phoned your family?'

'No.' I tilt my head back against the plastic bedstead and give him an expression that asks; why would I want to do a thing like that.

The following afternoon, a lady with a highlighted grey bob and an unplaceable European accent, wakes me up and tells me she's Dr Maslak the oncologist, but I can call her Valerie.

'Don't you want your family here?' She asks.

'I'll phone them when I know,' I say, sitting up in bed.

'Okay. I'm sorry to confirm, you do have Leukemia.'

My mouth feels dry, and my lips feel stiff.

She holds my gaze. Her lips are purple around the edges. 'It's a variety called acute myeloid leukemia. Basically...' Like the other doctor, she's talking but what she's saying is more like a series of foreboding verbal hieroglyphs strung together with English joiner words. 'The good thing is that we caught it now, so we can start treating it right away. If you have no objections, I want to start your first course of chemotherapy tomorrow.'

When she says chemotherapy, I look up to what I can see of my bleached blonde hair. This is happening so quickly. I feel like when I used to record pop music off the radio onto cassettes and a cassette would get a loop in it, then within the space of a second get all tangled up around the insides of the tape recorder and snap. That's what's happened to my life.

'Are you sure it's leukemia?' I ask Dr Valerie. I worry this could be one of those stories from a cheap gossip magazine, where someone is diagnosed with the wrong condition and ends up with both their arms chopped off for no reason.

'Yes, it's definite,' Dr Valerie says. 'I don't want to give you too much information now. I know this is a lot to take in. But here are some leaflets. This one's about chemotherapy, and this one's about acute myeloid leukemia, this one's about our hospital counselling service.'

When she's gone, I stare at the three leaflets laid out on the quilt in my lap. Eventually I pick up the booklet titled "*Understanding Acute Myeloid Leukemia*" with a picture of a moderately attractive guy standing in nature on the cover. I gaze noncommittally at pictures of purple and red blood cells with exotic alien names like lymphoblasts and neutrophils, and a clipart of someone having a needle stabbed into their back. I look at the page that says, "*Causes: radiation, smoking, benzene,*" none seem to relate much to my life. The worst thought of all is not that I'm dying, but that I'm going to have to tell my parents. If I'm really starting chemotherapy tomorrow, I'm going to have to tell them soon. I mentally concoct a situation where in the distant future I tell them, 'Oh yeah, I've been battling cancer for the last six months, but I'm fine now.' I visualise their bemused expressions. My mum's shrew-like face, unsure whether to land on anger or concern. My dad looking like he's smelt something bad, then looking at his blackberry.

'What's wrong?' My mum sounds flustered down the phone.

'What makes you think something's wrong?' I say, lying in bed in a hospital gown having a blood transfusion.

'Because you're calling,' she replies, '... the tone of your voice.'

'Okay, something is wrong. But I don't want you to freak out.'

'I'll decide whether to *freak out* or not when I know what it is,' she puts a sarcastic emphasis on the word "*Freak*," like it's some quirky modern turn of phrase.

'I'm in hospital,' I start.

'What've you done?' She demands.

'I've got cancer,' I blurt it out, more spitefully than I intended. 'Leukemia. The doctors just told me today.'

'Leukemia,' her voice mumbles. 'Are you sure?'

'Yes.' My lips start to go stiff.

'Where are you now?' She asks, the hubbub of a restaurant behind her.

'In hospital, um, I think it's the royal hospital in Whitechapel.'

'We're coming there now.'

'Okay,' I mumble, further surrendering control of my life.

I hear familiar voices in the corridor an hour later. They enter my hospital room as if violently teleported here from some champagne social. My mum's hair is in a slightly messy bun, and she's wearing her Burberry detective coat. My dad's top-quality hairpiece looks realistic but tousled, his shirt sleeves rolled up like he's one of the doctors here.

63

'Are you okay?' Her tone of voice would suggest disgust in other circumstances.

'Of course, I'm not!'

'How long have you known about this Kyle?' Asks my dad in his usual firm timbre.

'I only found out today!'

They draw up chairs next to my bed and prattle at me with drawn faces. When I tell them that I'm about to start chemotherapy, my mum remarks in a hushed voice, 'Well, we'll get an expert opinion before that happens.'

'I had a haematologist, oncologist person suck-out a bit of bone marrow yesterday and test it.'

'Yes, but this is the NHS. You know they can't afford ... we didn't get you medical insurance for nothing.' She lets out an awkward little laugh.

'I think your mothers saying you should get a second opinion,' my father states the obvious.

'Someone in Harley Street.' She leans towards me, giving me a whiff of Sancerre and *Roberto Cavalli*.

'From what the doctor was saying, I get the feeling it's kind of an emergency.' I clench my teeth.

'Do you want me to go and talk to this doctor?' She puts her hand on the quilt, having already decided to go talk to the doctor.

I slump forward in response, and my mother whispers that she'll go and talk to the doctor.

'She cares about you,' my dad says.

My mum re-enters the little room with an unfamiliar doctor in tow.

'Your mothers saying you'd like a second opinion. I can assure you they'd do the same tests and put you on the same course of chemotherapy.'

'It's not me who wants a second opinion,' I grumble. 'It's her.'

My mum gives me a look as if I'm being impudent.

64

In the end, we make a compromise. That my second bone marrow biopsy could happen at Harley Street. From there I can choose where I want to continue my treatment. Two especially depressing nuggets of information come out of this conversation. Firstly, just how much of an emergency they think my situation is. Secondly, that I'm going to be in hospital for the next few weeks, maybe months. After my parents leave, I look out at the familiar East London landmarks from a different angle to my window at home. The Gherkin glowing dark green against the orangey-grey sky.

I have the right side of my chest slit open and some sort of internal tap attached to one of my arteries, because as Doctor Valerie says, 'You might've heard stories about how much damage chemo can do to your veins.'

No, I hadn't heard these stories. It seems they're going to rot me from the inside, in a race to see if they can kill the cancer before they kill me. My parents bring me food in Tupperware boxes from an Italian restaurant. The next morning the Scottish nurse sticks a needle into the bit of my chest where the port was implanted. She attaches it to a bag of bright orange fluid hanging from an IV drip.

'Some people say they can taste it.' She smiles at me.

It's strange, I do get a taste in my mouth, like cough syrup. I lay there watching black and white Vivien Leigh films, from a DVD box-set James brought with my clothes. On the second day, between chemo infusions, I go into the toilet and try to cry, forcing my face into a frown. The last time I cried was when I got Ketamine in my eye, and before that I don't remember. I kick the little stainless-steel bin over and rip the empty toilet roll off the holder and throw it on the floor. Then I sit down on the closed lid of the toilet with my hands in my hair. I feel powerless, fed up with all the monotonous white and pastel hues and all the kindly nurses. Why me? Why not Milo? He's a much worse person.

I spend the next few weeks daydreaming melancholic scenarios. My triumphant recovery: making my way through the crowd at *Science Fiction* to frenzied applause. Or my last days lying in bed; all fashion-week-thin, bald, and green around the eyes. Doctor Valerie saying in her lispy accent, 'I'm sorry, there's nothing more we can do for you.'

I see a couple of people on the ward that look like that. I see them enough that I should say, "*hello*", but I don't. They feel like ghosts. Like seeing my own demise walking around, bald and skeletal in a dressing gown and slippers. When I think about death, I think about getting disqualified from a board game in the early rounds, and everyone else gets to keep playing, basically it's unfair. I don't think I've ever seriously thought about death before.

Other patients' rooms are filled with cards, and flowers, helium balloons, and pictures of relatives. I've kept mine bare, except for a few cards, so I can feel like I'm just passing through. I thought I'd get more visitors, but half my close friends claim to have a phobia of hospitals. I'm too proud to demand they come, and I try to assume the rest of the people I know think I'm too popular to visit. Kitten comes though, with a Yellow PVC bag filled with expensive eyeshadow palettes and Yves San Laurent lip glosses. I didn't know she was successful enough to be given this much free makeup. High off painkillers I help her to give me a glittery cancer-chic look, lots of dark purple shadow and holographic glitter.

Then I start to feel really sick. A different type of sickness to what I came here with, a stomach-churning, head-crushing g-force kind of sickness. As if this spaceship masquerading as a hospital is taking off, using some otherworldly anti-gravity device. They tweak my medication so that every day isn't like this. Still, I'm not able to eat the veal cutlets and Tiramisu my parents bring me.

The cross-hatched metal barrier flicks past the passenger window. The sky, a baby blue, a few clouds pasted on like the backdrop to a high school production of Oklahoma. Felix has already found radio Tijuana. He almost slaps me in the face, gesticulating wildly to some Mexican power ballad. His good mood contrasts with the last few days in San Diego. He had this darkness about him, wanting to spend all his time not doing very much in our sparse motel room. I asked him if it was because I'd complained about his drinking, but he said it wasn't that. I asked him if it was the motel getting broken into. He said it wasn't that either.

'I can't be Mr. Enthusiastic all the time,' he told me while pretending to meditate in a scuff-marked corner of the bedroom. 'I'm remembering things.'

So, I went and had a meal in a hipster coffee shop on my own and worried the thing he was remembering was that I'm the reason he almost died.

Now he's dancing in the car, to a sort of contemporary rhumba, wearing his horned baseball cap. The music trails off into a cartoonish Mexican voice, jabbering over a backing track. On one side of the car a huge motorbike overtakes us and on the other, a bright McDonalds 'M' peers over a breezeblock wall.

I pull my sunglasses down from my head, to shield me from the mid-afternoon sun and tell Felix, 'We're Thelma and Louise.'

'Who's Susan Sarandon and who's ...' he tries to remember the name of the other actress, knowing it's one of my favourite films.

'... Geena Davis?'

I remember when we watched Thelma and Louise. Me, Felix, and James wrapped up in quilts. Felix with his shot glass of wine. It seems like something from another life.

'I'm Susan Sarandon because I drive and I'm vaguely sensible.'

'I'm Geena Davis because I'm cute and easily influenced,' he winks, and sticks his hand out of the window, making a wave-like motion, cutting through the dusty heat.

Two huge trucks thunder past, the type with massive metal exhaust tubes and funfair lights.

I slow down as we head under a bridge with a big green sign that reads "*International Border 500m*". I start to get that feeling of possibility and trepidation that you get when you enter a new country.

'Wait! Pull over a moment.' Felix flails his arms around.

'We're almost there!'

'I want to leave something on this side of the border,' he says.

I glare at him and pull over into the last turn off. 'What is it? LSD?'

'No, I wouldn't leave that.' He frowns as I drive through a behind-the-scenes area of the border with lots of crisp packets and weeds. 'It's something metaphorical.'

'You made me pull over for something metaphorical! We're gonna have to go all the way back round now.'

'Ahhh.' He shrugs in that way like he's an elderly New-Yorker. 'Just pull over here, it won't take long.'

I begrudgingly pull into a layby. Felix clicks open the door and walks around the car into the sun-scorched shrubland. I get out too and cross my arms. I hear him counting, '8 ... 7 ... 6 ... 5 -' as he saunters off into the dry overgrown piece of nowhere. Then he suddenly starts screaming.

'Felix,' I say, worried he's been shot or bitten by a snake.

He takes a break from his loud, guttural, masculine scream, breathes in and starts again. He's just screaming off his own accord into the undergrowth. He breathes in and starts another howling, rasping scream that involves him ripping up part of a little dehydrated shrub and throwing it at a bigger shrub.

'Felix! What the hell!?' I shout.

'It's good, come and join me,' he calls back, and lets out a louder shriller scream to illustrate his point. He rips a little branch off something and hurls it ungracefully at the ground.

I think about how much of a better mood he's in, and about the guilt I still feel sometimes when I look at him. I glance around to see if anyone's watching. There's no one, so I go and join him. My first is more of a squawk than a scream. I'm a bit more self-conscious than Felix, who's rolling around, collapsing into the dried grass and weeds.

I have another large needle stuck through my back, into my hip bone. This time in a spacious modern art-filled Harley Street clinic. My parents accompany me for the consultation. It's in a big room with photos of land art on the walls. The oncologist has twinkly blue eyes and a Sigmund Freud beard. His verdict is that I continue to receive chemotherapy at the Royal, though he will personally advise them on the formula. Afterwards, my parents take me to a new Italian restaurant, and I only eat a quarter of my food, and fiddle with my glittery fedora while they talk about everything except cancer.

My dad and James carried all my wardrobes out to the car with an annoying camaraderie. I let out a little nasal sigh looking at the empty room with bits of holographic glitter rubbed into the carpet. Then I'm back in my parent's house, sitting on my old bed. The initials of all my school crushes still scratched into the headboard. I look at myself in the big square mirror. The same mirror that witnessed all my early-teenage hairstyles and private fashion shows. I look at the little scar near my collar bone from the port, and the bit of rash on my arm. I wonder if other people will notice how my face looks thinner and darker under the eyes. I catch myself rubbing my tongue around the inside of my mouth. The same motion popular among senile old men without teeth. My mouth is constantly dry, my lips chapped, no matter how much Pina Colada lip balm I put on. The worst thing is probably my hair.

A dumpy rosy-cheeked nurse passed by my room once, as I was arranging my bandana, 'We have some clippers if you want to buzz your hair down,' she offered.

I gave her a look of horror, tightening my doo-rag. It's me who gets to choose whether I walk around with a few balding strands of hair hanging from my scalp or not. I pull my fringe back to contemplate what it will look like, then set about searching my wardrobes for clippers.

'James is here!' My mum warbles upstairs.

I descend the staircase in a figure-hugging space suit made from gold padded lining fabric. My matching astronaut helmet under one arm, as if I'm just about to board the shuttle. For once I'm made up and ready to go in time.

'You're bald!' My mum accuses me.

'I have cancer,' I remind her.

James' heavily mascaraed eyes widen in his glasses when he sees me, rhinestones stuck to my forehead and scalp.

'You shaved your head,' he tells me.

'Yeah, I have cancer.'

'It looks good,' he attempts reassurance.

'It looks okay,' I correct him and pull a silver surgical mask onto my face. 'Let's go.' The mask is to protect my lowered immune system from a club full of bacteria. The space helmet is an extra precautionary measure. I put it on in the taxi to avoid the stunted conversation between me and James.

When we arrive at *Science Fiction*, I regret my decision to come almost immediately. I push my visor up and walk past the queue of vibrantly dressed queers. At the top of the stairs the bouncer makes a grunt, expressing that he's not just going to let us past. James starts mumbling something. The bouncer doesn't look impressed. So, I pull my mask down and say, 'It's me.'

'Okay,' he does an awkward flourish out of our way.

'I'm regretting this.' I squeeze James' gloved arm as we descend into booming electro-pop.

'You wanna go?' He turns to me. His serious expression paired with his huge blue lips makes me laugh.

'See how long I last. You can get me a cocktail.'

'You shaved your head,' Milo remarks insightfully, and grabs a hold of me to take a closer look.

'Yes,' I confirm the obvious.

He makes a little scrunched up, bee sting face and air kisses me.

Bobbi's hair is buzzed short after what looks like a recent bleach accident.

'We can be twins,' he shouts, hugging me and then poses next to me as the club photographer click-clacks at us.

'What cocktail?' James finally manages to ask me.

'Something strong,' I drawl. I don't know why I thought this would be a pleasant experience, the loud music and posturing gays worsened by my already sludgy disposition. I guess I just wanted to feel like myself. Instead, I'm cornered by people I only vaguely know, drunkenly asking questions about my personal health. After a while, I go and install myself at a table away from the speakers where I can do an unenthusiastic meet and greet.

'I like your shaved head,' says a guy with long curly brown hair, tribal stripes drawn on his cheeks with marker pen.

'Thanks. I preferred having hair.'

'Why'd you shave it off then?' He looks down at me, his eyes almost all pupil.

'Cancer,' I tut, for the zillionth time.

'Well, I still think it looks good.' Spinning lights flash over his face.

'If you want to talk to me, sit down, you're making me dizzy.' I stir my cocktail with the transparent plastic stirrer and attempt to remember where I've seen this guy before. 'Where do I know you from?'

'Some other lifetime.' he slides into the chair in front of me straightening his tight velour disco shirt. 'And this place, about a month ago. I told you; you got that scar from falling out of a tree.'

'Oh yeah, the psychic.' I draw out the words. 'Tell me something else.'

'I'm not a very good psychic.' He pulls his mouth into a wide frog smile. 'I can tell you're going to be okay.'

'Sure,' I mix a glass of mostly ice cubes. 'It would be nice if I could cut out the months in hospital.'

'I spent a lot of time in hospital when I was young.' He glances over at the cute gothic fashion boys, dancing nearby. 'I made my own language.'

'I watch a lot of old films where people smoke indoors.'

'Casablanca?'

'One's with Bette Davis in that no one's seen.' Resigned to the conversation, I ask him, 'Why were you in hospital?'

'Heart problems.' He leans forward, raising his voice over the music. 'I had my heart taken out and some dead person's heart sewn in.'

'That's quite extreme.' I stop stirring my drink. 'Really?'

'Yes, you want to see?' He starts unbuttoning his shirt.

'You are such a slut,' interrupts Moth.

'I'm just looking at his scar.' I look up at Moth, wearing a jacket that has lots of blonde hair extensions attached to it. His usual blue face paint highlighted with lots of white powder.

'That's what they all say.' He looks at the guy with the long hair and 70's shirt, then at me. 'James said I should visit you in hospital.'

'Sure.' I sip the dregs of my cocktail. 'It's the big one just down the road from here. The Royal.'

'Oh, okay.' He perches on the end of the bench.

'Anytime from the second of next month is good.'

'Can I visit?' Perks up the 70's guy. 'I'll bring you grapes.'

'I can't eat anything with a flavour,' I complain. 'I'm on biscuits and yoghurt.'

'I'll bring you biscuits!'

'If you have to,' I mumble.

'What's your real name?' His mouth twitches. 'I need it if I'm going to visit.'

'It's Kyle,' Moth slurs.

'Kyle Vancouver.' I draw the letters out sarcastically. 'Like the place in Canada.'

'Felix,' he says, shaking my limp hand. 'Like the cat.' He gets up before I can think of a good way to retract the offer.

'Why'd you tell him my name?' I ask Moth.

'Sorry,' he says, meekly looking at my bald head. 'You don't know him?'

'No!'

'Well, he was kind of cute,' Moth looks at me pleadingly.

I see I am now a representative of some debilitating disease to him. 'Moth, stop looking at me like that.'

'Sorry!' He looks away into the kaleidoscope of bodies and lights. 'Do you want a drink?'

'No.' I slide out from behind the table. 'I'm gonna find James. I'm going.'

'Isn't seafood dangerous for you?' I ask Felix outside a Ceviche stall with a roof made of leaves. I think I mean, isn't this specific seafood dangerous for you. Seafood that's been lying out in a busy polluted street in the Mexican sun.

'Everything's dangerous, Life's dangerous,' he says.

'But specifically, grimy seafood when you've got a heart condition.'

There's a big Mexican guy squeezed into a Chicago Bulls vest, compiling the Ceviches. He furrows his brow at our little spat in front of his store. The street is dusky with fumes and thick summer heat. Local women are strolling with bags, halter tops. The men wear jeans and caps. There are a few obvious tourists looking pink skinned, lost, and mildly uneasy. Some distant reggaeton plays from a distorted speaker amidst the shouts and car horns.

'I know what's okay for my body,' he insists. 'I live in it.'

'Maybe you should phone the doctors again.'

'Again! I didn't even phone them the first time!' He exclaims, then makes an expression like he didn't mean to say that.

'What!?'

'We should get a shot of Tequila before we talk about this.' He quickly pushes himself up onto one of the stools in front of the Cevicheria. 'Dos vasos de la tequila.'

The owner seems to just about understand his Spanish and pours tequila from a large plastic bottle into two full-size glasses. Felix pushes one over to me. I down it and glare at him.

'I just pretended to call them,' he says sheepishly. 'I didn't want to go home, and I felt like I was fine.'

I open my mouth and close it a few times.

'... And my memories have come back now.' He sips his shot.

I grab it off him and drink it too. The taste of the tequila is only palatable because it's weak. I continue to glare at him as he starts to look meeker, awkwardly adjusting his horned headgear.

'I just really wanted to do this trip with you," he whines.

'I guess you're just always going to do what you want. Whatever effect it has on your body ... or on me.'

'I'm serious when I say I can tell what's going to affect my body. It's connected to my brain.' He does some woo-woo gesture between his brain and his body. 'And I'm a bit psychic.'

'You're a bit of a dick head,' I tell him, too relaxed to be properly angry.

'I always thought I was more of a wanker.' He drinks the dregs of the tequila I took off him.

My mouth opens, about to say, you didn't seem to be connected to your body when you almost killed yourself. Then the thought re-enters my head that maybe it wasn't an accident. I close my mouth, realising that's not a conversation I want to have here.

'Look, to apologise for lying. We can go to a restaurant that you like, and I'll pay.'

I roll my eyes and tell him, 'I'm going to choose somewhere really expensive.'

'I wouldn't expect any less of you.'

We both hop off our stools, and I try to remember the directions to a hipster place I saw. The front of the shop open onto the street, with Japanese-Mexican fusion food.

'Sometimes I feel like you're keeping things from me.' I try to reprimand him.

'Sometimes I feel like you're keeping things from me too.' He looks at the side of my face as we walk.

Rather than enquire about what those things are, we both just leave it there. It's a bit too sunny to be really angry at him and I want to enjoy the feeling of being part of this alternative couple walking through Guadalajara. I feel like photos of Pete Doherty and Kate Moss walking through Glastonbury festival.

The nurse enters the room and utters a load of syllables which in my post nauseous state don't make a cohesive sentence.

'Sorry?' I put down my book about Elizabeth 1st.

'You've got a visitor: Felix,' she says.

I'm not sure who Felix is, but it could be some close friend whose day-name I've forgotten.

'Okay,' I say and within a minute, there he is, in his 70's shirt and red corduroy flares. His long brown hair pushed behind one ear.

'I brought you biscuits,' he says.

I look at him for a few seconds, trying to make sense of his appearance in my hospital room.

'Put them there,' I flap my hand at the bedside table. 'Do you always dress like that?'

'Yeah.' His plump lips pout. He places the pack of biscuits on my table. 'Except at work.'

'What's work?' I slur, unsure if I'm slurring because I'm tired or because I'm pretending to be disinterested.

'I dress up as a zombie and try to get tourists to come to the London Dungeon.'

'Oh, you're one of those,' I groan, remembering the over enthusiastic people outside London bridge station, wearing historical clothing and fake blood.

He's standing over my bed in the same way he was standing over me in the club.

'Do you only sit on command?' I ask and he mumbles some awkward vowel sounds before I point out the chair.

He scrapes it across the floor and pulls it up next to my bed so we're almost at eye level. In the hospital light I can see the small constellation of moles across his face.

'You're a hippy,' I say, limply picking apart the biscuit wrapper. 'Do you think you can heal cancer naturally?'

'I think if you imagine something happening hard enough, sometimes it happens.'

'I'm talking like herbs and diet and things.'

'I don't know. I'm not a proper hippy.' He pulls an awkward expression. 'I just get all my clothes from vintage shops.'

I think I mistook his approach in the club for confidence. In reality he has a twitchy, wide-eyed, lip-biting quality about him.

'... I used to have a problem finding any clothes that I liked. Even if I found something, I liked I'd have to go back to the shop like three times before I bought it.'

'I just buy everything and take back the things I don't like.' I let a bit of biscuit melt in my mouth, before swallowing it.

'I was watching this seventies film and I thought, rather than worrying about what to wear. I could just dress like I'm from the '70s all the time.'

I make a sort of snorty laugh at this and then my sinuses sting a bit. 'I like a bit of historical drag, but ...'

'I'm a pretend time-traveller,' he explains. 'Before the 70's clothes, I used to steal fake money from museums. My wallet was full of Roman and Tudor money.'

'I bet they liked that at the bar.'

'I don't usually *buy* drinks,' he reminds me of his little flask of absinthe.

'You tried to buy me a drink.'

'I wanted to get into the club,' he insists.

'If you want to be a club kid ...' I sit up in bed a little bit, '... some blue hair, some glitter, might help.'

'Maybe I don't want to be club kid.' He presses his knees against the bed and pushes the chair backwards slightly.

'Don't do that.'

'I thought club kids would be a bit wilder,' he complains

'You're disappointed we're not all drawing on our faces with marker pen?'

'Yeah, now that you mention it, there could be more breaking stuff too.'

'We're socialites, not arsonists.' I break off another bit of biscuit. 'They used to be a bit wilder when I started clubbing.'

'When did you start clubbing?' He asks. 'You make it sound like you're a veteran.'

'I am. I started when I was like 15.'

'They let you in when you were 15?'

'I was in drag.' I flap my hand as if this were obvious information.

'I wish I'd gone clubbing when I was 15,' he draws his mouth wide. I can see him eyeing the biscuits.

I'm still slowly eating my first one. I push them towards him. 'Have some.'

He ends up eating about half the pack, and I end up feeling drowsy and nauseous again.

'I need some time to myself now,' I tell him.

'Oh, okay.' He pulls his bag off the arm of the chair. It's covered in little badges that click against each other when he moves.

'Nice talking to you.' He pats the quilt near where my arm is, then stops in the doorway and asks, 'You want me to come again?'

'You're not a Christian, are you?' I hesitate.

'I think I'm kind of agnostic.' He presses his chin against the door.

'Then, sure.' I croak and lean back into my pillow feeling woozy.

I seem to have started down a course of picking up eccentric social pariahs as friends. There's an old lady I'd seen wearing a number of colourful party wigs on her bald irradiated scalp, as well as bright decade defying clothing ensembles. A neon flower pattern dress with a roll neck jumper and rave beads. A summer dress covered in pastel roses under a bright pink dressing gown. I complimented her in the corridor on a lilac wig with plaits in it.

'I discovered eBay!' She said, as if she were the founder. She showed me her room, filled with doilies, throws, and damaged Georgian figurines.

'I don't want to die in a white room,' she whispers in explanation of the decorations.

'You think you're going to die?' I ask, not having heard this from anyone else on the unit.

'Yes. The doctors want to do their thing so I'm going to let them. I enjoy the social element.' She gives me a devious expression.

'You're okay with that?'

'I've lived a long time, my body's worn out,' she says with mild disappointment. 'I'm going to have an orange funeral.' The wrinkles around her mouth ripple with a smile.

Sometimes I wonder if there is much difference between her and me, with my headscarves, and glitter around the eyes, and viewings of antiquated TV series'.

The second time Felix comes he brings plain round biscuits. I break a splinter off of one and let it melt into the roof of my mouth.

'How's Bette Davis?' He asks, his eyes following the trail of tubing from the IV drip down to the port in my chest.

'I'm reading about Elizabeth 1st - my fashion idol.' I gesture limply towards the massive book on my bedside table. 'When she died, they dressed up an effigy of her in expensive clothes and carried it around London on top of her coffin. That's what I want.'

'I want people in mascot costumes to carry mine, and they'll play *Octopus's Garden* by *The Beatles*.' He's wearing another polyester disco shirt, with a picture of some mountains across it in a beigey brown.

'That's very specific,' I say.

'When you're ill, you make funeral plans. It's reassuring.'

'I don't think I'm reassured by the idea of people dressed as animals carrying my dead body,' I let the biscuit slide down my throat. 'I'm not planning on dying.'

'Ever?' He jokes.

'Maybe when I'm fifty, on a four-poster bed with lots of white lace and professional mourners.' I look at my current bed and its generic light blue towelette quilt.

'Fifty is pretty young.'

'I don't think this makeup will look as good with wrinkles.'

'Maybe you'll have different makeup by the time you're fifty,' he says with an earnest encouragement.

'What I'm saying is, I don't want to be a fifty-year-old drag queen.'

'I think a fifty-year-old drag queen is a pretty good thing to be.' He pushes some of his hair behind one ear. 'You know *The Poison Ivy* in Brighton?'

'Yeah, and I know the drag queen you're going to say, and that is not what I aspire to be.'

'The one that does karaoke?'

'With one-colour-eyeshadow up to her eyebrows.' I role my eyes. 'I could've guessed you were from Brighton.'

'I'm from some village near Brighton.' He shifts position in the chair. 'I lived there earlier this year, but –'

'You're not coming all the way from Brighton, are you?'

'No, I'm living with my grandma at the moment in the wild west of London.'

'Cos, I do have people visiting me.' I gesticulate towards all my cards.

'Can I have a look?' He asks about the cards and flowers, decorating the window like some tragic birthday party.

'Sure, knock yourself out.'

He goes over and tilts a few of the cards forward to peer inside. I look at him from behind, his short slim body and his strange choice of clothes. He has a nice ass, but from this angle he could be a middle-aged female art teacher.

'You've got one from Boy George!' He picks it up and shows me as if I might not know.

'There's one from Kelly Osbourne too, if you're impressed by that kind of thing,' I boast in a lacklustre way.

'Had any chemo dreams?' He asks, putting down a card.

'What?' I ask, unfamiliar with this line of conversation.

'When I was in hospital, there was this girl.' He leans on the windowsill and rocks back and forth slightly. 'She was having lots of strange dreams during chemo. We used to share our nightmares together.'

'That sounds delightful,' I tell him. 'I don't dream.'

'What, like never!?' He stops rocking.

'I thought I had a dream once. I was dancing around Soho in just pearl necklaces and a pompadour wig. But I asked people and it turns out, it was reality.'

'You seriously don't dream?' He tilts his head.

'No,' I rebuff him, as if he's the odd one for having these internal night time cinematics. 'I actually used to think people were just making dreams up, and it was some conspiracy against me.'

'Mine were so bad I had to see a psychiatrist!'

'Like what?' I ask, mildly curious about this part of human existence I'm for some reason, not privy to.

'This thing with no face, cutting off my arms and legs.'

'Urgh.' I give him a little enacted shudder. 'Too many horror movies?'

'No horror movies. I was like six, maybe seven.' He looks at his fingers as if they'll tell him the age he was.

'That's pretty fucked up.' I press my cheek against the pillow so I'm looking at his face.

'I'm pretty fucked up,' he contorts his eyebrows in a debonair kind of way.

I'm starting to notice the other tourists. I mean, I'm starting to notice the other white people. My reaction is to avoid them as much as possible. Young people in various states of hippiedom and intoxication. Even worse, the embittered latter-middle-aged couples taking their unhappy marriages on a world tour. The wives adorned in boho attire that they wouldn't wear at home, bemoaning their sullen red-faced husbands.

'Jeff, you are embarrassing yourself in front of everyone,' says Jeff's wife, walking into the hotel.

Our eyes adjust as we head into our hotel-cum-hostel behind them. Jeff mumbles something, and I make eyes at Felix to make sure he's paying attention to this little telenovela.

'You know I have cancer!' Exclaims Jeff's wife. 'You are making my cancer worse!'

I squeeze Felix's wrist and try to stop myself from laughing. Then we have to get into the decades-old elevator with them. They pause and seethe for the time it takes the musty elevator to rattle up the shaft with our sweaty bodies inside. The lift judders to a stop and Felix flicks up the handle that opens the doors.

'If I ever get like that, I hope the cancer kills me,' I whisper to Felix.

He searches around his shorts for the keys. I get mine out my back pocket and unlock the door. The room has dirty beige walls with bright coloured paintings of markets on them. I see something black and crumpled in the middle of the bed. 'What is that?'

We both go over and exchange disturbed glances. There are no clothes strewn around the room this time, just the burnt figure in the centre of the quilt, dirtying the sheets. Bigger this time, about 40cm high, burnt completely black, the wings on its back still identifiable as wings. Felix lifts it up and turns it over, making his hands ashy.

'What does it mean?' I mumble.

Felix is lost in concentration, gazing at the burnt figure in his hands.

'What does it mean?' I ask again.

He looks up from the figure, distracted, 'I don't know.'

'Is someone following us?' I listen to myself; it sounds stupid. Someone following us all the way from Phoenix to Oaxaca just to leave a couple of barbecued ornaments in our hotel rooms. 'Why would someone follow us? Do you think it's some kind of threat?'

Felix is still deep in thought. He isn't adding anything to my one-sided discussion.

'What are you thinking?' I ask.

'Nothing.' He places the angel back onto the bed, a look of guilt crossing his face.

'This isn't you, is it?'

'No,' he objects, but doesn't say anything more.

'We need to tell the management and get out of here.'

The young guy from the reception kiosk, white shirt sleeves rolled up, comes to take a look. He doesn't look particularly impressed or mystified by the burnt offering on our bed.

'I talk to the cleaners,' he says.

'But someone's broken into our room!' I don't mention that the same thing happened back in Phoenix. I don't want to be an insane person jabbering about an international conspiracy against them.

'You and the cleaner are the only person that have key. What do you want me to do?'

'I don't know. Call the police. Give us another room. Make us feel like this hotel is actually safe,' I begin to rant, annoyed at him standing there, good-looking, hairy arms crossed.

'The police are no interested in this, and all our other room are full.'

That's how we come to be squashing our bags into the boot of our car. The sun shining down, overbearing, when an hour ago it seemed tropical and inviting. I'm not sure if Felix is just being quiet or giving me the silent treatment. Without me seeing, he's put the figure in a supermarket bag and wedged it into a space between our two backpacks.

'We're not taking it with us.' I pull it out and take it to the nearest rusty, fly-infested litter bin. The smell of rotten fruit and baby's nappies is pungent in the heat. I wedge it in, one of the wings snapping off in the process.

'Get in,' I call from the driver's seat.

Felix stares at the ground.

'Felix, get in the car!'

He peers at me as if I whispered it and he is hard of hearing. 'But all the hotels are around here.'

'We're not staying around here so some fucking banditos can kidnap us and cut our dicks off and send them to our families.'

'I don't think they're called banditos,' he mutters, looking down at the dust and stones.

'Felix!' I look at him sweaty and exasperated. 'Get in the car, please!'

After a silence, he hauls himself into the passenger seat.

We pass little flat-roofed shops in pastel colours, their names painted on in bold, '*Tienda*', '*Lavanderia*'. Trees line the pavement, the bottom of their trunks painted white.

'I don't know where we're going,' I tell him.

He's hiding his face. His hands in his hair.

'Are you angry at me?'

'No,' he says, 'I'm thinking.'

'I'm thinking someone's got a list of our travel itinerary and they're paying people to leave burnt religious ornaments in our hotel rooms!' I'm fidgeting with a bit of the steering wheel that's peeling off. 'Did you give anyone our travel details?'

'Probably just my grandma,' Felix tells me in a little voice that accompanies these moments when he hedgehogs inside himself.

An elderly couple in suits walk in front of the car, and I have to break. My mind is spinning off into numerous disturbing possibilities.

'You haven't done anything to upset anyone, have you? You bought acid on the dark web, right? You didn't buy anything else? Any assassins, any Ricin?'

'Kyle you're being crazy.' He gazes out the window at graffiti as I follow a dusty white bus into a backstreet.

'Of course I'm being crazy.' I look down at my knuckles, white from gripping the steering wheel too tight. 'What if it's the car!? What if someone's following our car?'

He waits a few seconds and in a whisper replies, 'Nobody's following our car.'

'How do you know?' I question him through gritted teeth.

'I don't know,' he replies. It sounds like the answer to a question in some other conversation he's having in his head. 'There's a hotel.' He looks through the rear window.

There's a fenced off courtyard with a red and white brick archway and a sign outside saying something about "*paradiso*" and "*fabuloso*".

'The kind of hotel where you wake up with a horse's head on your pillow!' I rant.

'That's Italy,' Felix says.

The third time Felix turns up I'm not particularly feeling like seeing anyone. But I don't have his number to cancel. He skulks into the room like some schoolkid late for class.

'Hi Kyle,' he mumbles, squeaking the blue chair loudly across the floor, 'Sorry.' His hair is tangled and there's something like woodchip in it. When his yellow duffle coat is off, he looks at me drowsily. There's a cut on his face and an almost petroleum-like smell of alcohol about him.

'You're drunk.' I edge to the other side of the bed.

'Only a bit. I did sleep.' When he opens his mouth, the smell makes me recoil further.

'Can you move back a bit,' I ask.

He makes a dejected expression, his tangled hair falling over one eye. The cut on his face, rising with the muscles of his cheek.

'Actually, can you go?'

'You want me to go?' He grumbles.

'Yeah. I'm having chemotherapy. I don't need some drunk slurring at me, smelling like a *Weatherspoons*.'

'Okay,' his voice cracks, and he quickly pulls his bag back over his shoulder. 'Sorry, bye.'

'Are you even supposed to drink with a heart transplant?'

'No.' He turns around to squint at me in bed. 'I don't do it that often, and I never drink that much.'

'It looks like you drank as much as you could.'

'My medicine makes it so I get drunk easy.' He scrunches his face up like this is a big problem.

'Great.' I roll my eyes.

'Someone spilt a cocktail on me.' He stands in front of the white wall and the pine-effect door, holding his backpack.

'You didn't think to maybe change your clothes?'

'I was rushing to see you,' he complains. 'Do you still want me to go?'

'Yes,' I confirm, allowing myself to sink down into the pillows. '... Wait, give me your number. If I want to see you, I'll call you.'

This really brightens up his stubbly, dirty face.

So, I state again, 'If!'

He searches around inside his bag. His phone is a chunky one with transparent orange casing, like people had half a decade ago. He looks up his number and writes it on the back of someone else's business card, that he retrieved from his bag.

'Just put it on the cupboard,' I tell him. He places it carefully next to the book about Queen Elizabeth the 1st, then edges toward the door.

My parents bring me a beef strudel in a Tupperware box and seem to be hiding their annoyance at how unappetised I am by it. They don't sit next to my bed like Felix does. They sit, one at each foot, as if they're at a meeting with a bed-ridden divorce lawyer. They wait until I eat a fork-full before the conversation starts.

'Dorothy sent me this shoot today.' My mum frowns without creasing her forehead. 'She seems to think she's working for Playboy.'

I lick one of the ulcers behind my lip. 'Playboy is pretty tame these days. What was so terrible about them?'

She leans towards the bed and whispers as if she's going to swear, 'Swimsuits with cut-outs. It wasn't even a swimwear shoot.'

'I think people should wear whatever they want whenever they want,' I shrug.

'I know you do,' my mum replies wistfully.

'What did you do today?' I croak at my dad who isn't really contributing to this stilted dialogue.

'Nothing much. A meeting with the Chinese.' I imagine my dad in a meeting room with the entire population of China trying to squash through the door. 'Are you keeping yourself occupied?'

I finish eating a tiny mouse-sized flake of strudel while trying to formulate a reply. 'I had a complimentary foot massage earlier.'

'They have a masseuse here?' My mum leans forward.

'No, it was one of those machines with the water.'

My mum nods briskly as if to say: "of course they don't have a masseuse here."

'Oh, and my friend Joan asked me to help her choose some outfits for the hospice.'

'The hospice,' my mum says, alarmed.

'She had the most extreme clashing outfits I've seen in my life laid out on her bed. A *Laura Ashley* dress with a neon pink bolero –'

I thought my mum would be amused by this, but she looks disturbed, 'How old is this Joan?'

'Seventy-something,' I say, ready to mention the other outfits. The floral nightie with the snot green polo-neck inside. The summer dress, 50s swim-hat, and orange rave tights she said she might like to be buried in.

'She's probably got Alzheimer's.' My mum finishes off what was supposed to be a witty anecdote.

Doctor Valerie opens the door and pokes half her body through.

'Hi, hi,' she greets my parents. 'Is now a good time to discuss your bloods?' She has bad news, and she wants to break it to me with my parents here.

I let out a stunted breath and say, 'Okay.'

She drags a chair in from outside, and my parents ready themselves with serious faces. Valerie presses her hands together and tells me, my white blood cells are up, lymphoblasts are down.

'We've spoken about this before briefly,' she says for the benefit of my parents. 'But I think now it's time to start considering a bone marrow transplant.'

'If he's recovering with chemotherapy, why does he need a bone marrow transplant?' My mum asks, flushed.

'Mum, the chemotherapy is putting it into remission, but it can come back.'

'At this point, it's Kyle's decision,' Valerie adjusts her necklace of big acrylic beads, her nails are painted post-box red and are chipped around the ends. 'I'm advising it because Kyle's leukemia has been quite difficult to treat. We've had to extend his course of chemotherapy a number of times.'

'Okay,' says my mum and looks at me with a pained expression.

'It's not as much of an invasive procedure as it sounds,' Valerie says to my mum and dad. 'It's quite similar to a blood transfusion but we'd basically be giving Kyle a new immune system. There are some dangers that I've already talked to Kyle about –'

'Dr Kyffin mentioned a bone marrow transplant,' my mum muses distractedly.

'If you want the transplant performed there, that's no problem,' Valerie says this to me as much as my mother. 'Actually, one of the reasons I wanted to bring this up while you were both here is, if this is the route we decide to take, we'll need to start looking for a donor.'

'You mean us?' My dad asks like an interviewer interjecting a politician.

'Possibly,' Valerie says. 'You have a sister too, don't you Kyle?'

'You're going to have lawyer blood,' says Milo on the phone.

'My sisters not a lawyer yet,' I tell him, half envious of my sister's success. 'She just studies and shops a lot.'

'Have you met any other gays in there?' He asks as if the oncology ward might be a cruising ground.

'No, my only friend is a mad old woman, and she's going to a hospice.' I flick the chemo line out of the way of my hand. 'She had lots of outfits laid out ready. A Laura Ashley dress with a neon pink fur bolero –'

'What's wrong with her?' Milo asks in camp concern.

'She's got leukemia, like me.'

'But you'll be okay,' he says as if I desperately needed reassuring. 'She's old. Older people die easier.'

The only one who appreciates my description of Joan's clashing deathbed couture is Felix.

'I want to meet her!' Felix laughs into the phone. His voice sounds different, maybe more adult when removed from his body.

'When are you bringing me biscuits next?'

'Tomorrow,' he says, audibly pleased at finding redemption.

He looks cleaner than last time, the drunken graze on the side of his face has faded a bit. He puts the usual packet of biscuits down on my bedside table and pulls a scarf from his bag.

'It's to apologise for being a drunk,' he says, his eyes deep and brown.

It's one of those silk ones with all the patterns of golden rope and gilded circles on it.

'Thanks, it's nice!' I say, surprised at his good taste

'It's *YMCA*,' he says, referring to the charity shop.

I begin to tie it around my head. 'Y'know, I can tie this in fifteen different ways. My favourite is *the front bun turban.*'

'Do that one.' He beams in his floral shirt and sleeveless jumper.

'Nah, I'm doing *the Egyptian Queen* for you.'

'You think I'm an *Egyptian Queen* kind of guy?' He sits down in his usual place and hugs his knees.

'You're a traveller, I mean backpacker.' I start organising the scarf on top of my head.

'A backpacker who hasn't actually been anywhere.' He starts levering off his battered *Doc Martin* boot.

'I assumed you'd been to Bali, Bangkok, all those places.'

'Nope. Just France on holiday when I was seven. I was planning on going to San Francisco last year.'

'Apparently the drag queens are shit there.' I tuck the last bit of the scarf in so that a little flourish hangs down at the side.

'Do you judge everywhere by its drag queens?'

'Yeah, I try to.' I inspect the headscarf in a little compact, the purple eyeshadow around my eyebrowless eyes makes me look like a heroin-chic-alien.

He plops his boots down on the rubber floor. 'How are things?'

'Don't ask.' I snap the compact shut. 'Tell me about this trip to San Francisco.'

'Well, I kind of missed the flight.'

'Wait, do you want to come on my walk with me? I'll give you a tour of the hospital.'

'I was living in a beach hut in Brighton, taking acid every day,' he tells me as we're leaving oncology. 'Maybe every other day.'

'Why?'

'Oh, I had a job at an old people's home. I lost it. I couldn't afford my rent. Some guy let me live in his beach hut.'

'No, why'd you take acid every other day.' I tighten my fur-trimmed dressing gown.

'Not like a full dose, sometimes half a tab, sometimes a quarter.'

We're walking down a yellow corridor with benches and white numbered doors.

'I mean, I enjoy a bit of LSD, but every other day seems kind of excessive.'

'I was going through something, having a bit of a spiritual experience, and I bought in bulk.' He shrugs and gives me a zany expression. 'Anyway, the day before I went to San Francisco I decided to take the last bit.'

'Obviously a good idea before air travel,' I mock him.

We turn the corner into a small atrium, then another corridor.

'It was quite a big last bit; giant plants, houses melting, everything turning into fractals. I thought there was a massive parade on, but I think it was just people walking down the street. Then I got really drunk and spent the night running into the sea with my ex-boyfriend. I missed the flight. So, I just went back to London to live with my Nan.' He pushes a bunch of hair behind one ear. 'I don't know if I believe things are *meant to be*, but it wasn't meant to be.'

'The children's ward.' I do a little gesture to present it to him. 'I'd like to bring to your attention to these beautiful murals of deformed woodland creatures in hot air balloons.'

He studies the lopsided bear, hedgehog, and rabbit, all in a hot air balloon painted onto a sky-blue corridor.

'Children's hospital murals are one of my favourite genres of art,' I tell him.

'There's one in Brighton of Bambi,' Felix says. 'He looks really happy, but all of his legs are broken.'

Two people in dark blue scrubs walk past having some very serious discussion. We move on past a notice board with photos of sickly children playing with toys. I catch a glimpse of me and

Felix in a window and realise the odd pair we must make. Me, head-scarfed with glitter eyeshadow, and Felix, with his Saturday Night Fever attire. On our own, we're strange, but together we're like Cher and Tom Cruise.

'Through those doors is one of the hospital's many scenic outdoor passages. If you're lucky you can see people with freshly amputated limbs smoking cigarettes.'

There's a sallow looking guy in a wheelchair with a saline solution taking a drag on a cigarette. I give him a nod.

'How come you live with your grandma?' I ask Felix.

'I thought you were giving me a tour.' He pouts, the wind blowing his hair back. We head through the sliding doors.

'I am, this is the main building. Now, why do you live with your grandma?'

'My mum kind of died and I never knew my dad.'

'Oh, sorry.' I regret being so persistent.

'Don't be, you didn't kill her.' He tries to be blasé.

We have to make way for an old man on a bed with a tube up his nose being pushed in the other direction. I make an executive decision to return to tour guide mode,

'This is the main corridor, our fifth avenue. And here's where the hospital radio station transmits Ace of Base songs from 9 am till 9 pm.'

'Mmm, Hospital food.' Felix sniffs.

'That's a sentence, I haven't heard before.'

'Can we?' He looks lovingly towards the busy, soupy cafeteria.

'The smell of food makes me want to vom at the moment,' I tell him. 'Here's the heart of the hospital, our *WHSmiths*.'

He snorts at my sarcasm and says, 'We should get some *Freddos* for the nurses.'

'Did they look like they wanted *Freddos*?'

'Everybody wants *Freddos*.' He shrugs. But when he sees the selection of budget chocolate frogs inside *WHSmiths* he doesn't look impressed. 'They've only got caramel *Freddos*.'

'What's wrong with caramel,' I ask.

'It's like *Creme Eggs*. It's too much.'

'Come on.' I roll my eyes and grab a handful.

'Okay.' he smiles scooping every caramel *Freddo* he can out of the space between the *Crunchies* and the *Curly Wurlies*. He heaps them into my arms, dropping a few on the floor. He scrabbles to pick them up. The check-out boy looks slightly worried. I'm not sure if it's us or the amount of *Freddos* we're dumping on the counter.

'They're for the nurses,' I rasp in an attempt to confound him further.

Felix helps the cashier scrape them all into a plastic bag

'There aren't that many nurses,' I tell him.

'We'll have to give some to the general public,' he says, gesturing to some people sat outside Costa coffee. 'Do you want a *Freddo*?'

'No, thank you.' A dumpy woman with bleached blonde hair piled up on top of her head waves him away.

'She didn't like that,' I remark.

'You should ask. People won't refuse a cancer patient.' He's already gearing up to offer someone else.

'I hate the general public,' I tell him.

'They hate themselves too, so you've got that in common.' Felix pushes the *Freddo* in the direction of an elderly Indian man who turns away in a perturbed manner. He drops it back in the bag, then withdraws another identical *Freddo* to thrust in the direction of a mother and child with matching black ponytails.

'Okay!' I grab it off him and turn to an elderly woman, on her own at a table with an empty cup of tea and a newspaper. 'Hiii, here's a chocolate bar, for you.'

'Oh, thank you very much.' She looks at the chocolate and looks at me with gratitude that far outweighs the 20p we paid for it.

'I used to flyer for a gay club on Old Compton Street,' I tell Felix before handing one to a cute guy in scrubs.

'What's this for?' He asks.

'It's for you,' I reply, pointing at him.

'Chocolate?' I ask a guy with a grey beard who could be in a British faction of the *Hell's Angels*.

'Sure,' he grunts, sticking it in the pocket of his leathers.

Before I can hand the bag back, Felix shouts, 'Free Chocolate!' In a manner that reminds me of Noddy Holder at the start of "*Merry Christmas Everyone*." Then we're handing *Freddos* out to a small gaggle of sickly, overweight and haggard human beings.

'What's this in aid of?' Asks a bug-eyed woman in a tabard.

'Love for our fellow human beings.' Felix squints aggressively.

It wasn't till I ended up in hospital that I realised there are people living in this vacuum-packed limbo between life and death. Not knowing if it'll be months or years before they get to return to that world of tube journeys, nightclubs, and supermarkets. Sometimes I feel like I'm no longer even human, I'm the subject of some sadistic medical experiment, or some extra-terrestrial under observation, unable to cope with earth's atmosphere. I have to keep tying my headscarf in new styles and keep sticking new constellations of glitter onto my face to retain some part of my identity. Keep reading my books about famous queens and watching increasingly obscure vintage diva movies. It's a hard point to be at, where the journey I've come on is as long and as full of white sheets and nausea as the journey ahead of me.

I notice how much more relaxed Felix is now when he visits me. He's slumped in the chair with his shiny geometric pattern sleeves rolled up.

'I didn't know you had tattoos.' I lean toward him.

The tattoos on his arms look like they were done with a cocktail stick while riding public transport. He's got a gay-arrow-symbol, something that looks like a squashed rat, and a smiley face bleeding into the skin at the crook of his elbow. On his other arm there's a wonky, badly coloured in Felix the cat.

'My ex-boyfriend did that when he was on acid,' he says.

'That figures.' I adjust the sweaty creased up sheet underneath me. 'Y'know you can get those fixed by a professional.'

'I like my crappy tattoos,' he complains, but doesn't seem to take offence. 'It's just a body. I don't mind it being a bit Frankensteiny.'

'It's not just a body. It's your body.'

'Some collection of atoms I call my body.'

I laugh at his blasé philosophy. But I think about my worries when they put the port in. How I'd have an ugly little scar under my once perfect unblemished ID magazine shoulder blade.

He asks me about where I've travelled as a club-kid. I tell him about taking MDMA in expensive New York hotel bars while dressed in a gold transparent burqa. Ending up in some recording studio in the Bronx full of rats. Getting the Paris metro covered head to toe in glitter and sequins. Getting thrown out of a boutique fancy dress shop in Harajuku on diazepam. We end up playing heads and bodies. We each draw a section of the body on a piece of paper and then fold it up and pass it on. When I unfold mine, it's got my head but with a lot of extra eyes. I can tell it's my head because Felix is a much better artist than his tattoos would suggest. The body has massive breast implants, nipple tassels, and a corset; I drew that. Then four hairy octopus tentacles and four alien Alexander McQueen platforms melting into the floor. He's tearing the paper out of the notebook for a second round, when I hear voices outside. Helium balloons of children's TV characters enter the room attached to some of my best friends. Together during daylight hours, they look like a mismatched glam rock band.

'Oh, you've already got a visitor.' Kitten holds a balloon of the pink power ranger.

'Hi,' I croak.

'We brought you balloons,' Bobbi states the obvious, his buzzcut now dyed neon yellow.

'Who's your friend?' Milo asks.

Felix sits up, looking uncertain.

'This is Felix,' I say, wondering whether I'm embarrassed by his presence at my bedside.

'Did I see you at Science Fiction drinking out of the tap in the bathroom,' Milo asks Felix.

'How you doing hun?' Asks James.

'Don't ask. Tell me what you've been up to.' I reply, seeing myself as they must see me: pallid, alien, and thin, wearing an old lady scarf that Felix gave me around my bald head.

'I think I'm gonna go.' Felix pulls his bag onto his shoulder.

'Okay, see ya,' I say uneasily, almost as if they'd walked in on us having sex. He bangs into Tamsin's *Minnie Mouse* balloon on the way out.

'Who was that?' Asks Tamsin, attempting to present herself as a boy, with a lot of foundation and the t-shirt of a metal band she's never listened to.

'Felix,' I say as if his name is explanation enough.

'I saw him in Science Fiction drinking out of the tap,' Milo reminds us. He's posing against the radiator with two helium balloons, one of a unicorn, and one of a princess. 'Where shall I put these?'

'Tie them over there. In the get-well-soon corner.' I wag my finger limply towards the cards and half dead flowers.

Kitten sits on the foot of my bed and is just about to say something, but Tamsin continues, 'Wait, that wasn't the guy with the ten-pound note. It was, wasn't it!'

'What ten-pound note?' Kitten budges up closer towards me.

'This guy wanted to buy Cosmo a drink and wrote his number on a ten-pound note ... So, you called him?' Tamsin raises the bit of skin where her drawn on eyebrow would normally reside.

'He sort of invited himself. He brings me biscuits,' I croak this summary of our relationship out, as if I'm under police questioning.

'We brought you balloons,' Milo echoes what Bobbi said a few seconds ago, tying the unicorn impractically to the window latch.

'Tell me stuff.' I pull my dressing gown closed.

'Rocco died,' Tamsin shouts. '—He didn't really, but his night did.'

'Ash is hosting this night at *Pegasus*,' Milo pipes up.

'That little place,' I sneer. 'Anybody go?'

There's a meek display of all the hands around the room. But I notice how unbothered I am by this little twink, superseding me.

'There was this amazing rave in an old bed shop some people are squatting in Peckham.' Bobbi plays with the streamers on his balloon. 'I got my tunnel caught on someone's bondage harness.' He turns so I can see his ear which now comprises of two dangling slices of scabbed over earlobe.

'Shit,' I say looking closer.

'It was a good night.' Kitten leans toward me. 'Except for this one, wandering around covered in blood.'

'They still have all the display beds,' says James. 'I got some good photos of everyone on ketamine on this giant bed.'

'How's your new housemate?' I ask him.

'Boring,' James whispers. 'He doesn't like the shopping channel!'

At first, I thought they were calling them *chicken buses* because people occasionally bring chickens on them. Now that I'm squashed into a row of six people, bumping about on vertical mountainous terrain, I realise why. The dumpy local woman next to me, dressed in bright traditional fabrics pushes me further into Felix. Contorted against the window, he smiles at me like this is all part of the experience. The woman is being squashed by an old man with a white cowboy hat and a stick. She moves part of her giant plastic basket onto my lap. It's filled with something that smells like cheese, wrapped in colourful local fabrics.

'We shouldn't have sold the car,' I mutter at Felix.

He's looking at the idyllic views of tree-covered hills and volcanoes. The midday sun boiling the sides of our faces through the window.

'Do you really want to be driving down a mountain?' He asks.

I nod emphatically, scratching a mosquito bite on my arm.

Felix turns back to the window, his horned hat on. 'I remember it being you who wanted to sell the car.'

'I was paranoid. I thought we were being followed.' I try to remember more of my motives. I look around at all the women in traditional dress, and the men in t-shirts and caps like they're all skateboarders. The only other foreigners are two really white girls with feathers in their blonde hair. They look like female members of the Manson family.

'It was too weird to be a coincidence though,' I tell myself as much as him.

The coach hits a rock and the lady squashes right into me, jamming the plastic basket into my ribs then mumbling something in a local dialect.

'The world is pretty weird,' replies Felix and squeezes my arm affectionately.

'You were freaked out the first time it happened,' I squint at him. 'How come you're fine now?'

He does a deep spiritual breath, taking in all the musty odour of the bus. 'I don't want to spend my life worrying.'

I can't tell if he's suggesting I stop worrying. I return to the topic I really want to complain about, 'We should've got the good bus.'

He holds up some nuts in a plastic bag for me to eat. I put the nuts in my mouth and almost bite my tongue as the bus hits another stone. I see someone's bag fly off the roof into oncoming traffic. We have to pull over, onto the edge of a precipice so the bus driver can go out and retrieve it. I give Felix a long look, meant to psychically transfer the message, *that could've been our bags*.

'You can choose the transport next time.' He pats my arm.

I'm not sure if he's trying to placate me or wind me up further. I look down at my arm and realise I've scratched the mosquito bite so much that it bled.

When I'm back at my parents, I think about Felix. I wonder what we'll talk about during this last course of chemotherapy. The hospital phoned me up to tell me my sister was a match for my bone marrow transplant. I phone her from the big brown leather sofa by the television.

'Don't worry about it,' she says. 'What kind of person would I be if I didn't?'

'Still, thank you,' I say.

Next, I'm back in Dr Kyffin's somewhat austere, land-art filled office with my parents. There are blood tests, another needle in my spine, fitness tests, even a psychiatrist, with thinning black hair and a brown leather case.

'Have you had any mental health problems in the past?' He asks.

I think about running around Soho in a thong and a pompadour wig but answer, 'No.'

'You'll have to take steroids which may cause weight gain.'

'That sounds annoying,' I tell him.

My new Hospital room has faux mahogany cupboards and magnolia walls. Glass doors, which with the press of a button fill up with opaque steam to shield you from the rest of the ward.

'Aren't you cold in here?' Felix asks, having just taken off his yellow duffle coat.

'I'm off chemo for a few days because I've got a temperature, so they left the heating off. It's a big hospital bed, get in, if you want.'

'Okay.' He undoes his *Doc Martens*.

When he gets in, we're squashed arm to arm. In my head I question what I'm doing, breaking our little chair and bed set up. He makes this dweeby smile at me to cut the tension.

'You have got a temperature!' He says.

'I know.' I sigh. 'This is supposed to be the recovery part of the journey.'

'Well, have some of my good health,' he says and grips onto my shoulder and makes a "*zzz*" sound.

'Thanks,' I drone. 'Tell me one of your stories. I'm not good at conversation today.'

'We could draw stuff with our eyes closed.' He reaches over the edge of the bed for his bag.

'No, tell me one of your stories.'

'What kind of story?' He wriggles, trying to get comfortable.

'I don't know, about taking acid in an old people's home.'

'Okay, that didn't happen,' he smiles, and his far apart eyes try to convey some message that maybe words can't. 'Do you want a sad one or a happy one?'

'I don't know, both?'

'Okay.' he muscles down into the bed like this is going to be a long story. Though when he's got comfortable it becomes evident, he hasn't even thought of which story he's going to tell me. 'Okay ... My favourite resident in the old people's home was this well-to-do woman. I mean she acted upper-class so most of the carers didn't like her. Her Alzheimer's wasn't as bad as a lot of the other patients. She just did things like, you'd bring her food, and she wouldn't touch it, then an hour later she'd say "*Why'd you bring me cold food? This place is a living hell.*"' he imitates a haughty British accent. 'She liked saying things were "*a living hell.*" She always talked to me about living in the south of Spain, and would say, "*I don't know why we ever left.*" Sometimes she'd accidentally say things in Spanish to people – Oh, you need to know what she looked like, she had big reddish-orange hair with a big grey parting and lots of silk scarves.'

'Nice,' I laugh.

Outside the opaque glass doors, someone is dragging something on wheels down the corridor.

'She looked like the kind of elderly woman, who goes on a cruise holiday around the Greek islands and isn't very impressed by it. Anyway, she'd teach me Spanish while she was watching her food go cold – Hablo un poquito Espanol, y ella es mi maestra.'

'What does that mean?' I ask. His face is close enough to mine that if I turn to look at him, we'd be touching. So, I just give him a sideways glance.

'I can speak some Spanish and she was my teacher.'

'So, what happened to her?'

'She was forgetting everything while she was teaching me. One day she'd basically taught me as much Spanish as she could remember. Then she remembered less than me. Then I got sacked and went to live in a beach hut.'

'That's sad,' I say, strangely moved by the story.

'So is Titanic.' He looks at me deadpan and we almost touch. His dark brown eyes, joking and serious. Then we're kissing. He presses his warm lips against mine a few times like neither of us are sure if it's okay. He moves his tongue against mine and then against the inside of my lip biting down lightly. I actually didn't see this coming.

'No biting, I've got ulcers,' I say in the place of a sexual come-on.

'Sure.' His face blurs. He grips onto my arm, fingers under my t-shirt sleeve.

I push my hand across his back. Feel the fabric of his acrylic shirt and his lips moving against mine. I pull away a moment. 'I shouldn't be kissing you. I've got a low immune system.'

'I've always got a low immune system.' He stays holding onto my arm.

'Yeah of course. Do you get ill often?'

'When I get ill, I get really ill. But I'm careful, I wear a coat.' He does this cheesy red lipped smile at me. 'Tell me something about you.'

'Okay ...' I think, my hand on his leg. I look at the haphazard arrangement of his eyebrow hairs. 'Okay. When I first ran away to London, I got this job flyering for *The Peach*. Walking up and down Old Compton Street wearing a lot of glitter and sequins. I thought the job was kind of beneath me. But it was all part of this rebellion against my parents.' I edge back a bit, so my face isn't right up against his, and pull the blanket to our waists. 'Most of the guys flyering on the street were kind of youth club gays: rainbow wristbands and purple emo hair. Then there were these two muscle-twinks, who flyered for *BoyBar*, in silver hot pants and angel wings. They had blonde hair and looked like twins. They were seventeen so they shouldn't really have been working there. They'd mince about with the *BoyBar* logo sprayed onto their chests.' I question why I'm telling him this lengthy anecdote so soon after we started making out. I kiss him.

'Yeah,' he says into my mouth, prompting me to continue.

'I remember them making some bitchy comments about my drag. They'd lord it over all the other flyerers on the street because they were better looking and more naked. I almost told the police they were underage. But I was underage too. Anyway, I had a better idea.'

He leans his head against the head of the bed, listening to me.

'I had these six-inch platform glitter boots. I basically stuck on a thong, covered my entire body in glitter and wore a massive pair of glittery angel wings. That night everyone went to *The Peach* and they gave me a job on the door.'

He laughs. 'Is there a moral to the story?'

'Yeah, I think so.' I look at him, wondering what the moral is. '– I'm not tall and I'm not muscly, but I can out dress anyone.'

Felix looks at me like he's just figured out the right combination of twists and turns to get all my coloured squares to fit into place. The look annoys me slightly, but I carry on kissing him. To me, he's like a Rubik's Cube that has more colours than it has sides. I've never understood Felix's intentions. In the outside world, I'd assume he wanted to fuck, but in here he's become enigmatic. I'd got to thinking maybe I was just a kooky game or an extended good deed. But no, it seems maybe he wanted me all along and somehow, he managed to make me want him too. I wonder if he knew what he was doing. If, like he said the first time he came to visit me, he imagined it hard enough that it actually happened. I didn't think my jaded little heart still did this kind of thing. Maybe it's the chemo messing with my hormones. But I don't have much time to ruminate on it because after that kiss I start to get really ill. Maybe because of the kiss I start to get ill. So ill that I don't have the strength to blame him.

I go to sleep with a slight temperature and a half-eaten meal on a tray and wake up paralysed by sickness. The kind that makes you feel like if you move a single digit you're going to throw up. Like when you're hungover and on a comedown, then you take a whole load of ketamine on top of all that. The room fills with doctors and nurses monitoring things, murmuring at me, their faces blurring into the lights. Their hands are on me, injecting something into my port. I'm back there in the UFO, being probed by strange annoying creatures dressed in navy blue. I feel like my soul is about to leave my body, as if it's just clinging to the throbbing pools around my thyroid and stomach and temples. Then I'm engulfed in a hot sticky blackness that whispers in my ear, "*You're going to die in this expensive hospital room. No more thoughts, no more memories, no more Kyle. Just emptiness.*"

I hear my mum's voice in the darkness telling one of the nurses, 'He was asking for someone called Felix.'

'Oh, his friend with the long brown hair,' says one of the nurses.

I don't even remember asking.

I lay there, my brain throbbing my skin burning up, thinking about unrelated things, World War two, a Madonna concert I was forced to go to, a drag queen's Siamese cats. All these things seem inextricably related and also evocative of my current state. Then Felix is there.

'I'm gonna die,' I hear my voice whine to the shadowy figure sat next to my bed.

'You're not going to die.' I feel the impact of his hand somewhere on the quilt.

'If you felt what I feel –' I hear my voice crumbling and distant.

There's a long pause where he just leaves his hand there, a flat weight on the sheet covering my arm.

'– I thought we'd get to meet up outside one day,' I add.

'We will,' his voice echoes like someone turned up the reverb.

'I'm dying.' I can't manage much more than the repetition of this grim reality.

'You're not dying,' his voice tells me, soft and close, almost convincing. 'I know you're not dying.'

'How?'

'I'm a bit psychic remember.'

'You're not,' I cough. I can't stop whooping and coughing. I cough so hard I almost wretch up some bile.

'I didn't tell you before 'cos you wouldn't believe me. But I know you're not going to die from this.'

I make a random grunt of disavowal.

'I'm gonna stay here a while,' he says. 'I'll just be in the corner reading.'

After a pause, I look at him and he comes into focus, his moles, the pores on his nose, his eyes a deep animal brown.

'Thanks.' I move my arm toward his hand. 'Can you get the bucket? I think I'm going to be sick now.'

He hesitates like he thought I was going to say something else. Maybe I was. But now my eyes blur and my throat spasms, I feel the bile surging hot and acrid down my throat. It burns my mouth as I push myself up to be sick into the cardboard bucket he's holding.

'Water,' I mumble. The orange phlegm is resting at the side of the bucket. I hear him go and get some from the tap. Everything has an echo as if we're in a church. I lay there, head sideways, mouth open like a dead fish. Not caring that the remainder of the bile is seeping out onto the pillow.

'Should I get a nurse?' He puts the water near my mouth.

I limply grasp the plastic cup. 'Maybe.'

Later, when the nurse has gone, I see him there in a chair in the corner of the room. Silhouetted against the window. He's reading a hardback book he said he got from *The Red Cross Shop*, titled, "*Age of Explorers.*" Maybe hours, maybe minutes later, I open my eyes and he's gone. There's something different about the room. Lit only by the streetlights and a few LEDs on monitors, there's a strange stillness. A silence you could almost swim in. I lean my head back into the pillow and notice some of the rawness in my brain and throat has gone. I said it was silent but looking up at the dark tiles of the ceiling, I hear something. I can't tell if it's a tone like a singing bowl or if it's a feeling inside my body. Then the

111

lights flash, they stutter on and off as if short-circuiting. Then there's something else in the room with me. I push myself backwards into the headboard. It looms over me, flickering like a hologram in shades of gold and pearl. A face, I can't tell if it's male or female, young or old. It holds its hands out as if it's reaching for me. It illuminates the room with a light like the walls of a swimming pool. Multiple pairs of thick feathered wings splay out from its back, shifting and undulating silently. My breath isn't leaving my lungs. It opens its lips as if to say something, but the only sound is the chime, I feel it like a vibration running through my body. Then it's gone and the room is dark again, just the fading negative of a face on my retina. I exhale in a quick forced breath. There's only a smell left, a bit like incense, a bit like the air after a foot of snow. I get out of bed for the first time in more than two days. My feet solid on the cold laminate floor, everything suddenly unfamiliar in how real it is. I slide open the door and see the large, framed photo of a spiral of stones in the sea and look down the corridor to the nurse's station. Everything is uncanny in how solid it is under the strip lighting. I get a strange urge to touch the magnolia walls to see if they're real. A nurse gets up from behind the nurse's station and comes over to ask me if I'm okay.

The air is thick with humidity and mosquitoes. I get out my big industrial repellent and attempt to re-spray my whole body while still walking.

'Are you sure that's good for the environment?' He asks.

'No.' I stand still, spraying my bitten and burnt legs. 'But it's good for not getting Malaria.' I feel like civilization is a long way behind us, the buses, street markets and hostels. Our Western clothes and bottled water seem out of place, faced with dense overgrowth alive with animals and oversize insects. I slap a mosquito the size of a spider on Felix's neck.

'Ow!'

'Mosquito,' I tell him.

'Sorry, I didn't think there'd be so many.' He's still wearing his horned hat, now a bit more bedraggled, missing some beads and fringe.

'As long as I can spray my whole body in poison every few minutes, I'm quite happy.' Despite my shoes being covered in dust and my t-shirt stained with sweat and jungle dirt, I am actually quite happy.

'What's that? More ruins?' Felix points up ahead.

'What?' I look around and then see something big and colourful amongst the trees.

We've seen roadside shrines here, little alcoves with a few candles and chipped statuettes of the virgin Mary or Jesus. But this is something else, a painted hut about the size of a shed, fronted with alcoves and concentric arches painted in bright clashing colours. Inside the alcoves are gaudy figurines of saints and angels, flanked by red tribute candles and the remains of tea lights.

'This is the best shrine ever!' Felix exclaims. He stands in the middle of the dirt track and just looks at it. The shrubs and vines behind it creep across its multicoloured roof and enmesh its arches. Little bits of mirrored glass glint in the sun.

'Have you got that torch?' I ask, looking at the dim interior and the concrete floor.

'Yeah.' He fishes about inside the pocket of his tie-dyed shorts. He hands me his keyring with a torch on and gets an "*I heart Bogota*" lighter out of the other pocket.

'Wow,' I murmur when we're both huddled inside.

The walls are alive with figures and flowers bursting out of the stucco. In the torchlight, the colours are blues and purples and reds. Some of the paint so thick it stands out from the wall. The details taper off into a small indoor sky, dotted with mirrored glass that glints in the torchlight like stars.

'This is amazing,' says Felix. 'How many people do you think get to see this?' He lights candles in the alcoves lining the two side walls.

There are more alcoves, with hand crafted angels inside, in a folk-art style. I don't say anything about burnt angel figurines in our hotel rooms. I squeeze the thought out of my mind and flick the torch from the back of Felix's tie-dye t-shirt to the main altar. There's a large angel figurine with a skull for a head, wearing what looks like a wedding dress. The alcove behind it erupts with fading fake flowers, and in front of it tealights and dusty photos.

114

'Oopps,' whispers Felix, accidentally spilling some wax while lighting a candle.

I shine the torch on the picture frames on the altar. Most seem to be of the same woman. Someone's mother, maybe grandmother. Pudgy with fluffy black coiffured hair. In most of the pictures, she's frowning.

'I think someone built this for her.' I turn the torch off and watch the candlelight make the colours on the walls flicker and sway. 'She's either a saint or her husband really wanted to do some painting.'

'Somebody liked her a lot.' Felix pulls his legs up into a meditation position, balanced on the bench. 'Do you mind if we're quiet for a bit?'

'Sure,' I whisper.

He closes his eyes, scrunches up his face. His expression straining to be placid.

'I don't think I ever told you ...' he says, snapping me out of a brief sleepy trance.

'Yeah?' I stifle a yawn.

'My mum used to say she was visited by angels. She was obsessed.' This is maybe the first time he's told me something about his childhood since waking up on that beach. 'Everything in our house was to do with angels, angel calendars, angel shrines, angel ornaments. She was trying to recreate the smell of an angel using essential oils.'

'Did she say what they looked like?' I lean forward in this multicoloured confession booth.

'Yeah, I forget though. I was young. I remember her saying they had more than one pair of wings.'

'Felix,' I whisper. There's silence except for the distant squawk of a bird. 'When I was really ill in Harley Street, after you came to visit, I thought I saw an angel – it had lots of pairs of wings.'

115

'Really?' His mouth is in a little 'o' shape. He comes across to my bench to join me, so we're both sitting next to each other, looking at the flickering multicoloured scene on the wall. 'You didn't tell me.'

'I didn't tell anyone. I thought it was a hallucination. I'm not a spiritual kind of person. I like high heels and Cher.'

'I think you can be spiritual and like *high heels and Cher* ... How did it happen?'

I tell him all about it while he sits there, legs pressed against mine.

'... I don't think that's a coincidence,' he utters.

'No.' I look at the painted birds, bits of tile glinting in their wings. 'What does it mean?'

'Does it have to mean something?' He pulls his mouth to the side. 'I always thought magic was an of-the-moment kind of thing. Like Deja-vu.'

'I think it means something.'

When we leave the shrine, I really notice how busy with insects and how sticky the air is. I wait a few minutes before bringing up what we're probably both thinking about,

'Those burnt angel ornaments we found in the hotel rooms. Did you think that was strange? You know, your mum being obsessed with angels?'

'Yeah, it did freak me out a bit.' He looks up at the parting in the foliage above us.

'Why didn't you say anything?'

'It didn't seem like the time.' He shrugs and kicks at the dirt.

'You don't think that had anything to do with your mum?'

'You think she's haunting us?'

'I'd hope your mum would have more sense than to leave bits of charcoal in our beds.'

He rubs against me. I feel very close to him right now. But that closeness reminds me that now his memory is back, I need to talk to him about what happened.

One night, I'm standing in the freezing cold outside the unit in my black fur lined dressing gown. It's a late afternoon in late November, and the streetlights are already on. The neat angular central London houses look like a film set. For this moment I don't care about the cold hanging static in the air, it's making me feel alive. I've made a decision that I never thought to make before. That I'm going to live. I'm going to have the bone marrow transplant, and I'm going to get better. This all sounds cliché even in my head, but I've got so much more life to live. I think of all the places I still have to visit and the things I still have to do, and I think about Felix. I look up at the orange light-pollution-sky. The cold breeze stinging my legs. The UFO lights of an airplane pass into a cloud. Before the future seemed predictable, maybe even depressing, tonight, it's a mystery.

My parents come to watch the bone marrow transplant even though I've told them it's going to be an anti-climax. My mum is set up to narrate the whole process,

'So, this is the bone marrow,' she begins, when the nurses bring the bag into the room. But that's about all she manages because that's about all there is to the operation. So, while we watch the dark red fluid sliding from the drip into my arm my mum opts for reminiscing about my childhood. The same things she usually reminisces about. The time I made a mountain of food at a wedding buffet, and my grandpa made me eat it all. When I cut my face falling out of a tree and refused to look in the mirror for a week. Me marauding the house in a towel and makeup pretending to be Tutankhamun. She asks my dad with each anecdote if he remembers it, and he gives a brief affirmative nod. When the nurse hooks up my second IV, my parents say their goodbyes. I feel like I should be doing something special to mark the occasion, but I can't think of anything, so I just turn on the tv and watch some episodes of *Sex in the City*.

'I'm not going to live as long,' I tell Felix drowsily, my mouth dry.

'How does that make you feel?' He asks. He's lying in bed next to me wearing a ringer t-shirt emblazoned with the word "*Daytripper*."

'A bit annoyed,' I shrug. I've been stuck in this room in isolation for the last four days, two of them with headaches and nausea. Now I'm just very sleepy with a dry mouth. 'I always said I was going to die at fifty. It's just now that might be the reality.'

'Well, this doesn't last forever either.' He gestures to the place in his chest where his transplanted heart is.

'I never asked you about that.' I swallow. 'How long do heart transplants last?'

'There's a guy still alive that got one in 1982. And I've got a pretty good one.'

'But what's the average?' I look at him concerned.

'About ten years,' he says.

I feel a blockage in my already musty throat.

Felix notices my consternation and adds, 'I'm not planning on dying anytime soon. If anything goes wrong, they can always –'

He mimes having his chest cut open and having another heart put in.

'But how does that make you feel? That you might only have – ' I do some flustered mathematics looking down at the quilt, '– Twenty years left.'

'I'm okay with it. I'm busy being here with you, now. Not being in a coffin twenty years in the future. How does it make me feel?' He muses. 'It makes me want to travel the world.'

'I wouldn't mind running away somewhere.'

'Come with me.' He wraps his arm around mine as if we might leave right now. 'I still have some money from my mum, and that's what I want to spend it on.'

'Maybe.' I don't want to commit to anything. I can tell how important this is to him. I've noted the failed trip to America and the books on world exploration. 'Where'd you want to go?'

'Oh, San Francisco, finally, and Area 51, you know the secret government base where they're hiding aliens.'

'I thought "*secret*" meant you can't go there,' I croak.

'There's this motel near there called *The Little A 'le'inn*. I want to go to South America too, see some ruins, take ayahuasca in the rainforest.'

'Of course.'

'The Sahara Desert, Morocco, Ancient Egypt. Oh, Greece too, Nepal, maybe India.'

'You want to go to a lot of places.' I stop him.

He catches his breath. 'Where do you want to go?'

'I don't know. Anywhere exotic where they don't hate gays.'

'There's a Greek island for gays called Mykonos. Jackie O used to go there."

We're all sat around the edge of this big exotic looking hut built for tourists to take hallucinogens in. Everyone's wrapped in patterned blankets, listening to this girl with dreadlocks talking about her dead brother.

'— I saw his ghost. It came into my room one night and just stood there with bandages on his wrists, as solid as I was.' She has Aladdin pants and a kaftan blouse and little trinkets tied to the end of her dreadlocks.

The People here are mostly Caucasian, dressed like they're from some try-hard post-apocalyptic society. I'm worried that the fact we're surrounded by white trash hippies means that we're probably also white trash hippies. There's tea lights and a not entirely pleasant incense that the shaman is wafting around the room with some dried leaves. Her face heavily wrinkled, a large pipe resting in her hand and a beaded hat over her black hair. I wonder if she's listening to the girl or thinking about what to make for lunch.

'— I looked at the trees and they were made of energy, and it was like I knew he'd gone back to that energy, and I was a part of that energy too. I felt everything that separates me from him dropping away.'

I look behind the girl at the light, fading through the emerald-green foliage. I look up at the roof made of leaves supported by long thin logs in a geometrical arrangement. The peaceful atmosphere reminds me not to be such a judgmental bitch.

'—And ... my little brother ... I didn't need him to be here anymore ... physically anyway,' her voice is stifled. 'It was okay for him not to be here. I could ...' she lets in a moaning inhale of breath, '... accept it.'

I refocus on her face, now red and blotchy.

'I'm finished,' she says.

'Thank you,' the shaman whispers in a thick dry accent, and after a pause begins singing something from the back of her throat and wafting the incense with some dried leaves. When she's finished, people wearing Aztec blankets get up to talk to the girl. She's still crying. Felix gets up and does an exaggerated yogic stretch. I figure now is the time to talk to him, while everyone is being honest, and before I think better of it.

'We need to talk.' I squeeze his arm.

'Sure.' He smiles, all casual travelling hippie, his hair tied back, a bandana around his neck and his orange geometric pattern shirt unbuttoned.

'Outside.'

'Okay,' he agrees, finding his sandals.

The bit I remember most from the trip last night, is climbing up the ladder to the treehouse where we're staying. The whole forest seemed to be alive, surging with glowing dots of electricity, forming fractals and patterns. The treehouse was dark, I felt like there were other living things there with me. I saw their faces in the dark, like Aztec masks, angular and reptilian. I felt the sleeping bag, the fabric like liquid in my hand. I sat down on it, cross legged like Felix does, eyes closed. The faces were still there behind my eyelids, growing, splitting into fractal patterns.

'Come with us ... Follow us,' I heard them whisper. The patterns undulating.

I got a feeling of vertigo, and everything started juddering. Then I opened my eyes, and I wasn't in the treehouse anymore. I was in the corner of the hospital room, with Felix lying in bed, the lights dimmed, his body littered with wires. I tried to move but I couldn't. I was stuck there, looking at his body.

I sit on a wooden bench facing into the darkening rainforest. He sits next to me, our knees touching.

'Tell me.' He prods me with his foot.

'We never really spoke about your heart attack.'

'We spoke about it a lot in America.'

'I mean.' I swipe a mosquito off my leg. 'I mean, why it happened.'

'Um,' he exhales.

I look into those big alien eyes. 'I don't know how to put this. But were you trying to ...'

'—Kill myself?' He finishes my sentence.

'Yeah?' I look into the dense translucent green of the jungle, the sound of strange insects and birds. 'Were you?'

'I was being reckless. I was drinking too much. I wasn't taking all my pills. But I don't think I was trying to kill myself.'

'You've got a heart transplant.' I look at the thick scar on his chest. 'Isn't drinking alcohol and not taking your pills more or less the same as trying to kill yourself?'

'Maybe.' He bites his lip, not looking away. 'Maybe.'

I didn't notice at first but he's crying. Felix cries silently, there's no loud sobs or moans, just tears forming on the rim of his eye and rolling down his cheek in silence. He's the only person who when he cries, I want to cry too. I hold him, the smell of his unwashed hair and his sweat and the sweet earthy forest.

'Why are you crying?'

'Because I regret it.' He sniffs. 'You know how I say I don't regret anything. Well, I regret that. I regret what I put you and my grandma through.'

'It's okay.' I keep holding him, squashing my head into his.

He takes some breaths in and smudges his tears away with his shirt sleeve. The Shaman has stopped singing, and people are leaving the huge, thatched hut.

'We're really good right now,' I tell him. 'I just need to know, if anything does go wrong between us, you won't do anything like that again.'

'No, I promise,' he mouths bitterly. 'I can feel myself changing.' He looks into my eyes with uncertainty at what it is he might be changing into.

I feel rotten. Like something so rotten its changed colour and started to meld with the surface beneath it. My body is sweaty, thin and fat in all the wrong places, a rash stippled across my forehead. It's one of those transitory states that from a doctor's point of view is probably a step towards health, but while you're in it is just annoying. My mum is having some inane battle in the hallway with a very large expensive bit of tinsel. I know exactly what she's doing because she's narrating the whole thing, using pretend curse words like *shucks* and *drat*. My dad seems to have decided that buying the tree is the end of his festive duties this year and can occasionally be seen in corridors eating little things like nuts and *Quality Streets*. I squash the sides of my pillow over my ears, so I don't have to hear her questioning why *they didn't put any blasted hooks on the end of this thing*. The fairy lights on my beauty table go out of focus, and I let my thoughts wander. There's a distant knock at the door which my mum answers.

She positions herself in my bedroom doorway. 'There's someone at the door for you.' And in a whispered tone, as if they might hear her from down the stairs and halfway across the house, 'He's dressed very strangely.'

'That's my boyfriend,' I tell her, and she gives me a look of concern. More concern than when my temperature was above one hundred.

Then Felix is in my bedroom, wearing some strange atrocity of a hat which completely clashes with everything else he's wearing, including itself. It's made of neon green wool with two points that hang down over his shoulders, an orange pom-pom on the end of one point, and a pink pom-pom on the end of the other.

'Heey.' His mouth stretches into a broad smile upon seeing me. He notices me noticing his hat and explains. 'I was at a hat sale.'

'Hat sale?' I rasp, unfamiliar with this concept.

'It wasn't just hats, it was a theatre clearance. But I only bought hats.' His eyes dart around the fixtures and fitting of my room. 'Here's your present!' He pulls it out from his yellow duffle coat. It's wrapped up in purple crepe paper and plastic ribbon. It jingles.

'Is it a hat?'

'Just open it.' He rocks on his heels in happy anticipation.

I limply tearing off the crepe paper. It's some sort of Chinese crown with intricate patterned beadwork, lined with pom poms. Beads and coins and fancy metalwork hanging down. He sits down on the bed next to me.

'You always get amazing presents!' I put it on over my stunted smattering of hair. 'I'll have to make a Chinese-style costume to go with it.'

'I think it's from Norway actually,' he says, untangling some of the beads.

'I think I've got something for you. But you'll have to find them.'

'Them?'

'There's a plastic box at the back of the bed. It's got headdresses on top. You've gotta move all the boxes to get to it though.'

He starts pulling all my wardrobes out from under the bed. He lifts a lid to see a tangled mass of bangles and cuffs and tries on a long gold spikey arm plate. I half cough half-laugh at his look of glee on seeing the amount of costume items I have.

'Is this it?' His torso is halfway under my bed. He hauls out a big see-through plastic box of tangled glitter fabric and feathers.

'Yeah. There's a pair of platforms in there. You'll know which ones.'

He pulls out a burlesque feather headpiece entangled with a Thai crown and then a pair of superhero platforms in red and silver glitter.

'Not those,' I croak.

He pulls out an embossed brown seventies platform shoe by the laces.

'Those.'

He holds them, with a look of disbelief, 'You're giving these to me!?'

'They're your decade,' I snort.

He jumps on me in gratitude causing me to exhale phlegm.

'Is your friend staying for dinner?' My mum calls up while I'm in my pajamas giving Felix a tour of my wardrobe.

My immediate reaction is to say no. But I turn to Felix who nods vigorously.

'Yeah, sure,' I let out a husky shout, and continue telling Felix about the pearl-encrusted playsuit I'm holding. '– I made it for the Met Ball. It has some horns covered in pearls that went with it. But they're somewhere broken in a taxi in Paris'

'What's this?' He asks, picking up a trophy with a little bronze figure in swimming trunks. He's one of those people who come to your house and pick everything up.

'Oh that ... I was captain of the school swim team.'

'Really?' He squints at me.

'My dad wanted me to be an Olympic swimmer. But –' I hold up a gold winged headpiece from my Hermes phase.

'I assumed you were the school gay,' he says.

'That too, but I didn't get bullied so badly because I did sports.' I swap his bobble hat for the gold feathered headpiece. 'Were you the gay kid.'

'I was the gay kid, the freak kid, the long hair kid, the everything kid.'

'You didn't like school?'

'I want to go back there –' he says '– with a baseball bat.'

'I left when I was sixteen.' I hold up the leotard that goes with the hat, gold plates on the chest, abdominals and crotch. '—It was boring.'

'We should wear these down to dinner!' Felix holds the gold plated leotard to his body.

'My parents have no sense of humour,' I mutter standing up. 'I wear sunglasses to dinner at the moment.'

Before we sat down at the table, I hadn't noticed that Felix was wearing a t-shirt with two giant magic mushrooms on it, with the words *"natural inspiration"* in bubble font. If this were a film, I imagine the camera would pan around our oval-shaped dining room table to show each person's expression. Me, with shaved peach fuzz hair and bug-eye sunglasses, picking at the Mushroom Kiev. Felix, cheek full of food with a large reproduction of a Cezanne landscape behind him, telling my mum the food is really good. My mum, trying not to look appalled at Felix's eating habbits and trying to think of a conversation starter. She almost says something, then thinks better of it. My dad is more interested in the food than any of this subtext. He'd possibly have a voice over of some internal monologue about a business deal.

'Do you do something creative like Kylian?' My mum begins.

'My life is kind of my art,' Felix says with food in his cheek.

'Oh, what do you do?' My mum asks faux-casually. Her chin on her palm, a bit of Kiev on the end of her fork, like the cover of a cookbook.

'He gets paid to pretend to be a Georgian zombie around London bridge.'

'Very funny.' My mum blinks at me. 'What do you really do?'

'That kind of is what I do. It's to advertise *The London Dungeon*.' Felix almost misses his mouth with a bit of mangetout. The comparison of my mum's eating and Felix's is hilarious to me.

'And you do this every day?' She asks.

'Three, four days a week.'

'Did you study acting?'

'I didn't study.' He pops a bit of Kiev into his mouth. 'I was a carer for old people in Brighton for a bit.'

'He lived in a beach hut by the sea,' I tell them proudly.

'I didn't think people lived in those.' My dad breaks his inner monologue to join us briefly.

'They don't. But houses are expensive in Brighton.' Felix chews enthusiastically. 'They're not quite long enough so I had to cut the end bit of the mattress off.'

'My goodness,' my mum says softly, as if I had brought a third world child to the table.

'I didn't notice you were wearing a t-shirt with giant magic mushrooms on,' I tell him heading back up the stairs.

'I don't think your parents cared.' He stretches his t-shirt out so he can look down at the psychedelic illustration. 'I got the feeling you wanted to shock them.'

'Yeah, maybe I did.' I flop down onto my bed.

He flops down next to me, and we just lay there for a while, my parents voices somewhere downstairs, almost inaudible.

'I got this feeling when we first met,' I tell him. 'Like we'd met before.'

'Me too,' he turns his head towards me, pushing his hair out of the way.

'You think we did?' I ask.

'No, I'd remember,' he insists, his face is squashed against the pillow. 'But I think things are connected in ways we don't see ... I mean the way we see things can't be the way they really are.'

'Why can't it?' I ask, lying on top of the duvet.

'Because it's filtered through our senses and our brains. Like colours, they're just our brains interpretation, they're not how it really is.' He kneads my hip like he's a cat.

'How is it really?'

'I don't know.' He makes a little bemused noise. 'Sometimes I imagine it like this giant floating disc with all the information that makes up the universe on. But it's much more jumbled than how we see it, and maybe some of the bits of you are closer to the bits of me than they seem. Does that make sense?'

'You think everything's on a giant CD-ROM.' I look across the pillow at him, sickly and sarcastic.

'It's a metaphor,' he tells me. 'I just think we're connected in ways we can't see.'

'I can see.' I look down at his hand near my crotch. 'You've taken a lot of acid though.'

'That's how I know nothing's real.' He looks at me, wide-eyed.

'Well, I'm real,' I hold his hand to show how solid I am.

Part 3

North Africa

I step out of the tube station into a premature summer's day, in an unfamiliar suburb of London. Two women walk past in big, folded fabric hats with a child in a suit. I'm wearing a PVC baseball cap over my patchy inch and a half of hair and a stripy short-sleeved polo neck. There's the hum of a lawnmower and the smell of freshly cut grass. Carbon dioxide and possibility in the air. I follow Felix's felt tip map to a cul-de-sac where the houses are squat brown semi-detacheds. A few bits of faded children's play equipment lie about in the street.

His grandma's house has a busy rectangle of garden with lots of daffodils and gnomes. The door knocker is shaped like a fist and there's stained glass suction cupped to the other side of the glass. Half a minute after knocking, I see a pastel-coloured dress on the other side moving stuff out of the way to open the door.

'Kyle?' Felix's grandma asks in a disarmingly girlish voice. Her long yellow-grey hair in a messy bun.

'Yeah!' I pull my mouth into a smile. 'Nice to meet you.'

Her handshake is a bit limp and distracted. She turns back into the house saying, 'Felix told me lots about you. Come in.'

I slip off my shoes and say, 'I like your garden.'

'Oh, thank you.' She rests her hand on a pile of magazines. 'Yes, I think it's important to have flowers.'

'And gnomes.' I step into the living room.

'Oh, well I like niknaks,' she says, looking around at all the angels and woodland creatures, crowding every surface like an overstocked charity shop. Something about the ornaments and the smell, like perfume and olive oil, makes me feel like I've been here before.

Felix appears on the stairs in a yellow and red striped t-shirt. He holds onto the banister and gives me that manic Cheshire-Cat smile, 'Wanna see my room?'

'I'm just taking this one in,' I tell them.

Felix's grandma surveys her trove of porcelain, murmuring, 'I've been planning a little spring clean.'

Felix snorts at this.

She passes him a jam jar with half-burnt joss sticks and says, 'These are yours.'

He gallops up the stairs like a kid who's excited to have a visitor. He holds the door open for me and wraps himself around me as I walk in. His room is like a museum maintained by a teenage stoner. Ethnic draperies and dusty cases of souvenirs. The wall behind his bed is covered in masks, dark wooden African masks, a gold Venetian mask, Japanese Noh masks, a couple of Indian dragon masks, a papier-mâché day of the dead skull. His desk seems to have everything except work on it. Fairy lights wrapped around cultural artefacts. A pyramid, a gold and black statuette of Osiris, a mini Persian rug, a Moroccan lamp, and an African carving with a big circular head.

'That's Africa,' he tells me.

'I thought you hadn't travelled much.'

'I haven't – most of this is charity shop.' He gestures to his collection of trans-continental tat. 'You know what I say, if you act like something has already happened, it will probably happen. I'll give you a tour – there's North America.' He gestures toward his windowsill, blind half rolled up. There's an out of scale approximation of New York, with an empire state building smaller than the statue of liberty. The statue of liberty has spawned two miniatures of itself. An old black and white photo of people from the 1800's next to a giant tree trunk, a half-evaporated snow dome with the Golden Gate Bridge inside, a shot glass with a highway 41 shield on it, and a miniature totem pole propping up a kitschy Las Vegas postcard covered in glitter. He shows me East Asia; a shelf attached with two big brackets to his orange bedroom wall. A length of the great wall, a red Japanese archway, and a geisha shaped like a Russian doll. Chinese good-luck trinkets on red strings are drawing-pinned to the shelf or weighed down by miniature pagodas.

In a cabinet, he shows me a special tribute to Norway. A straw reindeer held together with red ribbon, a curled 3D postcard of the Northern lights, some tiny multicoloured houses, and a Viking boat with a dragon at the helm. There's a troll ornament, a doll in blue and red native dress with discoloured skin, and some spider's web.

'How come Norway gets a whole shelf?'

'Um, because of the northern lights. Because of the Christmassy pagan vibe.' He reaches in for a postcard of a traditional Norwegian room with dark wood, embroidery, and fur rugs. 'If I ever go missing, look for me here.' He hands me the postcard. 'I bought most of this a long time ago. Actually, I got this the other day.' He picks up a papier-mâché day of the dead figurine. '*Red Cross shop.*'

'Cute,' I comment.

He puts it back on a rickety wooden stool, next to an Aztec figurine with a mouth full of jagged teeth. Propping up the stool is a giant Easter Island head, meant for garden decoration, and a half-empty bottle of tequila with a contorted Scorpion inside.

'You haven't been to any of these places?' I ask.

'Well ... no.' He shrugs. 'But there's this thing you can do when you really want something. You just surround yourself with it, imagine like it's already happened – down to the minutest detail. It's a way of sewing those seeds into the cosmos.'

'Which one's your favourite?'

'I don't know if it's my favourite. But this is good.' He reaches behind a model of a dusty NASA spaceship and a carving of an alien in the lotus position. He pulls out a carved wooden box, accidentally knocking over a globe with constellations marked on it. He leaves the globe on his crusty red carpet and opens the box. Inside is cotton wool and what looks like tiny bits of rock. He picks up a brown one between his thumb and finger. 'Guess what it is.'

'Um, a breadcrumb?'

'No, it's part of something.'

'I'm recovering from cancer; my brain isn't up to trivia.'

'It's Mars.' He flashes a look of pride at me with his thick eyebrows, 'the planet.'

I take it in my palm, and for a moment study his crumb of another world. 'I thought Mars was bigger?'

He rolls his eyes at my joke.

The three of us sit down at a small round table with lace effect laminate. Dinner is a vegetarian shepherd's pie and a salad with orange flowers in it. Felix's grandma dishes it up with a slightly arthritic shake while making apologies about the cheese on top being a bit burnt. Before she starts to eat, she looks at me concerned and says,

'Don't worry if you can't eat everything.'

'Has Felix been telling you about my health?'

'He doesn't tell me much. But you're looking very well.'

'My hairs still a bit –' I make an expression that shows how I feel about the mousey fluff under my baseball cap. 'But my appetites come back. Too much even.'

'You look like you've got space for a few puddings,' she tells me.

'I've been eating only puddings for the last three months.'

'Tell grandma what you do,' Felix says, his mouth full of lentils. 'She doesn't believe it's an actual job,'

'I kind of promote nightclubs and wear a lot of costumes.' I search my mind for a cross-generational description of my job.

'Like Felix?'

'No, I usually just walk around nightclubs dressed fancy. Make them seem more exciting than they actually are.'

'How do you get a job like that?' She asks as if a friend of hers might be interested.

'It's kind of ... you have to promote yourself. I've been in a few magazines, modelling.'

'Modelling.' She ogles and looks at Felix as if to say, she didn't know she was eating with royalty. 'Do you do the catwalk thing?'

'No, just photos – I'm short.' I glance at the Van Gogh print on the wall, going blue with age. 'Have you got any photo albums of Felix you're gonna show me?'

'Oh.' She fiddles with the fork handle. 'We haven't really.'

'Really?'

She looks distractedly at the few bits of sweet potato mash left on her plate.

'There was a fire,' Felix interjects. 'We kind of lost everything.'

'When? You never told me that.'

'When me and my mum lived in Brighton,' he stammers.

His grandma is still trying to compose herself by staring into her half-eaten plate of food. For a moment the wrinkles crisscrossing the corners of her mouth become more visible.

'Sorry.' I rub his foot under the table, realising I seem to have hit on exactly the wrong topic of conversation.

'You don't need to be sorry,' he says.

His grandma fumbles her way to her feet and mumbles, 'Trifle for dessert.'

After dinner, Felix's grandma tells me, 'There's a few photos on the mantelpiece.'

They're all in mismatched frames, one silver, one gold, one wood. There's a couple that must be Felix's mum. This ruddy-cheeked hippy woman with curly hair dyed maroon and lots of earrings.

'Here's baby Felix.' She hands me the framed photo to inspect. He's wrapped up in a yellow crochet blanket. The only hint that something's wrong is the tube going underneath the blanket.

'Cute,' I tell my boyfriend and his grandma. I get this feeling of loss from the photos. All the more tragic from the way they're posed next to the china birds. These cute little ornaments contrasted with all the things that can go wrong with a family. I pick up the other photo of Felix. A more recent one, in his usual 70s attire, holding a stick by a river, looking outdoorsy. The photo could've been taken in the '70s. It makes me wonder for a moment if my boyfriend could be a time-traveller.

'That's my mum, obviously.' Felix points to the pictures.

'She looks like your mum,' I tell him, trying to say the right thing. 'I would've liked to meet her.'

When his grandma goes to bed we spoon on the sofa. Some incense burning and an old horror film on TV with the volume down low.

'I should tell you something,' Felix murmurs.

'What is it?' I twist around slightly to talk to him.

'My mum died in that fire.' His face his blurred from the dark and its closeness,

'Oh,' I say.

'She took a load of pills and passed out. She was burning a load of candles in the living room,' he says this without much emotion. 'I was upstairs hiding in this tent in my bedroom when the firemen came.'

A dramatic voice comes muffled from the TV. I don't really know how to respond. 'You never told me.'

'No ... It was in all the newspapers because I was on *Children's Hospital*. They said she did it on purpose.' He swallows. 'I guess I didn't want you to see me as this tragic person.'

'I wouldn't have seen you like that,' I squeeze him.

'Cos people do. They think, *oh, that's why he's so crazy.*'

'I think you would've been crazy whatever happened in your life.'

We hold each other tight in the small space of the sofa. I feel the muscles in his back and the notches in his spine. He bites my lip, just enough to make me feel that throb in my abdomen. I push my tongue against his, we lock mouths, blocking out the TV and all the kitschy ornaments. I undo the button on his corduroy flares and begin to feel his hard dick through the fabric of his pants. He pulls away with a big pink smile on his face,

'Let's go to my room.'

'Okay,' I kiss him just next to his mouth, his cheeks flushed.

He takes my hand and leads me upstairs, our bare feet on the carpet.

The room is lit by the headlights of passing cars through a gap in the curtains. I wrap myself around his body, kissing, biting his lips. He breaks away,

'I wanna show you something.'

'No more souvenirs.'

'It's not a souvenir.' He bends down and fiddles with a plug socket. His erection showing through his unbuttoned fly. He flicks the switch on the wall and the whole room lights up. Multicoloured fairy lights wound around his bed frame, around all the miniature wonders of the world. Tiny white bulbs attached to his ceiling like stars. Before I can really look at the lights, he pushes me onto his bed and bites my neck. I kiss him hard and peel his vintage t-shirt off his flexing body, throw it on the floor. He pins me down by my wrists, bites and kisses my stomach. He eases my top off, chewing on my nipples, our bodies illuminated in a dim rainbow of fairy lights. I see all his sporadic homemade tattoos; the heart filled with arrows, a little alien head on his ribcage, two penises on his hip bent into the shape of a heart. He looks up at me, putting his mouth around my cock, trying to get it completely hard, brushing the shaft with his teeth. I lean my head into the bed frame and watch his long hair moving up and down. Short quick tinges of ecstasy shoot up my nervous system. I push my fingers through his hair, against his scalp. I pull him up so our chests touch, our arms grappling at each other's bodies as if we're in a rush. My warm skin against his – I try to hold him so tight that our bodies merge.

I arrange him so he's got a knee either side of me and push his cock, hard and hot into my mouth and suck it, faster and harder. I push it into the back of my throat so that I choke a bit and squeeze his ass. We fall down onto the bed, wrestling, biting, kissing each other's faces and necks. He grinds his cock against my ass. The globe next to the bed lights his pale naked body in blues and greens, his hair sticking to his flushed little face. He lets go to pull out a draw from his bedside table and rummages around inside.

'Sorry, I haven't got any lube, is this okay?' He opens a little travel pot of Vaseline with glitter crusted around the rim.

'Yeah,' I whisper. I feel a tightness in my stomach as he pushes his finger in and out of my asshole. I rub his hard cock and tilt my head back. 'Have you got a condom?'

'What flavour?' He grabs some from his draw and studies their packets. 'Banana, cherry, Pina Colada?'

'Pina colada of course.' I rip it open with my teeth and pull it down over his cock. I suck it, tasting the faint synthetic sweetness.

He pushes two fingers in and out of my ass, my cock tingling, becoming fully hard. I bite my lip. Then he holds onto my thighs and after some fumbling pushes his cock part way in. I gasp and suck in a breath from the pain of it being my first time in maybe 8 months.

'Are you okay?'

'Yeah,' I say and mould his ribcage with my fingertips. 'Just go slow at first.' I squeeze his nipples as he slowly pushes his cock inside of me. The pain turning to that feeling of warmth and cold that makes the hairs all over your body stand on end.

We turn over in the mess of quilt and bed cover. The contours of our bodies illuminated in a prism of tiny lights. I wrap my legs around him as he fucks me. We both look into each other's sweaty faces, lips parted. He breathes heavily into my mouth. The tips of his fingers push through my hair making my scalp tingle. I pant as my muscles tense around his hot cock, moving inside me. I grasp at his chest, feel the bump of his childhood scar. He looks at me concentrated and lets out little moans. He pulls his cock out of me, pulls the condom off, rubs his cock in his balled hand, his face scrunched up. Warm cum squirts onto my chest. He looks at me like he feels bad for cumming on me, but I smile. He starts to suck my cock, squeezing my balls, going fast, deep throating it. I push my hands through his curly hair and pull his head away.

'I don't think I'm gonna cum,' I look up at his red face.

'I'm gonna make you!' He goes down, ready to suck my dick again, but I roll over onto my side. I pull him down to face me so our dicks are touching. I straighten out the quilt and wrap his arms around me.

'I just want to lay here, like this,' I whisper over lowering breaths.

He kisses me on the lips. I haven't had sex in about eight months and right now I feel like I'm coming out of a swimming pool after 100 lengths

'Could you turn off my crazy lights?' He asks, and I fumble behind the bed for the switch and make all the pyramids, pagodas, and skyscrapers disappear. He spoons me and chews on my ear and says, 'I love you.' Then falls asleep, arms and legs splayed across mine.

This is one of those soft lit romantic moments from our relationship that could be cut and spliced into a montage with the following. The Valentine's Day when I was part delusional and suffering from Graft-Versus-Host disease, and Felix brought me homemade jelly. Jelly being about the most solid thing I could swallow. Meeting him dressed in Victorian zombie attire when he got out of work and eating vegan seafood in Soho square in the rain. Going to vintage shops and trying on the ski suits and 80's all-in-ones. Then suits in Oxford Street, making out as two yuppies in the changing rooms. The 3D cinema where he told me I should push the massive cut-out of James Bond over to fight patriarchy, then he pushed it over himself. A trip to Heathrow Airport where we drank gin and tonics. He told people we were involved in world music and were flying to Nepal. A picnic he made me have in Parliament square, where he told me, "One day all of this will be rubble," while smiling adorably. Then drinking *Koppenberg* out of goblets in an *Ikea* living room. Behind our television-set a missing wall with couples wheeling shopping trollies full of kids and flatpack furniture around.

'Does that look enjoyable to you?' I ask gesticulating to a young couple with a screaming baby and a distracted toddler.

'No, we're very lucky to be gay.' He leans into me. 'I wouldn't mind a little house somewhere though. With your wigs and my ornaments.'

Our car snakes along an empty road, the green light in the tower of a nearby mosque, glowing in the static darkness. Below it are a few basic sandstone houses. Leon is driving, trance playing at a low volume, the car, dusky with hash smoke. From the back seat, I see darkness through the windscreen. Behind us, the headlights of one other car in the distance.

Leon is the one with the dreadlocks who was rolling a joint on the steps of *Science Fiction* when me and Felix first met. I met him again at a squat near Gatwick Airport where Felix used to live. I felt like some royal family member visiting a community centre, sat on a half-collapsed sofa eating vegetarian mush. Some guy with a thick yellow beard strummed a guitar with five strings.

'So, you're one of those faggots that hand out drink tokens and pretend to be a celebrity,' Leon asked, stubbing a joint into his finished plate of food.

'Leon's a self-loathing gay,' Felix reassured me.

'Yeah, that just about describes my job,' I told him.

Now he's driving us in his Dad's desert rover. One of those stupid dreadlock rings in his hair. The contours of his face glowing from lit up symbols on the starship enterprise size dashboard.

'What was it like almost being dead?' Leon steers around a slight bend in the long empty road.

'I don't know.' Felix looks back at me to check. 'I don't really remember it.'

'He forgot the last year of his life when we were in America and didn't even tell the doctors,' I elaborate.

'Well, doctors don't know everything,' Leon says, glancing out the window at gravel and sand.

I'm going to tell him that actually doctors saved mine and Felix's lives, but I stop myself.

'Oh, look, Bedouin.' Leon nudges Felix and reverses with a swift crunch of tires and gravel.

A small structure made from dark red fabric is partly visible in the headlights. While we're staring at it a white car thwacks past at a crazy speed. It zooms into the distance, creating a sandstorm and quickly becoming a tiny blur of light.

'Where are they rushing off to?' I ask.

'Some people round here think they're in a racing game.' Leon shrugs.

'So, how long are you going to be here for?' Felix asks, his chequered headscarf tied like a doo-rag.

'Till we overthrow the government.' He takes a drag on a joint I didn't know he had. 'How long are you travelling the world for?'

'Till we've gone all the way round and back,' Felix says gleefully.

'Aren't you worried about your carbon footprint?' Leon asks.

No one answers, we're watching the headlights of the white car, emerging from the dust and speeding back up the road toward us.

'Fucking hell! Are they blind!?' I hear Leon sound worried for the first time. His hands grapple with the steering wheel. Headlights fill the windows. There's a huge crash and a painfully loud grating of metal. I'm flung to the side; friction burns on my hands from the seat belt. There's a thrusting of tyres as we careen into the desert. I see it all in flashes; sand filling the view from the windscreen. I twist my head around to see their headlights through the back window. The sound of tyres skidding on gravel. I see the outline of Felix gripping onto his seat as we accelerate up over a ridge of sand.

'They can't drive on this,' Leon shouts back to me.

'Is that something people do around here?' Asks Felix, out of breath.

'No,' Leon huffs. 'Be quiet. I'll drive us out into the desert.'

We bump around the desert for long enough that their headlights disappear and leave us in total darkness.

'Do you think that was homophobic?' Felix asks.

'How would they know we're gay?' He drags hard on his joint. 'If anything, it's people who don't like white guys with expensive cars.'

'But I think I saw them.' I lean forward against my seatbelt. 'The guy looked white and there was someone else wearing a hood.'

'How'd you see that?' Coughs Leon, toking too hard on his joint.

'Out, the back window.' I look out now and see just a bit of sky sprinkled with stars. 'I got part of their number plate too ... Could it be anything to do with you *bringing down the government*?'

'*Bringing down the government!?*' Leon says, confused and seemingly annoyed at me. He throws the butt of his joint out the window, filling the car with cold desert air. 'I was making that up. I basically just get stoned in the desert.'

'Oh,' I reply, feeling I shouldn't proposition Leon with any more theories on why weird white people would ram his Dad's car in the desert.

'Okay, let's go.' Leon starts up his sat-nav, then a robotic voice and an orange arrow guide us out of the desert. There are two pools of yellowish-grey nothingness, lit by the car's headlamps and Leon's trance music at a low volume.

'Are we going to phone the police?' I ask.

Leon cranes his head back to give me a look that says, *that's definitely not what he's going to do*. We drive over some desert shrubs and eventually reach the road. Leon gets out by a cafe, a few men gathered at a plastic table with cups of tea, passing a shisha pipe. He swears a lot then gets back in and bangs his face into the steering wheel and moans,

'My dad's going to be pissed!'

I'm covering the moles on Felix's face with a concealer stick in one of those old-timey central London pubs filled with dark-wood and yuppies. Felix has made an attempt at being a club kid in my red sequin dungarees. I'm wearing a sort of Georgian burlesque look: a ruff, my pearl covered leotard, and a pompadour wig. Some men in blue shirts and suits sit next to us are trying not to look at us while having some ultra-boring conversation about accounts and portfolios.

'I don't think it would be terrible if someone came in here and killed all these people,' I say, leaning back to take a look at the make-up on Felix's face.

'They just need some kind person to put a few drops of acid in their drinks,' Felix tells me.

'Arsenic,' I correct him, getting an eyeshadow palette out of my clutch.

'I'm serious!' He sips his half-pint of cider through a straw. 'If I was terminally ill, I would ask to visit the houses of parliament and spray LSD on everything.'

'I think we just need to kill 90% of the population.' I dab the brush into some glittery blue and tell him to close his eyes.

'You really don't like people, do you?' His eyelids flicker.

'How come you like them so much?' I blend blue into the corners of his eyes.

'Umm, 'cos I see that most people are like me.'

'Most people are not like you!' I laugh.

'I mean –' His eyes flitter while I try to paint them. '– They hurt, and they feel happy, and they're all just trying their best.'

'Those ones are trying too hard.' I get another brush to blend the blue out with some bright yellow.

The hotel bar we're headed to is famous for having the biggest disco ball in Europe. It's wedged awkwardly between the bar and the DJ booth, like some mirror covered Indiana Jones boulder. The DJ is playing banal jazzy electro pop, the signature music of Rocco's usually banal nights. The first person I see at the bar is Moth, face painted blue, wearing a short-sleeved tuxedo shirt with long black gloves, looking all *Star-Trek*-society-girl.

'Cosmo!' His eyes widen like he's greeting some long-lost friend he never thought he'd see again, who he never visited in hospital. He grips me in a tight hug.

I feel the fabric of his gloves pressing against my bare arms. To avoid any awkward soliloquies about how well I look and how worried he was, I say,

'This is my boyfriend.' For some reason I expect Felix to be shy. Maybe I want him to be shy, but he isn't.

He wraps Moth in the same calibre of hug Moth gave me and tells him that he looks like Audrey Hepburn.

'Have you ever actually seen Audrey Hepburn,' I ask Felix, accidentally banging my pompadour wig against part of the bar. 'He looks like Papa Smurf goes to the prom.'

'Drinks girls?' Moth asks, impervious to insults.

'I'll have a cider,' Felix grips onto the bar.

Moth looks at me like he needs a translation.

'He'll have a cocktail.'

'With berries in!' Felix adds, looking at what the smartly dressed people around the bar are drinking.

'I want that French Martini,' I say.

'Sophisticated,' says Moth and clicks camply with his fingers in the direction of the bar man. After he hands us the drinks, Moth says, 'Rupert Grint's coming.'

'Rupert, who?' I ask, pulling the drink from my mouth.

'He's Harry Potter.' Moth raises his eyebrows at my lack of knowledge.

'He's not Harry Potter. He's Harry Potter's ginger friend.' I raise my eyebrows back at him.

Felix is pulling demure little-black-dress-wearing socialites up onto the partial dance floor and grinding up against them to a remix of a remix. He's spilling a free vodka cocktail he got from the alcove reserved for club kids. His dance moves are like nothing I've ever seen before. It's like someone trapped inside a slow-motion hurricane. The kind of flailing of arms you might expect from someone on acid listening to Jefferson Airplane. He likes to involve the furnishings a lot too. He's currently hanging from one of the poles attached to the bar, his dungaree strap falling down, pouring the last of the cocktail into his mouth. A well-dressed couple look up at him, wondering if this is bourgeoise hedonism or worrying mania.

'Where'd you find that one?' Moth asks, leaning up against the DJ booth, so he can rub his leg against the male model DJing.

'Remember when you were asking to visit me in hospital.'

'That was him!? I thought he wasn't your type.' Moth moves his hand up the DJ's arm.

'I don't think he is a type.' I empty the last bit of French Martini into my mouth.

Moth laughs. At first, I think it's at me, but then I see the cute DJ tickling his wrist.

Felix leaves the small throng of dancers to wrap his arm around me and blink into my eyes.

'Where'd you get those moves?' I ask.

'I can't be too energetic.' He gestures to his transplanted heart. 'So, I had to think up a way of dancing that wouldn't give me a heart attack.' He demonstrates some of these moves at me. A bit like a mime of someone surfing then swatting away flies.

'Have you ever thought of going into choreography.'

'Are you making fun of me!' He slurs and tries to frown. 'I like my dancing!'

'I didn't say I didn't like it.'

His reaction to this is to sling my arm over his shoulder and drag me in the direction of the dance floor. He includes me in an offbeat tango, then bends me over backwards almost knocking my wig off. He hasn't drunk that much, but he is completely pissed. I dance for a while under the spinning white lights of the giant disco ball with Felix and a girl with a beehive full of flowers. Then I get a tap on the shoulder from a long-lacquered fingernail. It's Tamsin strapped into some bejewelled purple fetish armour.

'You look really well!' She says, leaning backwards to look at me.

'It's all concealer.' I take this opportunity to leave the dance floor.

'Did you come with James?' Asks Tamsin, twitching to be photographed.

'No, my boyfriend.' I nod in Felix's direction.

Tamsin studies Felix briefly and says, 'Rather you than me.'

'He has a condition where he gets drunk very easily.' I sort of defend Felix.

'I can see that.' She gives me a look of incredulity. 'Let's go for a fag.'

'I can't smoke right now, but I'll come out for some of that fresh London air. I'll get Felix. I don't trust him on his own.'

Felix is all slack-jawed and over-friendly with Tamsin. He grips onto her arm and marvels, 'So sparkly.'

She sticks a cigarette in his mouth and says, 'Come on kids.'

We exit through the black marble foyer, and I see paparazzi outside poised in their usual uniform of North Face jackets.

'Like the coats,' says Tamsin.

'Can I get a pic?' One calls.

I assume this is for some insinuation on the *3am Page*, that Harry Potter's friend is somehow caught up with Tamsin.

'Why not,' she says, her coat already dropping to her elbows.

'You too,' the paparazzi adds. So, I strike the same pose and we turn into moving statues while the cameras flash. Felix makes a vulgar pose with the cigarette hanging out the corner of his mouth, but they don't take any photos.

'Look, it's Jesus.' Tamsin points with her cigarette toward some street preacher using a little distorted amplifier to rant about hell and homos.

'Jesus has more taste; he's wearing Ben Sherman.' I wave my finger at the guy's baggy plaid shirt.

Felix takes a heavy drag on his cigarette and coughs,

'I'll go and have a look.' He strides over in the 70's platforms I gave him for Christmas.

'He doesn't seem like your type,' Tamsin says to me.

'I don't think he is a type,' I repeat.

'He's feral, that's what he is,' Tamsin snorts.

Felix is in front of the preacher, pretending to listen. He nods his head and shouts, 'Hallelujah.'

Tamsin is trying to tell me about Rocco's night at *Science Fiction* which isn't doing so well. Then I watch Felix grab one of the preacher's pamphlets. The man recoils as Felix lurches forward, trying to kiss him on the face.

'– It's mostly fag-hags,' Tamsin moans, 'biological women drinking WKD blue.'

I squeeze her bare arm and point in Felix's direction. He's now being shoved backwards by the preacher. He's stuffing a pamphlet into his own mouth. A serious-looking couple and a man in a suit watch, wondering whether they should intervene.

'I think we should go get him,' I tell Tamsin.

'We definitely shouldn't.' She stubs her cigarette out on the hotel wall then looks around for a cigarette bin. She doesn't find one so just flicks it into the street.

Felix is now jumping around, dungaree strap hanging down, half chewed up leaflet clenched in his hand, shouting inflammatory things about Jesus. 'Jesus was gay! Jesus was Chinese! Jesus was a paedophile!'

The preacher shouts at Felix as he strides away.

'I thought you liked Jesus.' I give him a look of reproach.

'I do,' Felix slurs, spitting out a bit of pamphlet. 'But that guy was a dick.'

In the elevator, Felix drops the other dungaree strap. He takes off his sweat-dampened shirt and balls it up in his hands.

'You gonna throw that at someone?' Tamsin asks, leaning against the elevator handrail.

'He's a pacifist,' I tell her.

'Yeah, I see that,' she jokes.

'Honey, you need to calm down a bit, this isn't –' The lift doors opens before I can think what this isn't. A man in a tuxedo ushers us politely through to the bar and dining area. It's currently filled with an echoey remix of *Insomnia* by *Faithless*. Within seconds Felix is back on the dancefloor, as if it's his job. He drags a chair into the middle of the floor and gyrates on it, trying to grab things off the ceiling and drinking someone else's drink. I feel I should be calming him down, but I don't have the energy. I worry he'll be lying on the floor in a few minutes, going into cardiac arrest.

'I didn't recognise you!' Says Rocco, dressed in a silver suit and silver shirt, somewhere between fashion editorial and game show host.

'I've worn this before,' I squawk.

We hug and kiss without touching.

'How does it feel to be back,' he asks, like a chirpy robot.

'Good, I guess.' I hold my wig in place. 'My energy isn't back completely.'

'Well, when it is – Lars has been asking after you.' Lars is the owner of *Science Fiction*.

'How's your night there going?' I ask him.

'Oh, don't ask me about that,' he groans and asks me what drink I want.

I tell him I'm good and head off to the toilet.

The toilets are brightly lit and heavily mirrored. You can watch yourself weeing from above and below in a thousand little mirror tiles. I wash my hands and try to touch up my cracked makeup under a light that shows every flaw down to the atom. Somewhere outside I hear a huge shattering crash. I wonder if they're doing some building or demolition work. Then I hear people's voices sounding alarmed.

Re-entering the bar, I expect to see some framed photo fallen off the wall. Tamsin points across the room, eyebrows raised. I don't realize what's happened straight away. Then I see it, the biggest disco ball in Europe, no longer attached to the ceiling.

'Your boyfriend!' She says lips pursed.

'I just saw him jump onto it,' Moth tells me.

I push through the people gathered around the disco ball. There are little shattered bits of mirror all over the floor. In the middle is Felix leaning against it unapologetically. All the tuxedoed bar staff are around him.

Felix sees me and slaps the glitter ball and whines, 'It fell on me.'

I grab him and pull him out by his arm through the crowd like an angry mother. I smile at the manager who is walking towards the scene of the crime we're fleeing. I pull Felix, sweaty and half naked toward the lift. It opens just in time, and out steps the actor that played Ron Weasley in the *Harry Potter* films. There's an exchange of glances. I smile at him. He looks at this cross-dressing Marie Antoinette dragging along a bedraggled hippy in red sequin dungarees and decides to smile back. Then we're in the lift and the doors are closing.

'What the hell did you do!' I growl. 'That's Rocco's job! We're never going to be allowed here again!'

'Sorry, I thought club kids were supposed to be wild.' He cowers, leaning into the elevator wall, seemingly shocked that I'm angry.

'Champagne and cocaine wild, not criminal damage wild.' I look at him in desperation.

'I'll go back and sort it out,' he says and tries to press the lift buttons to go back up.

'No, it costs thousands and thousands of pounds. We're leaving now!'

'I've got some money put away,' he slurs and waves his hand like its nothing.

The doors open and I clench his hand and walk through the black lobby, past the bouncer. I drop his hand as we walk in swift silence, past the departing paparazzi, away from the arch at the start of Chinatown, and toward the drunken tourists milling about Leicester square.

'It's a stupid place for stuck-up rich people anyway,' he argues.

'I know!' I hiss. 'But it's also my friend's job! I invited you there and you fucking destroy the place, and you can't even say sorry!'

'It's not your disco ball. Why don't I just go back and say sorry to them.'

'It's too late, you fucking idiot!' I scream at him. 'Just get the bus and go home!'

He plonks himself down on a concrete block next to a square of grass outside the cinema.

'Okay, let's have a drink on the bus. Calm down.'

'I'm not coming with you.' I look at him, as seriously as someone dressed like a Georgian clown can. 'Get some water and sober up.' I walk swiftly into the crowd away from him and wonder who I can phone at this time of night to let me stay at their house. I look back at him, leaning on the concrete block.

He looks like he's crying into the bush behind him, then I see he's throwing up.

I peer disinterestedly at another glimmering gold stall filled with lamps. Lamps suspended from the ceiling in so many different styles and shapes, it's like looking at sand through a microscope. Felix is across the narrow market street. I dodge out the way of a motorbike and a couple of women in colourful burqas.

'I want this,' he whines, stroking a stripey robe with a hood.

'Get it.' I shrug.

He shrugs too and walks on, stepping out the way of a donkey pulling a cart full of rugs.

'I feel like I already bought all my souvenirs before I left,' he tells me.

A man tries to pull us into a store filled with tiles and fridge magnets. Felix pulls me away by my arm.

'You were mad for souvenirs when we were in Mexico.'

'After a few markets, it starts to feel a bit empty.' He stops at a stall hung with hundreds of geometric patterned rugs. 'I'd like one of these for our place in Bethnal Green.'

'Would you,' I laugh, but maybe moving in together isn't such a crazy idea anymore. After moving in with my last boyfriend I vowed I would never move in with a boyfriend again. He was a young professional masquerading as a club kid. He liked taking cocaine and had a liquor cabinet with eleven types of gin in it.

Felix and I walk past shops with walls covered in thousands of pointy leather sandals. the leather smell mixing with dust, sweat, and spices. Other stalls filled with cones decorated to look like huge piles of turmeric and paprika.

'I get this weird feeling,' Felix says over the clatter and shouting. 'Like we're moving but really, we're always in the same place.'

'You bored of the travel?'

'I'm not bored,' he insists. 'Maybe it's just a little bit touristy here.' He looks over at some white twenty-somethings being pulled by a horse and cart. 'I wanna be like some travelling monk in the 1300s, walking to places no outsiders ever been before.'

We step out of the way of some bikes.

'Yeah, we have aeroplanes now,' I say, trying to remember our last flight.

'You used to be able to take a bus to India in the 60's,' he informs me.

'Sounds terrible,' I laugh, thinking of all the bus journeys we've had.

I point to a stall with a basket of what looks like dried antelope heads and a mess of flattened lizards. Then there's a guy with a load of chickens tied together. There's a wizened old man with a mat covered in creepy things, ostrich eggs, old photos, dried herbs, and dried animals. He makes some strange gesture at us. Then we're in a car park with dug up concrete and a few breezeblocks.

'Okay, wrong way,' says Felix.

I turn around, looking for a less occult route back than the way we just came. There's a white car with a massive dent across the side parked next to a few other cars. I step around the pile of rubble and look at the number plate.

'It's the same car,' I tell Felix, and he looks at me confused. 'The car from the desert! I think it's the same one.'

'Yeah, it's similar,' Felix says, trying to usher me back into the occult section of the market.

'No, I looked at the number plate,' I insist. 'It's the same car.'

'That was hundreds of miles away.' Felix stands next to me looking at the empty beat-up car.

'That's why I'm shocked.'

He crouches down, peering at the crumpled side of the car. I look through the window at its empty interior and grey seats. Felix looks at me, unsure, pulling his mouth to the side. 'Do you want me to throw a brick through the window?'

'No, I want to go back, where the people are.'

We head back, past baskets with big blocks of resin and dried leaves. We dodge motorbikes and a cart full of fruit. We head back to an area where there's silk scarves and Chinese tourists, the sun shining through slats of wood above us.

'Some kids from my school followed me in a white car once,' Felix says, outside a juice stall with huge mounds of fruit.

'At least they weren't trying to kill you.' I feel myself re-entering that paranoid state.

'Here it is,' says James, pointing across the lamp lit street to some big battered red metallic factory doors.

Outside are a group of twenty-somethings all wearing Uniqlo jumpers and grandpa coats, drinking out of cans. Inside are white walls and plastic wine glasses, a bar full of mini champagnes. People milling around stroking their chins at whatever's on the wall.

'Where's yours?' I ask, doing a little aerobic stretch in front of him in my silver sequin polo neck.

'Oh, 'round the corner. But I want a look at everyone's.'

We walk past a couple of Dandies with a woman in a tie-dye skirt, all musing over a large oil painting of a cartoon. We stop for a while in front of a circular podium with a pillar of bubbles coming out of it. A mass of transparent oily rainbows lit from underneath. I poke my finger into one and James does the same with his scratched-up orange nail. More bubbles replace the ones we burst, and I see the whole thing is moving, bubbles being pushed out of the base.

'Good I didn't bring Felix.' I say wiping my soapy finger on my trousers. 'Or that wouldn't be there anymore.'

We get to James' photos, in big, mismatched gold frames, depicting the everyday lives of people who dress alternatively. There's a goth girl who has a kid and works in a call centre. Tamsin in full drag, then in her daytime blend of genders, eating at the muffin shop in Bethnal Green. There's me on stage with my handheld mirror and me in a hospital bed with leukemia, the headscarf Felix got me and glitter around my eyes. The pictures are so big and glossy they almost look like they were staged.

'What do you think?' James asks me.

'It's a good idea, and you can see I have a good bone structure in both.' I pout.

We walk past a neon-pink mountain with little green skiers on it, then some envelopes and letters in frames on the wall.

'I'm sorry I wasn't there for you as much as I could've been,' he says in a voice that doesn't contain his usual camp irony.

'You were ... maybe I even pushed you away a bit.' I rub his arm with the hand holding the plastic wine glass. 'I had Felix.' I stop and look at a fractalized painting in dark blues and greens.

'You gonna move in with this one?' Goads James, standing in front of the painting looking at me.

'No, definitely not,' I say, moving on from my brief moment of art appreciation.

'Good, because my housemates moving to Berlin.'

I buy James a plastic flute of champagne to celebrate moving back in together.

'This is my muse,' James tells a woman with a monobrow and a bowl cut. 'He's the most vacuous person in London that's had a near-death experience.'

'I'm not vacuous.' I flap his comment away. 'I watch documentaries.'

'On the shopping channel,' James adds.

'Nat.' The girl shakes my hand. It may be the first hand I've shaken in about a year that doesn't belong to a member of the medical profession.

'What kind of art do you make Nat?' I repeat her name because it's funny and makes me think she's a giant gnat.

'I did the letters,' she says.

I look back into the gallery in case there's some giant letters I might've missed.

'I write letters to celebrities,' she elaborates.

'Oh. Who do you write to?' I wonder if I know them.

'Female singers. I write to them about politics, Amy Winehouse, Leona Lewis, Lily Allen.'

'I fucked Lily Allen's brother,' I tell her, remembering saying this once before. Even if it wasn't true then, it still sounds good.

'Cosmo's fucked loads of people,' James both boasts on my behalf and berates me.

On the way out, I role my eyes at the hipsters posturing outside. James twiddles the plastic champagne glass between his thumb and finger.

'You're in bitch mode tonight.'

'Am I?' I see why he might think that from my conversation with Nat. 'I don't get out much at the moment.'

'Some of us are going to your club, *Pegasus*, later if you want.'

'*Pegasus* is not my club. *Science Fiction* is my club.' I stand in the street with my hands in my pockets. 'Actually, Lars called me about putting a night on there for my birthday.'

'He plans ahead,' James says, showing he knows when my birthday is. '– And *Pegasus*, tonight?'

'I've got no energy.' I wilt into him. 'I'm still recovering. Can I stay at your, I mean *our* house?'

'The key.' He jangles it in my direction. 'But you have to drop it out the kitchen window so I can get in.'

160

Me and Felix are naked on a mattress in Leon's room at the squat. Felix just wiped the cum off my abdomen with his sock.

'I put these up when I was living here,' he points, sock in hand, at the hippie throws, hanging from every wall and across ceiling.

They cover everything including the window, billowing with the night breeze.

'We stole them from Camden Market after this shop sacked Leon.'

'There's a lot,' I reply.

'It reminds me of this tent I had in my bedroom as a kid. I was too ill to camp in the garden, so my mum put one up in there.'

'That's cute.' I swirl his few chest hairs and look at the wonky heart tattoo with the arrows through it.

'... When I was in there, I'd imagine I was travelling the world; Egypt, Mount Everest, Mars, another galaxy, the space between galaxies.' He tilts his head towards me, lit by a lamp on the floor with a red t-shirt over it. 'We need a room with lots of wall hangings.'

'I might be moving back in with James,' I tell him.

'Oh.' His face tenses.

'I know you wanted to move in together,' I lower my voice. 'But I've done that before, and it ended up with me and my ex hating each other.'

'Is this about the disco ball?'

'No.' I breath out.

Rocco didn't lose his job and apparently the damage was minimal.

'It's about familiarity breeding contempt,' I say.

'I just want some of that good stuff.' He puts on a bit of an American accent, to make his whining sound more comical than pitiful.

'You mean that heteronormative Ikea stuff?'

'If you have to put it like that – yes.'

'Not right now.' I lean my head back and look up at the throw behind us, depicting a tree with little birds on it. 'We can still travel the world together. That's better, right, than matching toothbrushes and a joint wardrobe?'

'Yeah, I guess.' He glares at me.

'Can you imagine us shacked up in a single bedroom in Bethnal Green, shopping at ASDA, dividing the bills?'

'Yeah, I can.' He tries to stare me out.

'Be glad that I don't want to fuck this up.' I put my hand on his chest.

I'm fastening the bedsheet over Felix's shoulder while he drinks from a novelty bottle of Ouzo shaped like a penis. Some echoey guitar music plays somewhere in the night outside. There are no cars trying to run us over, no angel ornaments, just me and him wearing togas made out of bedsheets, drinking in moderation. We head out into narrow cobbled streets lit by little upmarket shops, selling shawls and pottery. The buildings are all rectangular blocks covered in white plaster. It's one of those summer days, when you get drunk in the afternoon and then manage to stumble out again in the evening. We have to walk past the same shop selling souvlaki pita three times before we find the bar. Rainbow piano keys are painted on a board above the door. Inside are sofas and a dumpy American woman in her latter middle age singing show tunes by a piano. She sings *Viva Las Vegas* and accompanies it with little Liza-Minneliesque actions, such as shaking some imaginary dice in her fist, kissing it and rolling them out.

'We've got Zeus and Hermes over here.' She gestures towards us during her between-song spiel. 'What's the occasion?'

'Life!' Felix shouts, and when she asks for requests, he starts making a squawking sound and waving his hand about and screams out, '*Moonriver*! No, actually that one you like, *Nobody Does It Better.*'

She glances at the old gay in a red velvet smoking jacket behind the piano, and without the intermediary of conscious thought, he launches into the piano intro. I'm standing on the sofa in my toga, waving my cocktail about and singing almost as loud as her.

We arrive at a gay bar called *Jackie O's*, the sea splashing at the pavement outside. The place is like a nursing home for muscle gays with sunburn, but we hike up our togas and jump about, punching our fists in the air to some crappy house music. The woman who seems to be in charge gives us free glasses of prosecco and says, 'You guys are crazy.'

'We're just good time girls,' Felix squawks. He gives me his prosecco, to stop me worrying he'll give himself a heart attack. Then he goes and upsets a Greek drag queen by talking to her. We end up outside dancing on the pavement in the sea-spray. Felix's toga falls off, then we're making out on the cobbles in the seawater.

I light a damp cigarette from a pack I forgot buying. I lean out our hotel window and look at the moon; big and yellow, closer to the earth than usual. I breath in the tobacco and listen to the shush of the sea. I thought Felix had passed out, but he's propped up on the bed tangled in his wet toga.

'Did I ever tell you about the first time I saw you?' He slurs from the darkness.

'At *Science fiction*?' I close the window.

'Noo.' He beckons for me to come and join him.

I get on top of him with my wet toga and cigarette breath.

He strokes me and says, 'Just before I left Brighton there were some copies of *Boyz magazine* in a gay bar. I saw a picture of you in there. There's was something about you that felt so familiar. I thought I had to go to London and meet you.'

'Really?' I squeeze him and look into his face to check he's telling the truth. 'What was I wearing?'

'A ruff and some bondage harness covered in pearls.'

'What club?' I ask, to check against my exhaustive internal timeline of nights and outfits.

'Umm, some anniversary thing at *Pegasus.*'

'Yeah!' I look at him, remembering the exact outfit. 'How come you never told me?'

'I'm good at keeping secrets.' He pokes me in the chest with his finger. 'And I didn't want you to think I was a stalker.'

I link hands with him to stop him poking me. 'When we met, I felt like I'd met you before.'

'It's like that giant cosmic disc I told you about. Some of your bits are close to some of mine.'

'Your giant gold universal disc,' I snort.

'I didn't say it was gold.' He rests our hands on the damp tangle of bedsheet togas. 'But it can be.'

Felix turns up to the housewarming party first. He's dressed like a Caucasian member of the Jackson five. He pushes a bottle of wine into my hands and says, 'It's from the Ukraine.'

'Is the Ukraine known for its wines?' I ask. I'm wearing a silk robe in pastel-peach with lacey medieval sleeves and the kind of ribbed turban beloved by aging Hollywood spinsters. At a house party, you have to look like you've made an effort and no effort simultaneously.

Milo arrives an hour later, in a shaggy black fur coat and a sheer black turtleneck, with a gold ankh necklace.

'You're the one that knocked that disco ball down in the *W Hotel,*' he says, giving Felix the briefest of air hugs.

'If you've got a disco ball, I'll pull it down for you.' Felix winks and re-embraces Milo in a much more enthusiastic unwanted hug.

Milo's response is to hand Felix his coat and head towards the arrangement of glasses and alcohols on the kitchen diner.

'Is it cat?' Felix asks, dumping the coat on the back of a chair.

'It's mink.' Milo gives me another little hug and scans the room. 'Where is everyone?'

'It's nine-thirty. Sit down and tell me about this new boyfriend of yours.'

'Peter Rabbit? It's not a –' He makes a motion between me and Felix to indicate the word relationship. 'Just a drag protege and fuck buddy. Do you have Vermouth?' Milo perches himself on a stall at the diner while I open a few cupboards.

Felix offers to mix Milo a cocktail, to which he says a very decisive, 'No, thank you.'

'I know you like to pour it yourself.' I plonk the bottle of Vermouth on the diner, and Milo gets to work.

'Where's James?' He asks.

'James!' I call.

James comes out of his room wearing an 80's all-in-one with shoulder pads and hastily applied makeup.

'Aww, little Milo.' He comes and squashes Milo into a patronising hug, which Milo enjoys despite batting him away.

Felix seems to have appointed himself DJ, starting off with *The Spice Girls* then Janis Joplin. Kitten and Bobbi arrive, very high, looking like they've come out of some badly configured cloning device. Both with pink hair and rhinestones glued to their faces. Bobbi shows me that he's had his earlobe sewn back together. They gravitate towards Felix, identifying him as an accomplice in causing trouble. They cackle as he assists them in using every alcohol to make brown cocktails. There's a couple of James' butch female art friends with sporadic Felix-esque tattoos. Then some guys I invited because they were cute. One with braided hair and a basketball vest, the other wearing a translucent *Adidas* windbreaker and a gold crown of thorns. Felix decides to assist them in making cocktails.

'It's called a brown martini,' I hear him slur.

Me, Milo, and Bobbi look for pictures of dicks in James' coffee-table art books. Felix answers the door to Tamsin who is wearing a PVC bra under a fur trim coat, buttoned in the middle like she's in a 90's girl band. Moth turns up while I'm in my room, showing people all my wardrobes. His skin is a normal colour, and he's wearing a Versace silk shirt with a Hasidic Jewish hat, accompanied by the DJ from the hotel bar. They open a bottle of rosé champagne. There is some dispute between Milo and Felix over what song to play next. *White Rabbit* by *Jefferson Airplane* gets replaced with a female rapper saying the words, *pussy* and *ass*, a lot. Milo and the boy with the braids briefly gyrate on the coffee table in celebration.

All my favourite weirdos from London are crammed onto my L-plan sofa. Felix draped over the arm, his feet underneath my thigh. Milo cosies up to me, talking about our friend Prozac, who designed a couple of outfits for Kesha's latest tour.

'It's basically just fetish wear though,' he concludes.

'Sometimes I wish I'd done a fashion degree.' I rest my arm on Felix's legs.

'You think you need to? You've got contacts. And the stuff you make is actually good.'

I can overhear Moth asking Felix about his attire.

'I think I should've been born in the 60's.' Felix shouts. 'When would you have been born?'

'Two thousand five hundred and sixty-three,' Moth says in a camp drawl.

Kitten, Bobbi, Tamsin, and James' friend with the bowl cut are at the other end of the sofa, snorting something called Mephedrone. It makes you eat your own mouth and act like a *Warner Brothers* cartoon character. I watch Tamsin wrap her arms around James acting like they are great friends.

'Get some of your photos out,' I hear her say, enthusiastic at the prospect of seeing herself in print.

Felix has now started airing his views on the economy to the twinks. 'Money doesn't really exist,' he slurs, in reply to them talking about the earnings of a makeup artist friend. 'It just makes people do shit they don't really want to do.' He stresses his point by downing the rest of his cocktail. It isn't a massive amount; he's been drinking out of a shot glass in a failed attempt at moderation.

James drops his folders of photos in people's laps. Then there are people taking drugs, looking at photos of themselves taking drugs. There's one of Bobbi, in front of a dirt smeared night club wall, with green plaited hair, intricate tribal face paint, and a snorting straw sticking out of one nostril.

'You should make a book,' yaps Tamsin, looking at pictures of herself. A cute boy pushing a £5 note into her bra, and a pornographic pose on top of the bar at *Pegasus*.

'Look at you guys.' Milo nudges me to look at a photo of me and my ex-boyfriend behind a DJ desk, white nostrils, big smiles, arms around each other.

'Urgh,' I say, shielding it from Felix who leans in to have a look.

'I liked him!' Milo exclaims.

'Yeah, he was fun when he was high.'

'Is that Ryan?' Felix says, really close up to my ear.

'Yup,' I tell him while turning the page. There's another photo of me and Ryan, this time in an embrace on the dance floor at *Science Fiction*.

'James! What is this tribute to me and Ryan all about?'

'They're nice photos,' he says.

'Can we burn them?' Felix burps.

Kitten wedges herself between me and Felix. '– Urgh, that dick head."

'You introduced me to him!'

Tamsin is telling James to get the camera out now.

'I'm ready for my close up,' she says, undoing her bra in the centre and posing, grinding her teeth androgenous, with her made up face and boys' chest.

'Where's the blender?' Asks Felix.

'No, gurl, please,' I say jokingly.

'I'm gonna make a punch, everybody's gonna love it.' He's lying on the non-drug covered half of the coffee table.

'People can make their own drinks.'

'It's going to be a special punch. Come on Bobbi.' Felix reaches across in the direction of Bobbi.

Bobbi shrugs and seems like he's going to help but is a bit too high to leave the sofa.

'Don't encourage him,' I tell Bobbi, as Felix rolls off the coffee table and stumbles in the direction of the kitchen diner.

'I met him before once.' Bobbi tells me, running his hand through his pink mohawk.

'Yeah?'

'He was in the toilet at *The Peach.* I think he was trying to write the song that was playing on himself with marker pen. I think I helped him.'

'Yeah, that's Felix,' I say, hearing him in the background, opening and closing cupboards.

The door plays its midi version of *La Cucaracha.* I get up to answer, tightening my silk robe. Rocco is on the other side of the door, wearing a suit and a shirt all in tartan.

'Happy birthday!' He hugs me.

'It's not my birthday, babe.'

'Oh,' he says unfazed, 'I brought you Japanese vodka.'

'Have you been to Japan?'

'No.' He briefly contemplates putting the vodka down with the mess of other beverages and the blender that Felix is plugging in. Instead, he primly carries it over to the coffee table, amidst hyena-like shrieks and cackles.

'Aren't you supposed to be at work.' Tamsin points her acrylic nail at him. She's now almost completely naked, posing for what has turned into a porn shoot.

'Weren't you supposed to be there too?' Rocco replies.

'Oh, was I? Sorry!' She looks like she genuinely didn't know, but also laughs maniacally instead of apologising.

'It's ending anyway.' Rocco gives a disinterested flick of the wrist. 'I'm going to New York for a bit to start a fashion line.'

'I didn't know you designed clothes,' says the twink with the braids.

'I don't,' says Rocco, very into giving one-word answers at the moment. Milo's latest female rapper stops midline and *Spice up Your Life* comes on. Then Felix gets tangled up with the chord to the blender and pulls a load of stuff onto the floor, then falls over himself.

'Is that your boyfriend?' Asks Rocco.

James already seems to be sorting it out, putting on his camp, serious voice. Rocco asks if there are any shot glasses for the vodka. I look at the remains of a few of Felix's septic miniature drinks on the coffee table.

'I'll go and wash them up.' I pick them up on my fingers.

Felix and James are cleaning up. Felix trying to save some of the pureed fruit.

'I'm not impressed.' I look down at him.

'I wasn't trying to impress you.' He squints.

Tamsin and Milo contort on the coffee table to Christina Aguilera. I assume from the lull in Hijinks that Felix has passed out in my bed. The doorbell plays La Cucaracha, and I buzz up some more guests. They turn out to be Ash, in a purple fur coat and metal choker, and this new club kid called Peter Rabbit, wearing a leather jacket and black lederhosen. I'm surprised at how friendly I am with Ash.

'Guess who I was on the phone to earlier?' He says in a high, nasal voice.

'Cher?'

171

'Amanda Lepore. She's going to perform at *Pegasus*.' He places his hand on the drinks table.

'Why?'

'Obviously because I'm hosting a legendary night there. Urgh, what's that?' He lifts his hand from the kitchen work surface with some of Felix's fruit mush on it.

'My boyfriend's cocktail.'

'Did he really rip that disco ball out of the ceiling at *The W hotel*?' Ash looks over at the raucousness happening around the coffee table.

'I wouldn't say rip. But yeah.'

'Where is he?' Ash sounds interested to meet him.

'Asleep, I hope ... I'll go and check.'

When I open my bedroom door, I see a lot of costume items, pulled out of boxes, and Felix tangled up in them on the floor. He's wearing two tiaras and is mostly naked with lipstick and face paint all over his face. He reaches his arms out to me,

'Kyle!' He slurs gleefully

'Felix,' I say in monotone.

Felix seems to have attacked Kitten with the lipstick as well as himself. She's sitting next to him, the neon pink swirls and smears on her face contrasting with her skin tone and usually perfect makeup.

'He seems a lot happier now,' she says.

'He's barely conscious.' I pick up some oversized bug eye sunglasses from the floor before they get broken.

'Conscious enough to be offended.' He grabs my leg and looks up at me, cute and bedraggled.

I pull my leg away and sit on the side of the bed. 'Is this about us not moving in together?'

'It's not about anything,' he says, with a drunken pitch shift. 'Nothing's about anything.'

'Did you have to get so fucking wasted?' I put the bug-eyed sunglasses on top of my turban. 'You have a heart transplant.'

'I was drinking out of little glasses,' he complains.

'Maybe you should be drinking out of no glasses.'

'Nurghhhhh.' He makes an inebriated sound of disagreement and pushes his head, tiara and tangled hair into my lap.

Kitten tries to subtly leave the room.

'It kind of makes you into an asshole.' I stroke his hair. 'Why don't you go to sleep for a bit.'

He makes a moany little sound while rubbing his head in my lap.

'I'll go and get some water.' I stand up and allow his head to drop onto the bed.

In the bathroom, Kitten tells me, 'He said he doesn't think your friends like him.' One of her false eyelashes is hanging off.

'Some of them don't,' I state the facts. 'He doesn't exactly make a good impression.'

'You used to be a mess too,' she says.

I note in her tone of voice that she misses those times, but I'm sure I was a mess in an entertaining socially conscious way. And I think I'm glad I'm not a mess anymore. Still, I have to drink the last of the Japanese vodka to forget how drunk Felix is.

A track about fashion is blaring out, and there are drinks everywhere. I put on my big bug-eye sunglasses and dance with Ash and the boy with the gold crown of thorns. I try to return to being a wild club-kid, rather than a cancer patient or Felix's carer. I shrug off the robe to reveal a bejewelled bodysuit underneath. There's a moment where we start making out as a three, but to my credit I leave them to it. I go and drape myself over the coffee table and pop olives into my mouth. I look at Milo, Tamsin, and Rocco bitching intensely on the sofa.

'So, what are you going to call your new night at *Science Fiction*?' Asks Rocco, sitting in the armchair.

'I'm just doing that one-off birthday takeover of your night.'

'But Lars is going to ask you.' He shrugs like it doesn't bother him.

'You think?' I say, excited at the idea of my own flagship night at *Science Fiction*.

'Don't fuck it up like he did.' Tamsin nods toward Rocco.

'Things have a short shelf life these days.' He flaps his hand.

'*Flasher Slasher* was going for three years,' Kitten adds.

'I don't know if my future is hosting club nights.' I pop an olive into my mouth.

'I'll do it,' says Milo.

Then Felix makes his return to the party, like some horror film monster that had died suddenly rising out of the lake. He drags my duvet with him, wearing multiple head pieces, his face a mess of makeup and face paint.

'I thought you were sleepy,' I hint at him to go back to bed.

'No, just drunk,' Felix says squashing past people, including an annoyed looking Milo. Felix perches himself on the edge of the TV stand, knocking over a few empty shot glasses.

'Do you try to ruin every party you go to.' Milo turns to him.

'I try to make them interesting,' Felix slurs.

'Last time I looked in the dictionary the definition of interesting wasn't a drunk hippie in a duvet knocking over glasses.' Milo turns away like this is the end of the matter.

'The last time you looked in a dictionary was never,' Felix laughs at his own humour.

Milo rolls his eyes, and Felix roles his tongue into a tube.

'Just because he's your boyfriend, I'm not going to pretend like it's fine,' Milo tells me.

'Get along or don't talk to each other.' I make a frustrated gesticulation with my lacey medieval sleeves.

'I'm sorry,' slurs Felix, getting up to give Milo a hug.

'Get the fuck off me!' Milo Shrieks batting Felix away.

Felix sits back down and seems to go back inside his duvet cocoon. Then he grabs a nearby glass of Ukrainian red wine and flings the contents at Milo, some of the spray landing on Peter Rabbit's white t-shirt and lederhosen. Milo stands up and screeches with queeny exasperation.

'Right, that's it! Felix!' I pull him out of the duvet by his hand and drag him with me to the bathroom and slam the door shut.

'What the hell was that!?' I rasp at him.

'He's a dick,' Felix whines.

I can hear Milo in the other room screeching.

'I know he's a dick!' I position myself against the mirror. 'He's also one of my best friends.'

'Why would you be friends with someone like that?' Felix sits on the toilet, half naked, covered in face paint.

'What is this about?'

'It's about your friends treating me like shit.'

'If you weren't acting like shit. Maybe they wouldn't treat you like it.' I lean against the mirror, my face feeling hot. 'Every time I take you out, you embarrass me,'

'Maybe you shouldn't be so easily embarrassed.' He glares, his eyes big and pink.

'It's like you don't care what people think of you,' I say.

'I don't.' He continues to glare at me.

'Well, if I was one of my friends. I would wonder why the fuck we're going out.' I glare back at him.

He looks down at his hands, smeared with face paint. 'Sometimes I think you're different from them. And sometimes I think you're not.'

'What's that supposed to mean?'

'Sometimes I think you're still that arrogant person I met outside *Science Fiction*,' he spits it out, like he doesn't want to say it, but he can't stop himself.

'I should ask you to leave,' I huff.

'I was leaving anyway,' he says, neither of us able to look at the other.

One of the classic photos of my childhood is me standing in front of the giant statues of Osiris in the Karnak temple. White polo shirt and striped shorts, my legs far apart in the sand as if I've come to conquer. My mother is looking distractedly at something out of frame. The statues of Osiris look so perfect they could be a fiberglass recreation at a theme park, with their crossed arms and wrapped beards.

I studied ancient Egypt at primary school where we made wonky canopic jars out of papier-mâché. Mine was a blue and gold, glitter glue Anubis with googly eyes. I wanted to be Tutankhamun, I didn't mind dying young. I just liked the image of myself in a sparkly white pleated loincloth with gold jewellery, being fed figs, and telling slaves to go build more pyramids.

My parents would occasionally indulge my hobbies if I wasn't too precocious about them. Not walking around the house half naked with a towel on my head and my mum's eyeliner, spouting facts about mummification. Or wrapping all my cuddly toys in toilet paper with bits of my mum's jewellery as amulets and making a funerary procession with them to the oven where they were entombed until my mum decided to cook. When my mum told me we were going on a cruise up the Nile that summer, I almost peed myself. I ran into every room of the house screaming, 'Yes, yes, yes!' And jumping on sofas and beds. Felix said he had the same obsession. When he was in hospital as a child, he'd make little books written in his own made-up hieroglyphs.

I pay an old man in a kaftan to take a photo of us, back where I stood about 15 years ago. Both sweaty, Felix in his ringer t-shirt and headscarf, making demented open-mouthed expressions. Me in my bug-eye sunglasses, trying to look fashion editorial. The statues of Osiris are just as massive and mystical. I'll put it in a frame next to the old one when I get back and impress James with my artistic sensibilities. We leave the bit of the temple with all the Osiris statues and head back into a hall filled with huge hieroglyph covered pillars. The late afternoon paints the ruins a deep orange. There are barely any other tourists about. I like these moments with Felix, silently walking through these ancient places. I watch him trace the indentation of a hieroglyph in one of the pillars. I realise he's probably going to move in with me and James when I get back. I was so occupied with Felix's recovery that I can't even remember the last time I saw James. I don't think I've called him while I've been away. I don't think I've called my parents either.

'Have you written to your grandma?' I put my finger into a hieroglyph of a bird with a circle on its head.

'I think I sent some postcards,' he scrunches up his nose.

'I'll send that photo to my parents,' I tell him.

'Take some more.' He poses suggestively against one of the pillars. 'I'm not very good at staying in contact with people when I'm not in the same place as them. Is that bad?'

'I'm not good at staying in contact with people when I'm in the same place as them.' I say, thinking about James.

'Just give them some souvenirs from my room when you get back.'

We look up at the pillars, shadows lengthening in the late afternoon sun. Big sections of hieroglyphs missing, smoothed over with terracotta coloured cement.

'Are you going back to your grandma's?' I ask.

'I don't know.' He shrugs.

'I mean ...' I stop and push my sunglasses onto my baseball cap. '... You can move in with me and James, if you want.'

'Nah,' he says, sauntering off toward the engraved walls at the back of the hall. A few seconds later he turns back, smiling. 'Yeah, of course. I'd love to.'

James has gone away on a photographic errand to Berlin. I'm here disinterestedly doing some little fashion sketches in an old spiral-bound notebook. Jotting down names and ideas for my new club night. The shopping channel is trying to sell me little animal-shaped hole punches. A Bryl-creamed man in a purple shirt excitedly punching away at pieces of pastel coloured paper, shouting that you can use them to decorate cards or even as confetti. I think for a while what it would be like to fuck him on a mound of these little confetti shapes. Little pink horses and rabbits stuck to our sweating bodies on the shopping channel studio floor. I see the streetlights come on, through the blinds, and I pause for a long time over the little sketch I've done, a long-legged figure wearing a re-imagined version of my glittery armour.

My thoughts don't stay where I want them to. I start thinking about all the things Felix has been through, wondering if they excuse him throwing wine in my friend's face. He told me he spent his childhood feeling more like an experiment than a person. He said he was just coming out of that feeling when the fire happened. His mum was having a break down, arranging ornaments on the living room floor and talking about Jesus. He had a tent in his bedroom because he couldn't go camping. He went and hid in there and imagined he was in Egypt or Norway. That's where the firemen found him, they said the tent might've saved his life. He said he blacked the whole thing out.

I must have fallen asleep. I wake up to my ringtone with my head wedged into the sofa arm. I see Felix's name on the screen with a little cartoon picture of a cat's face and push the phone to the other side of the coffee table. I let it keep bleeping and vibrating till it goes to answer-phone. I look at it for a few seconds, and it starts ringing again. Remembering how persistent Felix can be, I groggily pick up the phone and carry it to the kitchen. I put it in an oven glove and shut it in the cutlery drawer. It keeps ringing, a muted midi version of Bolero rattling against our knives and forks. Felix has tried to call a few times and left a message saying he's "*sorry for being a dick*" and telling me to "*call him.*" But I haven't received this kind of torrent of attempted communication. I assume he's drunk.

Eventually, the ringing ends in the muffled chime of a text message. I go and retrieve it from the oven glove. The message says in block capitals, "*LOOK OUT THE WINDOW.*" Knowing what Felix is capable of, this sentence immediately fills me with fear. I hoist up the blinds and look out into the street. On the grass verge below is Leon, holding a guitar plugged into an amp decorated with fairy lights. Next to him is Felix, holding a microphone and wearing a gold ruffled prom shirt. He sees me in the kitchen window and jabs at Leon's arm and Leon begins to play some distorted guitar chords, his dreadlocks hanging over his face. Then Felix sings into the scratchy low-quality microphone,

'*Nobody does it better ...*' His baritone voice has an awkward adolescence about it, but he doesn't sing badly.

I curse him for involving me in this scene that I feel he stole from some rom-com. But I still open the window and lean on the faucet to get a better view, like someone waiting patiently for carol singers to stop. I can tell from the light in the window below that the neighbours are watching as well. I've never been serenaded before. I see there's a sort of kamikaze embarrassment about it. Having to sit and watch as your private relationship is turned into a Broadway show. I curse him, looking up at me, hair tucked behind one ear, singing earnestly, lit by fairy lights. Curse him for knowing exactly how to embarrass me and for knowing the perfect song to sing.

When he's finished, he quickly says, 'Sorry, Kyle.' And plonks the microphone down on the amp. There's a squeal of feedback.

'I guess you want to come up?' I shout.

'If that's okay.' he shouts back.

'What about Leon?'

'He's going to pick up some weed.' Leon slaps Felix's arm for his lack of subtlety.

I press the unlock button to let him in and mutter, "*fuck*" to myself. If James was here, I might make more of a show of being angry at Felix. Instead, I allow Felix to start making out with me as soon as he's meekly muttered, 'Sorry.'

'You're an asshole,' I say when he breaks away, but I say it in the same tone as a compliment.

'I know. I got insecure, then I got drunk. More drunk than I meant to. I'm not good at controlling it sometimes.' Rather than sitting at one of the kitchen-diner stools he sits on the kitchen floor and looks up at me.

'Maybe you shouldn't be drinking at all,' I tell him.

'I hoped you wouldn't say that.' He sucks one lip underneath the other.

'Because it's true.' I join him on the floor tiles. 'I'm tired of feeling like I'm your carer. I spoke to my doctor, and he said it's amazing you're still alive. I don't want to worry that you're going to die.'

182

'I'm sorry.' He reaches across and limply touches my knee, trying to look into my eyes. 'Since we've been together, I don't feel like drinking so much. I used to not be so bothered if I died, and I thought that was kind of enlightened.'

'How's that enlightened?'

'Not being attached to anything ...' He sounds like he's going to make a list, but he can't think of any more points. '... But you make me attached. You make me want to look after myself.'

'You should look after yourself for yourself.' I look at him disappointed. I don't want his health to be dependent on me. 'Sometimes you seem so confident, and sometimes you seem so insecure.'

'I'm both.' His lips move bitterly. 'More the second one if you have to know. I feel like your friends are never going to like me.'

'I thought you didn't care what people thought of you.'

'Maybe, I care when they're your friends.' He looks at me from under lank brown curls.

'I'm one of them, and I like you.' I push myself up off the kitchen floor. 'I want to show you something.' I go into my recently organised bedroom, I open the dresser drawer and get my wallet out, then hop back into the kitchen. For a moment I worry that I've lost what I'm looking for. I find it folded up behind the little cut out of my picture from *ID magazine*. I pull out a ten-pound note and stick it into his hand. I watch with hesitation as he unfolds it. He's confused, then he turns it over and sees where he wrote his phone number on the bottom about a year ago. He presses his hand into his face and takes a long-distorted breath, then gets up and wraps himself tight around me and sobs. I feel like I should do something, maybe cry, but I'm not much of a crier, so I just wrap my arms around him.

The taxi drops us off, our bags full of hummus and flatbread. A sign over the entrance reads, "*Welcome to Tranquility Beach*" in peeling sky blue letters. Beyond the sign are the shadows of a few dishevelled beach huts, dotted uniformly on the sands. I shine my torch at the thatched rooves as we make our way down the rocks with our plastic bags. The night is warm and still, the only light other than the torch is the planetarium of stars above us. He dumps the bag in the doorway of our hut and fumbles around in his pocket for the key.

'I've got it.' I twist the key in the stiff rusty lock.

The sea shushes in the dark behind us, and there's the smell of damp wood. I kick the door open and drop the shopping bag by the small round table. I'm just about to throw myself down on the bed when Felix shines the torch into the room, and I see something on the bed. I think maybe it's just clothes. But, no, there's a group of small dark objects resting on the old red blanket.

'Shit.' I hear my voice murmur.

Felix continues to shine the torch at the burnt angel ornaments arranged on the bed, and more on the shelf behind it.

'Shit,' I repeat. 'Who would do this? We have to get out of here.' I turn to Felix, just standing there, gaping with the torch and shopping bag in his hands. 'Felix!'

He shines the torch at me, and I have to force him to lower it.

'It doesn't look like they've taken anything,' he answers.

'Someone's following us, tracking us around the world.' I reach for my bag. 'We should go. Get to a phone, call a taxi.'

Felix just stands there, shining the torch at the burnt figurines.

'The phones are far,' he says, as if in a trance.

I take the torch out of his hand to stop him examining the ornaments. I shine it at the dirty beige walls, then at him. 'You can stay here, but I'm not.'

'Okay.' He pulls his bag out from behind the bed.

The door clangs shut with all the little burnt angels still inside. The sea behind us, I point the torchlight across the sands toward the road.

'I can't believe this is happening,' I call backwards. He doesn't reply. 'Can you?'

'Yes.' His voice is just audible over the sea.

'What do you mean?'

'You know when we were talking about my mum and her angels.' I hear his footsteps stop.

'Let's keep walking.' I swing the torch around at him, then notice lights coming down the road.

'—And I said maybe she's haunting us.' His voice is slow, like he thinks we're just having a casual conversation on the beach.

'You think we should wave this down,' I call back, ambling toward the road.

The car is getting close. Probably people heading for the resorts further up. The car stops and in the headlights I see something that stops my breath. I quickly turn back toward the beach, grabbing for Felix's arm, managing to get part of his bag.

'It's the same car!' My voice is muted in the desert air. I saw the dent in the bumper, the same as in the street in Morocco. I start to stumble back down the rocks under the weight of my backpack. I hear the car door open. I realise we don't have much to protect ourselves, except a few bits of wood and some kitchen knives back at the hut.

I hear Felix's muffled yell and turn around to see a man in a grey suit pushing him to the ground. Then in the headlights, I see the shadow of another man rounding the car. I don't have time to react. He punches me in the stomach and there's no breath. Then he's pushing me onto the ground too. There's dirt from the road in my mouth. I struggle. I can hear Felix struggling too. The guy manages to pull my bag off. I grab at his suit, but he pulls my hands back down, his knee in my spine.

'Who the fuck are you? Why are you doing this?' I shout.

Felix is shouting too, 'You're not real! You can't do this! You're not real.' Then muffled sounds.

The guy is pulling something like a cable tie around my hands, and I'm trying to bite him or kick him. Looking up into the headlights, I see Felix's legs as he's forced into the car. Then I'm being forced onto my feet, my arms twisted.

'You fucking psycho!' I resist as he forces me into the boot.

He slams the top down, and I'm in darkness. The engine vibrates into motion and the car is moving with us inside.

I lie there tasting the blood and dirt inside my mouth, listening to the tires on the gravel. I try to think who these people could be and what they want with us. It must be Felix they want. They must be the same people that left the angels in the rooms. They must be powerful if they can follow us through so many countries. The car stops. I hear the doors open, there's a struggle, muffled voices, and then silence again.

I squirm, trying to pull my hands out of the cable tie in the humid darkness. I force my back up into the roof of the boot and attempt to push it open. But it's pointless. I just lie on my side, in the dark. My heart, beating in anticipation. Are they trying to get some information out of Felix? I always thought there was something he was hiding from me. But none of the ideas that come into my head seem rational. Could it be something to do with drugs? His mother saw an angel before he was born. He claims to have psychic abilities. Is he something more than human? Are these people like the men in black. Then, I think about Felix's 70's clothes and wonder if he's a time traveller. These thoughts make my hairs stand on end and my stomach feel strange. Am I really considering that someone with terrible tattoos who lives with his grandma has the ability to time travel? I try to calm my mind.

The boot of the car is thrust open. It fills with dusty desert air. I'm momentarily blinded by a torch shining in my face. I don't see what the guy looks like, he forces me to my feet, and I get a headrush. He walks me to the outline of a concrete bunker surrounded by empty desert.

'Are you going to tell me who you are?' My voice spits, strained and camp.

There's no reply, just him forcing me to the metal door of the bunker.

'Do you speak English?' I ask.

No reply. I've always found people respond to insults, so I try to think of one. But he's pushing me into a white tiled room with strip lighting. It's not what I expected. I see a figure in a white robe, splattered with blood. It looks unreal in the bright light. I see its hands, grey, thick with veins, placing a knife down on a silver tray. My body is both stiff and numb, my mouth barely breathing. I see Felix's naked body on a bed, smeared with blood. I lunge for the person in the robe. The man in the suit grabs my arm, and I crash into the silver medical tray. As I'm being forced to the ground, I see dark clotted blood and something like guts on the medical tray. Then my face is being pushed into the white floor tiles.

Part 4

Asia

We're on my bed, Felix in his banana pants, me in some pink transparent boxers. His big old atlas open between us. We're like two gay demi-Gods, looking down at all the desserts, seas, and mountains. The late morning sun coming in under the blinds. Felix traces a line up the Nile and around the Sinai desert into Israel.

'Do we have to go to the middle east?' I look at the trajectory of his finger.

'We don't have to go anywhere,' he says.

'Well let's skip this bit.' I circle most of the map with my finger. 'I've heard they can be quite sassy toward gay people.'

'We'll just go to Mecca then.'

'Isn't that –'

I must look concerned because he squeezes my arm and says, 'I'm joking, you have to be Muslim to go to Mecca. We need to stop over somewhere to make the flight to India cheap though.'

'India.' I think of crowds, and beggars with milky eyes.

'Do you like any country where people have a different skin colour to you?' Felix squints, and I make an open-mouthed, offended expression.

'I'm not racist! I just don't want a stomach infection.' I hear someone at the door as Felix is turning the page of the atlas.

James stands there, in a yellow polo neck, with a suitcase and backpack. He looks surprised for a moment at seeing me and Felix back together.

'Let me put on some clothes so I can hug you.' I pull on my silk robe, tiptoe through and give him a hug.

'You did your hair,' he says, sticking his hand into my newly bleached quiff.

'Actually, Felix did it.'

'Tell me about that.' He shrugs his backpack off.

'He came and serenaded me.'

'Oh –' James gives me a look that's filled with questions.

'Did you get me anything from Deutschland?'

'Lemme see.' He heaves his backpack onto the kitchen diner chair. He starts to pull little bottles of German spirits out of a side pocket and piles them into my hands.

'Wow, thanks. I'll hide them in here.' I open the drawer below the cutlery. 'Felix isn't drinking spirits anymore ... his idea.'

'You too?' James gets the cafetière out of another cupboard.

'No.' I frown at him. 'I know moderation.'

'Oh, do you? You never introduced me.'

'We're not close, but I know her.' I lean back against the work surface and stretch out my arms showing the full opulence of this big-sleeved silk robe I've taken to wearing most of every day.

Felix comes and joins us in pants and socks, his big collared shirt open. 'Sorry if I was an asshole at the party.'

James makes a priestly gesture of forgiveness and asks me, 'You want coffee?'

'If it's that good stuff from Columbia,' I say, sitting on a stool, twizzling.

'It can be. Felix?'

'A little bit.'

'I thought you didn't drink coffee.' I poke Felix with my foot.

'I do when James asks.' He leans suggestively on the counter.

James fills the kettle and asks, 'Whose parties have you been wrecking while I've been away?'

'We're planning our world tour,' Felix says.

'How far around the world?'

'Vladivostok.' Felix smiles.

'Vladi-what?' I twizzle round on the stool to look at him.

'We're catching the Trans-Siberian express there.'

'Do you know what the Trans-Siberian express is?' James looks at me, cafetière in hand like a 1950's catalogue model.

'It's a train.' I adjust the tie on my silk robe.

'The longest train journey in the world,' he goads me.

Later I pirouette apprehensively into James' room, it resembles a gallery of rejected photos and vintage *Ken* dolls. He's on the computer adjusting some colour wheels next to a photo of some German Goths, their hair gelled into massive double mohawks.

'You're so motivated,' I tell him.

'I love my work.' He twists around in his office chair.

'Taking pictures of goths?' I say as if that is all he does.

'Goths from around the world. Actually, that would be a good series.'

'I've already got your next photo series planned. You're going to travel around the world with me and Felix.'

'Definitely not.' He laughs. 'Is this trip actually happening?'

'Yes.' I cross my lacey medieval sleeves. 'We're starting in December, to avoid the winter.'

'How long?'

'Maybe 6 months.' I pick a *Ken* doll up, off his chest of drawers.

'You just moved in.' His forehead furrows.

'I don't want to move out. I'll pay some of the rent. I'll find someone to sublet to.'

'I'll find someone to sublet to.' James pulls his mouth to the side. 'Are you sure you want to travel the world for six months though?'

'We've been talking about it since I was in hospital. We're going to drive down the West Coast from San Francisco.' I ramble as if I'm being accused of something. 'Who wouldn't want to do that? I'll send you postcards!'

The first job I return to is DJing at *Burger Bar*. The club in Soho with the kleptomaniac decorations, everything upholstered in worn red velvet. I'm in the same pulpit with the same chipped paintwork. Only this time I feel good about being there. I'm wearing a rib cage made of mirror tiles over a shiny jumpsuit, playing a remix of *All or Nothing* by *Cher*.

'I thought you were dead,' a girl with a mound of platinum curls squawks at me.

'Nope.' I hold the headphones to one of my ears.

The next person to sidle up to the booth is Milo. He catches me in a moment of lapsed self-awareness. I'm flinging my mirror covered hands out in the direction of the dance floor.

'Cosmo ... gurl ... Kyle!' He barks. He's wearing a black embroidered catsuit with deep burgundy lipstick smudged across his face. 'What are you on, can I have some?'

'White wine and Cher.' I shake the empty glass at him.

'Sure.' He purses his lips together. Then his eyes flicker with the remembrance of the point he was going to bring up. 'You're not really going to travel around the world with that psycho, are you?' He asks as if it's a joke I've been making.

'I am actually.' I guide him over to the side of the booth where I can hear him better. 'We're going on an international gay bar crawl.'

'Oh honey, please don't.' He knits his eyebrows. 'I think you're in a very destructive relationship, and you need intervention.'

'I know you don't like him.' I look at Milo's petulant face, disco lights flashing across it. 'But he makes me laugh, and he kind of saved my life.'

'He makes you laugh,' Milo repeats, emphasising the fickleness of the statement. 'How long are you going for?'

'Maybe six months,' I try to say it quick enough that he'll ignore it and move on to the next subject.

'Six months!' Milo squawks. 'Six months with –' He searches for the right insult to describe Felix. '– With Charles Manson Jr.'

Lars, the owner of *Science Fiction*, gives me a bag of flyers. I can't stop myself from getting them out on the tube and looking at them. My disembodied head covered in mirror-glass and sequins, with rings around it like the planet Saturn. *Arcade 3000* written at the top in a trippy mulicoloured font and "*Cosmo birthday special*" at the bottom. I wave some in Felix's direction when he comes to visit.

'Give me some?' He snatches them out of my hand, then returns his attention to my beauty table, now covered in maps, notes, and travel guides. My room has become a sort of office, with transitory purpose and lax dress codes. Me on my bed wearing my pastel-peach robe, sending emails to DJs and performers. Felix wearing a floral pattern shirt in fluorescent pinks and oranges with corduroy flares, planning our route across the world.

'Peru,' he says. He repeats the word a few more times, trying to get my attention.

'Do they have gay bars?' I ask, focusing on the email I'm about to send to a DJ friend.

'Peru? I don't think so.' He puffs up one cheek.

'Where's the next place with gay bars?'

'Ummm probably Brazil.'

'We should go to more places with gay bars.' I press send on the email and start up another one to a photographer from *Boyz* magazine.

'Maybe *you* should choose some places.' Felix twists around on his cushioned stool.

'I'm busy.'

There's a pause, I type a few words.

'I don't feel like we're connecting at the moment,' Felix whines.

I sigh, then push the computer away. 'I'm just busy at the moment.'

He comes and sits down on the bed next to me. He leans his head into my shoulder blade, and I shut my laptop realising I'm not going to get any work done.

'What do you want for your birthday?' He asks.

'I don't know.' I push my hand through his hair. 'You could do something about this.'

'Do what?' His eyes look up toward his mass of brown hair.

'Maybe something a bit more modern.' I push his hair back, so I can imagine him with emo hair, a quiff, even a buzz cut.

He gives me a curious look. What style could turn him into the kind of boyfriend I could be photographed with, behind DJ decks and on red carpets.

'— Something shorter. Maybe add some colour. I like a guy with blue hair.'

I wake up in my own sweat with a feeling of terror. A strange sensation, like a vibration, running through my body. It's not the room I expected to wake up in. There are scratchy blankets and peach-coloured walls. White light shining through big lattice windows, covered by drapes. The bed creaks as I edge up onto my elbows. I try to push my mind back to what caused this feeling of horror. Where's Felix? I turn to his side of the bed and there's no one there, just a tangle of blankets. I remind myself we're travelling; he isn't in hospital anymore. I pull myself out of bed. I slip my bare feet into boots and pull on my jeans, hoodie, red hiking jacket. I peek through the drapes at snow tipped mountains reaching down into vast rubble covered slopes.

There's a sign on the door in Indian and English writing. I open it into a courtyard, frayed prayer flags flapping in the breeze, turquoise walls, and a wild tangled area of foliage. A sandwich board with badly printed photos advertises curries and flat breads. My feet seem to know where to go before my brain does. I walk out onto a dusty path cut into the hillside and hold my breath as I look at the massive valley below, veins of water running through it. I'm very high up, empty roads and uninhabited paths cut into a steep sandy rock face. My bare skin rubs against the inside of my boots. The wind makes me wince and hug myself, I hear voices on it, soft and discordant, like children chanting. On the other side of the valley, a few clouds make shadows on the mountains.

Concrete stairs merge with the rocky outcrop. At first, there is a handrail, with tangled faded prayer flags strung along it. Then there's just the rock to cling onto. The crumbling brick steps fading into the hillside, the chanting getting louder. At the top of the slope is an old building. The white and red paint, worn and dirty, as if it's in the process of returning itself to nature. The feeling of fear has mostly faded, leaving behind uncertainty. Where am I going and is Felix there? The building is a few stories high. I follow the weather-beaten wall round. There are rows of worn bronze prayer wheels, covered in foreign writing. Then an entrance made of dark ancient wood. I listen to my footsteps on the stone as I step inside, hugging myself. Inside are faded murals of meditating figures, a white one in the lotus position with lots of arms, a yellow buddha surrounded by a wall of praying people. The dark corridor fills with the smell of sandalwood, the melancholic chanting close. I wonder if I'm supposed to be here. I walk past a room with a pile of parchment and a picture of the Dalai Lama. Then I jump, seeing rows of young monks in a heavily decorated room, reading simultaneously from books. Lots of little shoes outside the room.

Wonky steps lead to a concrete terrace. Worn-out signs in an embossed font warn me to watch my head. Standing on top of the building, I see a monk sitting on the edge of the roof top. A lone figure in yellow, facing an almost cloudless sky. I step across a mandala drawn into the old stone. The children's chanting muted by the vastness of the landscape. When I'm closer I see, it's not a monk, it's Felix. He's sitting cross-legged in his yellow duffle coat, his neon hat blowing in the breeze. I lean on a pole strung with prayer flags and look down at him, his eyes shut. There's no barrier at the edge of the building, just the valley and the sky.

'What is it?' Says Felix, without opening his eyes.

'You weren't there when I woke up. I thought something had happened.'

'I thought something had happened too.' His voice is quiet. 'That's why I'm trying to –' He makes some flakey gesture.

'Trying to what?' I hug the pole. 'Are you going to finish that sentence.'

'Trying to meditate!'

I sit down next to him and marvel wordlessly at the postcard view in front of us.

'So big,' I prompt him to talk.

He breathes in and out slowly. 'I used to do this thing when I lived in that beach hut. I used to sit on the pebbles in the morning and meditate. I'd make everything disappear, the sea, the sky, the beach, my body. Then when I was finished, I'd create it all over again.' He pauses like I'm supposed to have some kind of reaction to this.

'Where were we before here?' I ask.

'What do you remember?' He looks at me confused, his lips parted.

'Umm.' I search my brain, fuzzy from just waking up.

The monks are still chanting below. I can't have forgotten. This can't be a *Felix waking up on the beach in San Francisco* scenario. My eyes go out of focus as I look at the mountains. I vaguely remember waiting in a crowd to take a photo of Felix on the bench outside the Taj Mahal. Felix lying down in an erotic pose and asking if he looks like Princess Diana.

'Delhi?' I look at him for confirmation, but he keeps his eyes fixed on the valley below. I try and delve deeper. There's another blurry memory, like a second of video footage, us flapping around on a pink lilo with mud on our faces. 'The Dead Sea?'

He looks at me with an inconclusive tilt of his head.

I open the door and see my boyfriend's face, juxtaposed with blue curly hair, cut short-ish so it hangs to one side.

'Happy Birthday,' he says. He's wearing a black and white ringer t-shirt with those sequin dungarees that he permanently borrowed off me. 'You like it?' His moles and far apart eyes take on a renewed beauty. He's almost like another person.

'Yeah!' I reach out and touch a strand to check its real. 'I'm just surprised.'

'Good, I like to surprise.' He gives me a quick chaffinch peck on the cheek. I can tell James is craning his neck from his stool behind the kitchen table, wondering what Felix has done. Felix looks at the glass of Cava in my hand.

'James made me breakfast.' I take his shoulder and mutter. 'It was supposed to be a champagne breakfast, but he thinks Cava is Champagne.'

'Oh, poor you.' Felix hugs me.

'You can have a thimble full,'

'Wow!' Says James, his long legs arranged on the stool like a crane fly. 'I thought the 70's look was a permanent thing.'

'Nothing's permanent,' Felix tells him.

'You're so profound,' James replies.

I go and get the sherry glass that I got for Felix to drink from. But actually, the only thing I've seen him drinking recently is a bottle of non-alcoholic wine while we all watched *Thelma and Louise*.

'You wanna go anywhere today?' He sips the Cava.

'No, I think I'll just stay in and screw.' I wink overtly at my new visually improved boyfriend.

'Oh! I've got something else for you!' Felix hums a little fanfare and pulls an envelope from his pocket and hands it to me. It's covered in glittery stickers of ponies. Inside is another envelope with an American airways insignia on it. 'They came in the post yesterday!' The look on his face is one of absolute unparalleled excitement.

I take the tickets out of the envelope and look at our names on them in bold pixelated capitals, *Vancouver, Kyle*, and *Gunston, Felix*.

'No going back now.' I fan myself with them.

I filled the club with every shiny decoration and lighting fixture I could find, dust-covered and decaying, in musty cupboards and under boxes of fliers for previous nights. I collect a few of the flyers up for when I ask James to help me create a club kid museum. I hook a cluster of about thirty disco balls in different sizes and states to the ceiling. There's a full church window of gobos and gels, beaming spinning and strobing from every angle and alcove, creating a sort of disco grotto. I go around the club switching them all on. They jerk and rotate for an audience of me, Felix, and two bar staff.

In the green room, Felix pushes hard on my abdomen with his knee, pulling at the corseting of my new suit of armour. He gives it a few swift yanks, grunting and puffing his blue hair out of his face.

'Ow!' I yelp feeling a bit of skin getting caught.

"You said you wanted it tight.' He holds his tongue between his teeth as he ties the strings at the front.

I notice a few spots where the blue Directions hair dye has bled into his skin. I adjust the messy knot he's tied and push it inside the mirror tile covered chest plate. I look at myself and Felix in a mirror propped up against some lockers. I look like a medieval knight that had a child with a disco ball. Felix is wearing some gold dungarees I dug out for him and my gold Hermes hat.

'We're a club kid power couple.' I practice posing against him for the gay media.

He sprawls across the mottled velvet sofa with his latest travel book. I wonder if he now fits into my life the way I need him to. I climb the dingy stairwell onto the roof where I can pace with a cigarette looking out at the skyline. The moon blurred by cloud.

Fast forward two hours and Felix is forcing me, half-drunk, out of the green room. The DJ playing *God Save the Queen* for my entrance. There are flashing lights and gurning club kids. I'm getting handed champagne. Then there's a rolled-up note in my nose and something that stings like MDMA going into my nostril. Moth is in front of me, blue-faced, looking like a member of some post-apocalyptic tribe, passing the tray of drugs onto the next person.

'Are you going to open that?' Kitten staggers into me, pointing at the champagne.

Some guy with green hair, so high his eyes are closed is telling me how glad he is I'm alive. I see a photographer in the crowd trying to get a picture of me, so I climb over the pink-haired boy onto the bar. I wrap my leg around one of the poles supporting the bar and pose like a porn actor. Then I hold the champagne where my crotch is and let the cork burst out and scream,

'Happy Birthday, me!' All the lights reflecting off my armour, champagne spraying over the crowd.

I walk down the corridor to the smoking area with people following me, and people jumping out the way. I feel like Michael Jackson in those press clips, where you see him walking, surrounded by a crowd of masked children, minders, and well-wishers.

'Hey!' Says a guy with a good jawline and a black quiff, the air filled with tobacco.

'Hey, have you got a cigarette?' I ask.

He gets out a pack of Vogue slims.

'I always buy those,' I tell him, pulling one out.

'You don't remember me, do you?' He shouts over the burble and chatter.

Some people are helping a guy wearing a lot of yellow faux fur to climb over the wall.

'I don't know anyone,' I shout back, looking for a light.

'I gave you MDMA at *Burger Bar*, we went back to yours.' He lights my cigarette and I jab it at him in recognition. The goth boy I pulled just before I got diagnosed with cancer. Just a bit older and a lot hotter.

'You got—'

'— Hotter?' He says, his voice deep and Northern.

'— Taller.' I tap cigarette ash into a plant.

We end up going to the toilet and doing MDMA again, cut up with his library card. He looks at me with his mascaraed eyelashes and good jawline and starts kissing me. It's an erotic, frantic, MDMA kiss.

After about twenty seconds I tell him, 'I've got a boyfriend.'

'Monogamous?' He asks.

'Well ...' I pause.

He smiles about to pin me against the cubicle wall.

'Yeah, I think it is.' I scratch a bit of glitter of his face that transferred from my mouth to his and open the cubicle door.

Felix is sitting in one of the sinks. He's talking to one of the twinks from my house party, the one who had the gold crown of thorns. He now has an intricate gold halo. I expect him to look freaked out by whatever Felix is saying, but instead, he laughs and says,

'Yeah, I totally get that.'

'Oi, boyfriend,' Felix calls. He only looks slightly suspicious of me and the black-haired guy. 'Having a good time?'

What kind of person asks if you're having a good time, when you're so high that one of your eyes is spinning backwards into your head? Then I remember, he's sober. I hear the intro to paper planes by MIA,

'I love this song! Give me a piggyback!'

He heaves me and my armour onto his back and gallops through all the noise and lights. Gurning costumed people dive out of the way. We topple onto the dancefloor and Felix starts making out with me amongst everyone's legs.

I had to stop the bouncers throwing a naked guy out. He'd ripped the rainbow flag off the bar and proceeded to gyrate on it in just his pants. I'm wearing it as a cape now, like a gay Britannia, surveying the battlefield. Mirror balls ripped from the ceiling, wires hanging out, the floor covered in costume items and broken glass. Suddenly Lars is in front of me, with his crew cut and crooked smile, looking like a daddy from a porn film.

'This place is a mess!' His camp voice informs me.

'Sorry,' I clench my teeth and glance at some toilet roll smeared on the wall.

'I didn't say it was a bad thing.' He puts his hand on my shoulder to steady himself. He's got the manner of someone who's spent the last few hours taking meth in a sauna.

'This is my boyfriend Felix,' I change the subject, and pull Felix over by his dungaree strap.

'I'm the owner of this shit hole.' Lars gives Felix a firm handshake.

'One of the best shit holes in London,' Felix shouts over the music.

'I'm just passing through,' Lars mumbles. 'Let's sort out your pay.'

Me and Felix follow him to the office, the lights flashing over his bomber jacket. The green room is like a Hieronymus Bosch painting done in glitter glue. A large portion of the club straddling the two sofas. A mandala of half snorted lines covering the glass table. We step over them, then stand side by side in the office, my vision going in and out of focus. Lars hands me some money from the safe. He hands some money to Felix too, just because he's high.

'How about making this a permanent thing?' Lars says.

'Yeah,' I drool, trying not to chew my own teeth.

'We're going away.' Felix prods me with the £20 notes Lars gave him.

'Oh yeah. We're travelling around the world for like —'

'— Six months,' Felix finishes my sentence. 'In November.'

Lars pulls a disappointed face that shows this doesn't fit with his plans. He asks Felix if he wants a job on the door, which for some reason fills me with dread. I try to send him some psychic message about not mixing business and pleasure. But he's already saying,

'£12 an hour. You can start on Friday.'

There's a derelict monument with two huge eyes painted on, covered with the remains of prayer flags. The rest of our group are up ahead, spinning big dark-metal prayer wheels. Felix pulls me on by the sleeve. I look at him all rosy red in his neon hat and hiking gear. I don't have any words, just damp exhaustion. I take in the sights of the village. A little goat biting a bit of dry grass out of a stone wall, some children in old jumpers playing in the back of a truck, a Nepalese woman in silver aviators haranguing the other hikers.

'Laka hostel, good drink, good eat, good sleep,' she repeats for me and Felix.

'Sorry, we're all already booked somewhere,' Felix says sweeping me away from her as she begins to try and tell us the names of nearby mountains.

Making my last trundling steps I look down at the gravel and concentrate on the sore spot on my back.

'We did it!' Felix squeezes my abdomen through layers of coat.

I fumble to undo my backpack, my fingers stiff from the cold. I shrug it off, so it hits the stone floor. The earth seems to sigh with me, shadows rising up the mountains in the peachy glow of early evening. Following the others, I drag my bag through a doorway under a hand-painted hostel sign. Felix swaps money for a key and listens to instructions supplied using about 10 words of English. I catch my reflection in a dusty mirror. At first, I don't recognise myself, all red and sweaty in the dim electric light. I collapse onto one of the single beds in our little rustic shack, ecstatic and exhausted. I look up at dark beams of wood and breath in the cold earthy smell. Felix drops down next to me and pulls his neon hat off. I allow my body to roll into his, with a crinkle of hiking jackets. He pushes his lips into mine and unzips my jacket.

'I wanna tell James, I actually did it.' I smile, Felix's arms around my body, inside the jacket. 'I still haven't written to anyone.'

He gives his New Yorker shrug. Then seeing my look of concern, says, 'I saw a phone box outside.' He pushes his cold hands under my jumper, against my sweaty, worn-out body.

'I need a shower.' I heave myself up off the bed.

He lays there tired and horny in his hiking jacket.

We eat curry off metal plates with different compartments for rice, potato, beans, spinach, and chutney. The place is more like a medieval basement than a restaurant, the earthy smell mixing with the spices being cooked.

'We should socialise,' Felix says at the end of the meal, sucking at his fermented malt drink.

'Should we?' I ask looking at the only other people in the restaurant, an unironic group of crust hippies chatting in the corner, the sound of their conversation mixing with the portable TV behind the counter.

Felix is already getting up to talk to them.

'Did you hike with that guitar?' I hear him ask.

'Yeah, it's only small,' says an American surfer accent. 'Got a drum too. We just stuff all the clothes in it and stick it in the bag.'

I've realised Felix is actually the sociable one, while I'm more of a jaded networker. Still, I follow him over and let him introduce me to these youth hostel dregs.

'Amber.' An Australian girl with greasy ginger hair and a head-wrap shakes my hand.

I can imagine her family saying, "*oh Amber's so adventurous, guess where she is right now!*"

'What brings you to the Himalayas?' Asks the guy who introduced himself as Caleb, casually thrumming his fingers against the drum.

'Everything.' Felix slurps his drink.

'We're on a world tour.' I sit on a worn-out wooden stool

'Flying?' Asks Amber, lit from above by a dim electric light.

'Mostly by land.' Felix moves his finger across the tablecloth, as if tracing our route on a map. 'Mexico, Peru, Brazil ...'

'Is that safe?' Asks the guy with the guitar, who looks like Caleb's twin.

'Yeah,' Felix says, starting to take on a surfer tone of voice.

'Other than someone trying to ram our car in the Sahara Desert, and someone leaving burnt ornaments in our rooms, yeah,'

'Burnt ornaments?' Caleb repeats.

'Of angels, in Arizona and Mexico –' I try to think if there were any more places.

'– And Egypt,' Felix says, slurping his drink.

'Creepy,' says Amber.

'What brings *you* to the Himalayas?' Felix asks.

'Consciousness expansion, touching the void,' Caleb reels off.

'Secret teachings hidden in the mountains,' continues his twin brother plucking at the guitar.

I must be making a face because Felix says,

'Kyle hates anything spiritual.'

'I did an Ayahuasca ceremony!' I squawk.

'Okay, okay, sorry.' Felix leans his head on my shoulder and smiles up at me.

After a round of paint stripper flavoured shots, the guitar comes out and Felix joins them in singing a rowdy mantra. I decide to pull on my coat and go for a walk in the night air. I look up at the sky, filled with paint splatter stars, black spaces where in daylight there would be mountains. I get out a little keyring torch that I bought with *Rishikesh* written on the side. I flash it about the rocky ground and stone walls.

The hippies reminded me of all the friends that I haven't seen for the last few months. There's a battered metal phone on a stand outside the hostel reception. The plastic receiver is cold against my ear. Rather than a dial tone I hear static. I scoop some coins out of my pocket and push one into the little slot. It clatters inside and then the static continues.

'Hello?' I whisper into the mouthpiece. A second later I hear my own voice back. I put a few more coins in, but there's just static.

'Hello, hello, hello,' I say, and hear my voice back. The words fading into the night, along with the chanting and guitar. An elderly Nepalese man talks loudly in a nearby hut.

The door to the bedroom creaks open and a shaft of torchlight enters the room. I hear Felix take his clothes off, then he gets into bed. He wraps his limbs around me and leans his face against mine.

'You said we saw those burnt angels in Egypt,' I mumble

'Yeah.' He turns around so we're facing each other.

I lay there in the dark with my head pressed against his. I'm remembering the hut in Egypt, flashing the torch around the wall of burnt angels.

'How did I forget about that?'

'Maybe we both tried to forget about it.' He kisses my forehead.

207

I lie in the darkness his limbs heavy on top of me.

'How did I forget?' I whisper, as much for myself as for him.

'Maybe the same way I forgot about being in hospital.' He yawns.

I wait for him to say more but then I just hear little wheezy snores. For the first time since San Francisco, I'm thinking about going home.

We did a joint interview with *Boyz* magazine in the office at *Science Fiction*. Me in a pearl-encrusted jumpsuit with a white lace shirt underneath. Felix in his gold ruffle shirt, sitting cross-legged on the desk, his hair a faded blue mess. A man in a check shirt called Alan sat with a dictaphone asking us questions. I felt like some previous incarnation of myself probably would've slept with him.

'How did you meet?' He started.

'In hospital,' I answered.

Felix gave me a look as if to say, *that's not how we met.*

'I was dying from cancer. And he's got a heart transplant.'

'Sounds like a movie,' Alan commented enthusiastically.

'They're making a movie of it. Tilda Swinton is playing me,' I told him.

'Who would play you Felix?' Alan turned to Felix with the dictaphone as if parodying an interviewer.

'Will Smith?' Felix said.

It gave me a slightly septic feeling, to see my relationship trotted out in the gay press as an example of homo-romantic success. It was a 2D rendition of who we are, and I didn't like being the straight man in Felix's anarchic avant-garde comedy. I've never for a moment been confused for a straight man.

'What might people not know about you?' The next question reads in bold neon letters.

'Kyle was captain of his school swim team,' Felix laughed.

'Yeah, I'm mad for sports,' I said sarcastically. But in writing it looks like I'm totally serious.

'What annoys you about the other one?' The next column asks, with images of us in bubbles.

'He breaks stuff and sweats in his sleep,' I answered.

'He puts me down,' said Felix.

'What can we expect next from you guys?'

'I'm working on a major new club night and going on an international gay bar crawl with Felix.'

'I'm gonna blow up parliament.' Felix said.

'We can't print that,' tutted Alan.

'Okay, I'm going to take twenty microdots of LSD.'

'We can't print that either.'

'I'm starting a school in Africa?'

Alan looked unhappy.

'Okay, I'm going to travel the world too,' he said, reluctantly sensible.

Felix loves being in that little ticket booth at Science Fiction. Being as much of a freak as he can, with people assuming he's an up-and-coming wild child of London's gay scene. He straddles the chair in his dungarees, trying to give people counselling and life advice while they're on MDMA. He's also started wearing novelty hairbands, with the ears of some lesser-known blue Pokémon. He brings decorations to hang from inside the booth, bunting and fairy lights in the shape of strawberries, and he tells people facts from the travel books he's reading. I should be happy for him, but I'm not. I get the same feeling I got when all my friends walked in on us in the hospital room. Except this time, the entire London gay scene has walked in on us. I guess if I dig deep enough into my cruel club-kid heart, what I'm trying to say is, he embarrasses me. He hangs around with anyone who'll talk to him. There's a guy who would probably be cute if he didn't jump around like some *Jim Henson* puppet while wearing an adult Babygro. Then there's the guy with the multicoloured dreadlocks. I could tell Felix would befriend him, Felix sniffs people with dreadlocks out like an Alsatian sniffs out narcotics. Occasionally this guy will manage an interesting look, but it's totally chance. He seems to just throw the first thing he sees onto his body, a blow-up backpack with a rainbow crop top and a slinky for a necklace, or a neon green fur coat with a body stocking and a miniature bowler hat. He's also partial to spirit gumming children's glitter stickers all over his face. Once, when I was hosting a night and talking to Mick Jagger's son, the dreadlock guy and Felix, appeared out of nowhere, half-naked, covered in glitter stickers. They jumped and danced around us like leprechauns. Both trying to tell me a story about how they lost their clothes on the way here.

Me and James are both watching the man from the shopping channel demonstrating his little animal-shaped hole punches.

'I hate this guy,' I tell James.

'You know him?' Asks James, stretched out in the armchair, legs halfway across the floor. He's wearing an argyle cycling top and suede trousers.

'I know him enough to know that he's an asshole.' I grab the control and click to the next channel, it's *The Outdoors Hour*.

A woman in tweeds is interacting with a woman whose heavily made-up face suggests she very rarely goes outdoors. They're fawning over a display of backpacks in a rainbow of muted colours.

'I think I'm supposed to buy one of those,' I say out the side of my mouth.

'For your international gay bar crawl.'

'Yeah, Felix gave me a list of stuff to get – I like the purple one.'

'Are you actually going to buy something off the shopping channel!?' James asks as I consider the backpack.

I consider everything purchasing it entails. Filling it with clothes and toiletries and heading off on a plane with Felix for six months. Backpacking through the mountains in Peru. Dragging it through the streets in India wearing crumpled clothes. Not hosting the amazing new night at Science Fiction.

I watch as they do a demonstration, where they fill the bag with books, and bottles of water, and some bricks. Then they get one of the cameramen to put it on.

'I can't do it James!' I whine.

'I know.' He gestures at the forced frivolity on the TV screen. 'You should just get one from a camping shop.'

'No, I mean, I don't think I can travel round the world with him.' I grit my teeth.

'You already bought the tickets.' James visibly resists telling me *I told you so*.

'I'm a terrible person.' I push my head into my splayed fingers and feel the heaviness of what I'm saying.

'Only sometimes.' James gets up and sits next to me, squeezing my shoulder. 'Couldn't you just do part of it?'

'I've just recovered from leukemia. I'll have to come back for appointments. And there's my career.'

'True.' James leans on me, looking into my eyes, trying to make me tell him the real reason.

'I love him, but –' I sound like I'm pleading with James.

'I think Felix is great, but I never thought you were a great couple.' James tries to reassure me.

'I love him,' I insist. 'He saved my life!'

212

'You know, when I was with Liam, he helped me so much with my photography,' James starts talking about his ex. 'The camera I'm using is his old camera. But I couldn't have stayed together with him.'

'I wasn't talking about breaking up with him, just the world trip,' I'm gripping a chunk of sofa. James edges away, like he's said too much. 'Maybe I *was* talking about breaking up with him. I don't know. I don't want to hurt him. It's like, thanks for being there when I was dying, but could you go away now?'

'Allow me to be Oprah for a moment.' James looks at me with an honest expression. 'I always thought it was more hurtful to stay with someone when you don't want to be with them.'

I feel my lower lip protruding far out from my face, my mind going blank. The people on the shopping channel are still nattering about backpacks. I grab the control and switch them off and let out a noise, probably too loud to be a sigh.

'We've got tickets to America,' I say.

'Just America?' James asks.

'Yeah.'

'Just go to America then.' James massages my shoulder.

I groan and lean into him and try to think of excuses for being such a terrible person: Felix's drinking and destructiveness, my cancer check-up on Wednesday. People think I'm good, and I'm brave because I survived cancer. Like there's something redemptive in being a survivour. But there are bad people who survive things. While I'm on the tube, on the way to my check-up, I imagine shooting everyone at point-blank range, all the miserable commuters, struggling through their banal lives. I shoot two men in suits discussing business outside of the workplace. I shoot a woman with clean pastel clothes and her boyfriend with his stupid beard. I shoot some teenage girls from Germany and some dowdy woman with a wolf on her t-shirt. I walk along the platform and imagine myself ploughing them down, blood, brains, and intestines splattering the tube station walls.

'Are you getting back to things?' Dr Kyffin asks at the end of our brief consultation. He looks unsure what kind of things it is I might be getting back to.

'Yeah, doing some DJing.' I sit there, looking at all his books, wearing far too many sequin items for a cancer check-up. 'Planning a trip around the world with my boyfriend.'

'When are you going?' His beard twitches.

'In a couple of months.'

'That's probably not a good idea,' he says.

'Hello ... hello,' the phone echoes my voice back, the same as the one in Nepal. Near the phone is a shop, with elephant covered hareem pants fading in the boiling sun. The smell of incense and pollution in the air.

'Stupid phone,' I say, and the phone plays my insult back like it was a recording. I mash the receiver back down and head into the hostel.

My eyes take time to adjust to being inside. Half-assed mandala murals on the walls and some kind of tribal house music playing. I lean against the payphone by the front desk which also echoed my voice back. A statue with an angry dragon face and pointed Thai crown watches me. The air conditioner puffs at me, drying sweat to my skin.

'The phone outside doesn't work either,' I tell the receptionist, a plump guy in a *Dolce & Gabbana* t-shirt.

He's surrounded by aging souvenirs and old posters for tours of Chiang Mai.

'Maybe is bad number,' he says, taking the crumpled piece of paper from my hand. He looks at James' number.

'Could I try using the reception phone.' I point to it, just behind the desk. 'I can pay.'

'Reception phone? Oh no, sorry.' He laughs awkwardly.

'Just for a few minutes,' I plead. 'It's kind of an emergency.'

'Is for staff only.' His face starts to turn stern.

I walk to our room, past hippy-jocks playing pool, some Manson sisters getting chatted up by a guy with his greasy hair in a bun. Felix is sat on a pillow in front of the windowed doors that lead to our little concrete balcony. He's meditating, half-naked with a towel wrapped around his waist, his hair wet. I head into the bathroom and peal my sweaty clothes off. I jerk the shower handle and slap a couple of mosquitoes dead against the already mosquito plastered tiles. I watch the water dribbling over my skin and realise I feel isolated. It's been just me and Felix for so long, I think I'm starting to snap. I've even started blaming my bad memory on him. The way India blurs into Israel. I can't remember the last flight we took and I'm normally the kind of person who can remember exactly what they were wearing a year ago, down to the diamante horns and *MAC* silver-strobe lipstick. I think I miss the diamante horns and MAC silver-strobe lipstick.

I make a disgruntled expression at myself in the cracked mirror. My roots are a couple of inches now. I try combing my hair back and over to the side, in a new style. Then I notice something in the bin. Something dark black in amongst the toilet paper. I reach down and pull it out with my wet hand, a sudden fear tingling through my body. It's a burnt figure with wings, the ash coming off onto my hand. My throat tightens looking at the melted details of its face and praying hands. Along with the fear, memories start to appear from that leaky sealed off place in my mind, like misty hungover recollections. There's me and Felix with the torch pacing away from the beach hut. Then car headlights, a man's shadow grabbing Felix. Then I'm struggling in the gravel, someone's on top of me. I look at myself in the mirror holding the angel, my mouth taut. Felix must've found it and tried to hide it. I wrap the towel around my waist and walk across the tiled floor to where he's meditating. I hold the burnt angel to my chest, ready to confront him, his face scrunched up in concentration. I've always felt like he was hiding something from me. I pause there a moment, looking down at him. Then I walk back to the bathroom and put the figure back in the bin. I step into my sandals and head for the hostel computer.

That evening, I'm on one side of the bed arranging the contents of my bag. Felix is hanging off the end of the bed, reading a book. The ceiling fan spins with a rhythm of clicks and whirrs, motes of dust floating in the orange light. I clip the bag closed and try to order my thoughts.

'I remember the attack,' I decide to tell him.

He doesn't ask what attack. He just says, 'What do you remember about it?'

'How was your check-up?' Felix's voice sounds chirpy and adolescent down the phone.

'I still don't have cancer.' I pause, fiddling with a glitter eyeliner from my beauty table.

'But?'

'The doctor said I shouldn't be travelling around the world.'

'Well, we knew he'd say that.' Felix laughs.

'I think I agree with him.' I grip the eyeliner in my hand.

'We've got flights booked!' Felix starts to sound worried.

'I've got check-ups, I've got medicine to pick up – my immune system,' I reel off fragments of my mental script that I created before this conversation.

'I thought you were just going to fly back a couple of times,' he stammers.

I vaguely remember saying that, in some flakey conversation when I was planning my night, and he was planning our world tour.

'We've already booked the flights,' he repeats.

'I can pay you back for the flights.' I look at my tense expression in my beauty-table mirror

'What's this really about?' His voice is strained.

'It about my health,'

'Your health,' he scoffs.

'Felix –'

'We need to talk about this properly.' The strain in his voice is turning to anger. 'I'm coming over.'

'I've got to get ready for hosting *Arcade 3000*,' I make excuses. 'We can talk tomorrow.'

'No,' his voice cracks. 'I'm coming over now.'

'Don't!'

I'm not sure if he heard me because now there's just the engagement tone ringing in my ear. I know it's not fair, but I'm not ready to talk to him, especially if he's angry. I look down and see the glitter eyeliner I was fiddling with has leaked all over my hand.

The doorbell starts playing 'La Cucaracha' while I'm halfway through doing my makeup. It's probably Felix. I'm half glad he's come now, rather than drunk and lairy at *Science Fiction*. I meet James in the lounge. I half hope he'll pick up the door phone, but he gestures for me to do it.

'Kyle!' Felix barks into the phone.

'Yes,' I answer.

'Let me in!'

'Are you drunk?'

'Yesss, very very drunk!'

I put the phone down like he did on me.

'He's drunk,' I tell James.

'Did you expect him not to be?'

La Cucaracha starts up again.

'This isn't the way I want to talk about this!' I tell the phone.

'This is the way I want to talk about this,' he burps into the speaker accompanied by a scrabbling sound. 'Let me in you dick head!'

'I don't respond to being called a dick head.'

'You just did.'

'I'm not letting you in, so you can smash up my apartment. Come back when you're sober.' I smash the phone into the receiver a few times. *La Cucaracha* starts playing again, so I pull the wire out of the phone.

'He's not going to go away,' James says. Then he looks at me.

I'm shaking, my eyes starting to blur.

'This is fucking up my makeup!' I head for my bedroom to put pressed powder under my eyes.

A few minutes later there are Felix sized knocks on our apartment door. Someone must've let him in.

'Kyle–' James poses in my doorway, watching me trying to apply liquid eyeliner. 'You're being –'

'– Immature? Pathetic? I know.' I get some eyeliner where I don't want it and let out a moan. 'We're both too angry, and he's drunk! It's pointless talking now.'

'Why are you angry?' He asks.

'I don't know!' I put down the eyeliner brush.

The little rhythmic knocks continue in the background. James stands there, trying to stare at me till I answer. The knocks stop, and I hear raised voices, the neighbours and my drunk boyfriend.

'Okay, I'll deal with it this one time.' James flaps his arms about. I'm unable to tell if he's being camp and funny, or camp and annoyed. I hear him open and close the front door.

I quickly finish off the black line around my eye. I look at my half made-up face and feel like a stupid child. This couldn't have gone any worse. It's almost like I'm trying to destroy my own relationship. I wonder if that is what I'm trying to do. I should just calm down, go out there and talk to him. But what would I say?

Sorry, I can't go on your dream trip around the world. Sorry, I don't think I'm in love with you anymore. These are the sort of things that are hard enough to tell a sober person. I look at my sad drag queen eyes, red and sparkly. Part of me wants to just run out there and say, *Fuck it! I don't care about anything, let's get on that plane to San Francisco!* Instead, I just watch myself soullessly blending black eyeshadow around the crease of my eyelid.

James comes back in about ten minutes later and looks at me looking at myself in the mirror.

'Next time, I'm just going to let him in,' he says in his serious voice.

I go to *Science Fiction* and drunkenly try to talk to people and move my body in a way that somewhat resembles dancing. Then I leave as early as I can, without saying goodbye to anyone. I wake up in the early afternoon and stare at my egg chair and my wig heads and feel terrible, inside and out. It's almost 6PM by the time I summon up the guts to get on the tube and go see Felix. I hold onto the yellow metal bar with my sunglasses on and the residue of makeup, trying to avoid human interaction.

His grandma answers the door and looks happy to see me, but then doesn't seem to know what to say.

'Is Felix in?' I ask the obvious.

'He's in his room.' She ushers me in. 'Did you two have an argument?'

'Sort of,' I sigh, my arms hanging limp.

His curtains are pulled shut. The room looks like it's been ransacked. The Arc de Triomphe is on the floor and one of the Statues of Liberty has been knocked over, its torch snapped off. I go to pick it up.

'Leave my stuff alone,' he croaks.

I notice him lying flat out on the bed, two empty miniature bottles of wine on his bedside table.

'Sorry.' I move my hand away.

'You know what my friends said ...' He picks at his quilt. 'They said, "*That club kid is too in love with himself to be in love with you.*"'

I look bleakly at him. He stares up at the ceiling.

'Which friends?' I ask.

'I told them, "*You don't know him like I do.*"'

'I do love you Felix,' I say, getting down on the floor next to his bed, rather than standing awkwardly in the middle of his room. I sweep some ornaments and socks out of the way.

'If you loved me enough, you'd go with me,' he complains, sounding like a kid.

'That's not how it works,' I tell the side of his face.

'Why not.' He moves his lips bitterly. 'It's how it worked when you'd just recovered. It's how it worked before you started pretending to be a celebrity again'

'Before I spoke to the doctor.' I lean on the quilt, trying to get him to look at me.

'Don't pretend that's the reason you're not going,' he says, still focused on the ceiling.

'It's one of the reasons.'

'What are the others?' I see a teardrop forming in his eye.

I want him to look at me. If he looks at me things will be different. He still loves me. I don't want him not to love me. I try to explain how I feel,

'When I was lying in hospital with cancer, there was only one person I could really talk to. There's was only one person I wanted to see.' My lips quiver with the emotion in those words. 'That was you.'

He pauses and breaths at the ceiling. 'I preferred you when you had cancer.'

'Fuck you.' I get up from where I was kneeling next to his bed. All the things in his room blurring with anger and sadness. 'I'm going!' I stand there by the door. Part of me hoping he'll apologise. That he'll plead with me to stay.

'Go then,' he rasps, his face red. He pushes himself off the bed to look at me with his far apart alien eyes.

'This is over,' I croak. I turn and walk out of his room.

I heave my backpack through the doorway and look back at Felix. A dim outline of a body, under a quilt. I try to pull the door shut slowly so I don't wake him. He lets out a little moan and turns in bed. I pause and bite my lip, but he's still asleep. I wait there a bit longer, a pang of guilt between my heart and my stomach. Then I pull the door till it closes with a little click. I'm in the dim strip lit corridor, a small statue of a figure with a Thai crown on the floor. An American accent somewhere downstairs, the smell of disinfectant, the windows dotted with rain.

'Checking out?' Asks the *Dolce & Gabbana* man behind reception.

Two Manson sisters are on the sofa talking in hushed tones.

'No, my friend's still in the room.' I hold onto my backpack straps. 'I'm just going away for a few days,'

'No problem. See you –' He searches for the last word. '– Later.'

I try to remember how to say *thank you* or *goodbye* in Thai, but just repeat, 'see you later,' and get a bit trapped in the hostel door as I step out.

The street is wet and desolate, the neon signs on the shops reflected in the asphalt. The rain is starting to fall hard. I pull up the hood of my purple hoodie. The only other people on the street are a couple of prostitutes in miniskirts, sheltering under the battered awning of a shop. A few white guys with American accents walk with wet t-shirts. I pass a couple of tuk-tuks, one driver smoking, another reading a paper. I pick up as much pace as I can with my giant backpack. Some distant Thai pop music combines with the dribble of rain off a shop roof. My mind asks if I'm doing the right thing. If I'm leaving him in danger. But if he's in danger, I was in danger too, and I wouldn't have known if I hadn't spotted that burnt figurine.

There's a taxi parked by a corrugated metal fence.

'How much to the airport, Suvarnabhumi?' I try to pronounce it, shielding myself from the rain.

'Get in,' says the driver, in his short-sleeved shirt.

'How much?' I ask.

He tells me some ridiculous price in a kindly manner. I give him a price that is above what I think I should pay; I'm too sleepy to haggle.

'Six hundred Baht,' he tells me, as if I'm being unreasonable.

'Five hundred Baht,' I say.

He plucks a cigarette packet out of his pocket, looks at it and nods, then gets out to help me with my bag.

I rub sleep from my eyes and slump into the torn-up taxi seat, a confused English boy in a foreign country, cigarette smoke and a dusty leather smell. The taxi joins sparse dawn traffic, the wind starting to beat at pylons and spindly roadside trees. I try to think about what I'll do when I get back. Visit a few people, maybe Milo, definitely James. Maybe I'll even visit my family, make sure they're still there going about their daily lives. I try to think about what I'll do when I get back, to cancel out the other thoughts. Thoughts about what Felix has been hiding from me and how long he's been hiding it. Was it just the last few months? Or the whole holiday? Or our whole relationship? Maybe I should've locked the door at the hostel and said, "*We're not leaving this room until you tell me what's happening!*" We're being followed by people who leave burnt angels in our hotel rooms, people in a white car, people who attacked us. I remember being pulled off the ground and forced into the car boot. I make an expression of disbelief. It seems so extreme. I double check the misty part of my brain that the memory came out of, to see if it's real. I'm there in the boot of the car with my hands tied behind my back and grit in my mouth. I want to go back and shake Felix awake and shout, "*How did I forget this? Why didn't we report it? How did we get away?*" I feel alone. Like I'm putting together a puzzle that I'm missing half the pieces to. I search the leaky sealed off place in my mind for memories, but it's like trying to find something when I don't know what I'm looking for. I remember what he said in Nepal, when I asked him how I forgot, "*The same way I forgot about being in hospital.*" The window wipers squeak, and the taxi speeds down the motorway, just a few other cars and rickshaws on the road. What if he really does have psychic powers? What if he wiped my memory? My mind goes back to the conspiracy theories, that he's a paranormal wonder kid and some international agency is after him. But I would've seen more evidence than just him telling me, I fell out of a tree when I was young. That he's a time traveller, with his 70's clothes and no pictures of his childhood. I Look out the window at the rain-blurred lights of the airport. The decorative plants outside the terminal blowing as if they are underwater.

I walk along the travellator like an avatar in a role player game, somebody else pressing the forward arrow. A shrill Thai voice making announcements over a tannoy. I go about all the normal things, check-in, security, spraying perfume onto myself. I sit down with a cardboard cup of cappuccino and some expensive crumb of Western food. The morning sun beginning to illuminate the thick bundles of cloud. Rain blows horizontally across floor to ceiling windows, the airplanes swaying on the runway. I'm sitting under an advert for a jeweller with a picture of a big gold ring. It makes me think of Felix's "*giant gold disc.*" I sip the coffee, and in my mind, I place the things that have happened around the gold disc. The burnt angels in America, Mexico, Egypt, and now Thailand. Felix waking up with no memory in San Francisco. Me not remembering the attack. The car following us in Morocco, then turning up in Egypt. How did we get away? I see it again, being grabbed and pushed onto a white tiled floor. Felix is on a bed covered in blood. They killed him, but somehow, he's still lying asleep in our hostel bedroom. And the answer is there; we didn't get away.

I stand up, unsteady, all the families, their bags and trollies around me. I feel a twinge in my stomach and a tautness in my throat. I'm going mad, some kind of joint schizophrenia. Something crashes into the ceiling, blown off by the stormy weather. The scratchy shrill voice over the tannoy makes an announcement in Thai and English, about a plane to Singapore being delayed. I have to get away from all these people, to somewhere I can listen to my own thoughts. I start to march through the disordered metal benches, children crying and adults complaining about delayed flights. I hadn't noticed quite how filled with delays the departures board is. Then the announcement calls out that my flight to London is delayed due to adverse weather conditions. It doesn't matter. My brain just repeats that last scary thought. We didn't get away.

James' crotch in his stupid tweed trousers is standing in the way of the television. He's standing there with his hands on his hips, trying to get me to look away from the shopping channel. I make swiping motions to get him to move.

'I'm going to a party later,' he starts.

'*Joan Rivers' Jewellery Hour* just started.' I make some more swiping gestures at him.

'I want you to come with me,' he continues.

'Sounds terrible,' I groan.

He sits down next to me, one leg over the other. I'm in some jogging bottoms I didn't even know I had and a neon smiley-face t-shirt that I don't even like. Next to me is a small melted tub of ice cream that I've been eating with the small end of a medicine spoon. I think you should comfort eat after a break-up, but you shouldn't let emotionally induced weight gain impede the next stage of the breakup, sleeping with hot guys. I try to watch Joan's giant collagen filled lips giving a description of the bracelet that she's sliding around her wrist.

'When I broke up with Liam, you forced me to go to *The Peach* the day after,' James argues.

'That was different,' I murmur, more interested in Joan and her bracelet.

'Different how?' James edges into my personal space.

'You were moping around the flat,' I say.

He makes a gesture toward me and the ice cream pot.

'Moping around ... *around*!' I elaborate making a circling motion with my finger. 'You were doing it in lots of different areas. It was bringing me down. I'm just doing it in one area.'

'Well, honey, it's kind of bringing me down too.' He rubs my arm to show he's not being a bitch. 'I thought you broke up with him because you were planning on starting a new club night. Not so you could watch the shopping channel all day.'

'I broke up with him because he said he wished I had cancer.' I switch off the TV and give James a long doleful look. 'Where'd you wanna go?'

'That rave at the bed shop.'

'A rave,' I say in disgust, collapsing back into the sofa, lifting the remote control.

'A rave with a giant bed and lots of cute gays,' he adds.

I fondle the remote control and remember how depressed I am over the whole Felix thing. James takes the remote out of my hand.

'Pleeease.' He drums his long legs against the coffee table and looks at me with a Disney smile. 'Pleeeeeease.'

'Okay! But I'm dressing down.' Of course, dressing down for me is wearing a gold sequin onesie and gold motocross armour. I do some minimal black and gold makeup too.

'Do we have to go?' I say, looking out the front door at the rain, dripping and pouring.

'The taxi's here,' says James, pushing me through the doorway, putting up his umbrella.

'Okay, I'm getting a hat.' I run back upstairs and spend about five minutes looking for that Hermes hat I leant Felix. When I finally get into the taxi James visibly suppresses his annoyance.

'Everybody ready,' the driver asks sarcastically.

The thunderclaps, and the window wipers start up, and we're heading to South East London. I look at my twinky demi-God reflection in the rain-beaded window and try to decide if I'm in the middle of a breakdown or not.

We pull up at an industrial estate, rain pooling up in the uneven concrete of the car park. I can see a line of bleak wilting party people, queuing around the side of the building. They are sheltering from the rain, under a bit of overhanging corrugated roof, in their neon crop tops and cyborg fashions

'We're not waiting outside,' I tell James, who is readying himself to walk into the pouring rain, in his mustard-coloured jumpsuit and string vest. 'I'll make some phone calls.' I search through my phone book. Through a couple of phone calls, I get someone to come to the door and scan the car park for us.

'There!' I say pleased with myself.

We run through the rain, me holding onto my gold hat by the wings. I hug the person who meets us, an Indian guy with a green mohawk, wearing post-apocalyptic attire. He goes on about how "*banging*" the party is and the "*bass drop*" on the last tune. Me and James nod like we can relate to that kind of thing. Inside smells like sweat and smoke-machines. It's just how you'd imagine the back of a bed shop that's been occupied by stoners to look. A few ceiling tiles dangling, vibrating from the thudding trance music, some holes in the drywall, a random picture of Shiva.

'Where'd you buy the gold?' The guys asks, looking at my attire.

'I made it,' I tell him, bored of being asked where I got my clothes every time I go out.

'Wow, can you make me one?' He says with the enthusiasm of someone who has double dropped.

'Yeah, have you got £1000?'

'Kind of steep,' the guy shouts, loud enough to be heard over the music.

'It's my job,' I tell him.

James jumps in, asking the guy if he knows where to get MD.

'I've got x-boxes,' he whisper-shouts over the throbbing trance beat. 'Three for twenty.' He gestures us into a shadowy corner, near a neon wall hanging of a bush baby.

James looks at me.

'I don't know if I want pills,' I tell both of them. 'I just want to get so drunk I don't feel anything ever again.'

James makes disappointed eyes at me.

'Okay, four for twenty,' I say.

'Fine,' says the guy. He adjusts something in the pocket of his black and green hippy hoodie.

'Have you got a tenner?' James asks me.

'I don't even know if I want any.' I readjust one of the straps on the armour.

The guy looks at us as if to say, *just hurry up and buy them.* So, I say I'll get James a drink.

As we're entering the main room James slips two triangular pills into my hand, and I stick them in my sock. The place is packed. The crowd spattered with lasers and smoke. Bits of stretched out neon fishnet on the walls. Repetitive spacey music blaring, slightly distorted from a mass of speakers. James looks at me with enthusiasm, bopping up and down on the balls of his feet to the thud-thud-thud of the music.

'I'll get some drinks,' I tell him, shaking my head. I walk across the muddied office carpet, to the bar. The lights reflect off my gold sequins. I realise people don't usually wear sequins to raves. Then I wonder if I should host a sequin rave some time. Then I wonder if I should host any parties ever again. If I should seal all my costumes off in some low-cost storage vault and disappear. Strangely this is the idea that fills me with most joy at the moment.

My parents and friends wondering, "*Where's Kyle? Where's Cosmo?*" While I'm wearing black polo necks and suit jackets, working in a milliners in New York. The second most joyful idea is downing as much alcohol as possible.

The rave bar only has cans of *Strongbow* or *Red Stripe*. I go for two cans of *Strongbow*. The barman gives me them with plastic cups on top.

'You used to be captain of the school swimming team,' the guy next to me, blurts out. He has transparent purple tubes for hair

'Did you go to Surrey Manor?' I shout over the music, uninterested.

'No! I read the interview in *Boyz* magazine.'

'Oh, that thing,' I say, distracted for a moment by the purple space-age symbols on his hoodie. 'Did you think we were a good couple?'

'Yeah, sure, you guys seemed fun,' he says, awkward and stilted.

I notice he has really good clear skin, the way some geeks do.

'We just broke up,' I tell him and pour cider into my mouth.

'Oh, sorry –' he starts.

'Don't be,' I shout.

He stutters something into his *Red Stripe*.

I down a load more cider and tell him in a very loud whisper, 'My friend forced me to come here.'

'You don't like it?' He asks, blinking, his eyes covered in neon paint.

'I don't like anything at the moment.'

'Do you like Ketamine?' He looks at me wide eyed.

I'm about to say, "*Is the Pope a Catholic?*" But instead, I touch his space age wizard sleeve and say, 'It's about the only thing that would make me happy at the moment.'

I down the rest of the cider, while he racks up massive lines in a bean bag area, surrounded by hippy wall hangings. The

Ketamine stings my nostril and drips down the back of my throat. I spill the guy's drink on the bean bags. Then I become really enamoured with what I'm wearing, stroking the sequins under the dark spinning lights. He starts stroking my arm too.

A blue haired girl from a group of people nearby lumbers over and asks in what seems like slow motion, 'Are you that Cosmo, club kid?'

I hesitate for a very long time. Then tell her, in slow motion, 'I don't think so.'

Me and the guy press our faces into the bean bags.

'I'm such an asshole,' I say.

He says I'm not an asshole in an unconvincing manner. Then he's kissing me, sloppily, but I've already drifted too far across the galaxy to stop him. At some point, I find the other can of cider, like some ancient forgotten treasure amongst the bean bags. I break off from the mouth licking to down the whole thing, pouring a lot onto my top. Then I stumble in the direction of a nearby balcony, part of the bean bag attached to me. I almost tip my drink onto the rain drenched mass of people below. I slump over the edge, looking at the dance floor, a mix of dirt and dayglo colours, smoke, disco lights and green lasers all surging to this distorted bass. I see myself from above, fucked-up and alone, no longer part of this two-person unit. I'm not acting any better than he was at that hotel bar. I wonder if any of the reasons I broke up with him were real reasons. Maybe I was just a bit unnerved, embarrassed even, to love someone like him. Someone who fucks up my public image with their zany, dorky, reckless free spirit. I grab one of the pills and slap it into my mouth, like it's emergency medication for anaphylactic shock.

Someone on the stairway tries to talk to me, but I can see my friends at the bottom, probably talking about me. They stop shouting over the music as soon as I stagger over. Kitten and Bobbi look like pink versions of the people from *The Matrix*, and James looks like someone who buys all their clothes in the reduced section at the vintage shop.

'How's things,' gurns Kitten, in that up-front way of hers.

'I'm building up to throwing myself off that balcony.' I lean on Bobbi and sort of vomit out the words.

'I don't think it would kill you,' Kitten laughs.

'Good, horribly injured is enough. I need more alcohol.' I try to pick the one who offends me least to take to the bar. I scoop Bobbi in the direction of the bar, my hand on his sweaty back.

'I don't know why James thinks taking me out and gossiping about me will cheer me up.'

Bobbi gives me an awkward expression. He has pink horns and a pink PVC crop jacket. I stand on my tiptoes to look over the crowd at the bar. It's now sinking into a pile of empty cans, all vibrating with the burr-burr-burr of the bass.

'Umm ...' Bobbi tweaks the piercing on the tip of his ear. 'Why'd you guys break up?'

I step into a free space close to the bar.

'Did you think we were a good couple?' I ask him, maybe rhetorically.

'Yes. Weird – but good.' I must give him a look of disbelief because he starts trying to gurn out an explanation. '– like chips dipped in milkshake.'

'Yeah,' I snort reaching for a space at the bar. 'Me and Felix were totally chips and milkshake.'

'Chips dipped in milkshake are good,' Bobbi insists. A bit of black light illuminates the pink swirls on his face.

'If you're gross.' I pull him towards the bar with me. 'Would you want chips and milkshake all the time?'

He looks at me with his pierced cheeks puffed up. I push my finger into one to deflate it.

'I told him I couldn't travel the world with him, and he told me he preferred me when I had cancer.'

'I'm sure he didn't mean it,' Bobbi tries to talk louder than the music.

'I think I preferred him when I had cancer too!' I shout.

The bar guy is asking what I want so I get us both ciders.

The music has turned to a sort of electro tribal, the lasers circling to the beat. I wonder if I need to take the other pill.

'You preferred him when you had cancer?' Bobbi repeats.

'Yeah, it was easier when there was none of this outside world getting in the way. When it was just me and him in hospital.' I make a drunken gesture at the outside world and start dancing.

Bobbi dances too, in his disorientated staccato manner. 'Do you love him?'

'Yeah, of course.' I move my arms in a cross between rave and vogue.

'Do you want to fuck him?'

'Maybe.'

'Sounds like you should talk,' Bobbi says.

I fling my hands into the lasers, not caring about smashing up the gold armour, or the sequin onesie filling with sweat. Me and my friends are squashed into the mass of bodies and smoke. Lights reflect off the sequins on my arms. The Ecstasy surging into my heart, filling me with possibility. Kitten makes an expression like I'm being crazy, so I dance even crazier. The bass drops and I jump, the juddering strobe light, stop-framing my wild flailing limbs. I jump and dance through the crowd, away from my friends. The crowd multiplies and blurs, a kaleidoscope of lights and smoke. I don't know if I'm smiling or gurning. I dance as hard as I can, as if it will permanently shake all the mental baggage out of me. I make a wild noise at some people I don't know. For a moment I'm that kid who just moved to London again. I get pushed into a group of hippies. A girl with a short ginger fringe puts an orange glow bracelet on my wrist. Her gay friend dressed in an elf hoodie, sways with neon dots on his face. There are two twins with a well-honed rave dancing style, one juggles some kind of glowing nun chucks. I make sure to dance crazier than any of them. Leaping, slamming my hands into the tunnels created by the smoke and lasers.

I notice my phone vibrating in my pocket. I stumble and push my way off the dance floor, looking at the screen. It's a number I don't know. According to my call log, it's already rung five times. I stagger toward a corridor with a neon painting of a butterfly hanging from the way. My phone starts ringing again in my hand. The same number. I can't hear it over the music, it's just vibrating in my hand. I press answer, and there's this little voice saying my name.

'Helloooo,' I say in a stupid voice and press my head against the corridor wall.

The voice down the phone rasps something back in a silly voice.

'Sorry?' I say.

'Is that Kyle?' The voice asks.

'This is Cosmo, Kyle, Cosmo,' I laugh, looking close up at the chipped white wall.

'Kyle, its Felix's grandma.'

I stop and pull my face away from the wall.

'Felix had an accident. He's in hospital. I'm there now.'

The high turns to panic.

'What kind of accident?' My lips blather, looking from the dirty corridor wall to the group of people sitting on the floor.

'His heart stopped beating.'

She keeps saying things, something about an operation, something about life support, but my mind isn't hearing it as cohesive sentences.

'Where are you? I'm coming now!' I feel all the sweat from dancing, turning cold.

She gives me the name of the hospital. I have to ask her to say it a second time because I'm not really listening. Then I run for the exit. Images of this person I love flooding my brain. I push the backdoor open into heavy rain, lit by a security light. I'm running for a taxi that's just leaving. I wave my hands. It stops and there's no passenger, so I open the door.

'Can you take me to the hospital,' I hear myself stumble over the words, my heart like a balloon in my chest. 'Northwick Park, Harrow.'

There are so many emotions flooding my mind as I walk into the strip-lit reception, people staring at me in my sweat-dried sequin jumpsuit and gold armour. The receptionist is a girl with an innocent face and blonde hair with roots.

'I need to find a patient who's just come in.' I'm jittery from the Ecstasy. '— My boyfriend, he's had a heart attack.'

'What's his name.' She looks tired and only mildly concerned.
'Felix Gunston.'

She does some rapid typing and says she can't see him on the system. She asks me how you spell Gunston. Then she says she still can't see him. My heart grasps at the possibility that the whole phone call was some kind of mistake or prank.

'I'll call his grandma.' I get out my phone and Felix's grandma answers. She tells me in a flustered voice to come to ECU. The receptionist shows me where that is, with a sparkly nail on a laminated colour coded map. The map is very effervescent and hard to concentrate on.

I walk swiftly down corridors, little zip-zaps and flickers around the edge of my vision. The corridors seem to pull themselves along like a train. Drawn, serious faces look at me, attached to people in nightgowns and surgical robes. I start to unfasten the armour. I figure the more normal I can look, the better. I must've already lost the hat at the rave. I get in the lift with a stout woman who stares at my clothes.

'Hi,' I say.

'Hi,' her voice echoes back.

Then I walk through scratched red double-doors. Everything has a strange electricity to it. Before the guy behind the desk can talk to me, Felix's grandma is standing up, and I'm hugging her. She's wearing a faded red coat, and her eyes are tired and watery.

'How bad is it?' I hear my voice.

'It's bad,' she says, the wrinkles around her mouth downturned from her own honesty.

'I'm sorry,' I mumble. I feel like if it wasn't for the Ecstasy I might cry. 'I'm so sorry.'

I end up on the departures side of the airport. Crowds of passengers clamouring around information desks, murmuring and shouting. The floor to ceiling windows are crisscrossed with rain, bits of street furniture and plants blowing across the road outside. Wet people are setting up camp all across the marble effect floor, like a well-off refugee camp. I step in the gaps between families, seeing things more like a camcorder than someone who's actually there. My brain is so filled with thoughts it feels like it's going to implode. They come in gasps. *Did Felix really die? How did he come back? Did someone wipe my memories?*

I look at all the stranded passenger's faces, and it brings me back to reality for a few seconds. Then my thoughts spin off again. *Did we both die?* Is this some kind of purgatory we're trapped in, with dead phone lines, and typhoons to stop me from leaving? All the people copied in, like CGI crowds in a film. But they're too detailed, too alive. A large middle eastern man sits cross legged explaining something to his wife with a lot of head nodding and slicing hand gestures. Their three children crawling over the luggage, eating prawn crackers. They're real, down to the man's comb over. People don't just die and come back to life. I search for the first solid memory since the attack. It's him meditating on the monastery wall in India. Me waking up with that feeling of horror. Did I just make up these memories of him getting killed? Was it a dream? It seems so much more solid than vague pictures of us at the Taj Mahal or on lilos on the Dead Sea. It seems more solid than the things I told him about his recovery. Him in a wheelchair in his grandma's lounge, him getting physical therapy. I start to realise there's either something very wrong with the world or something very wrong with my mind. I walk faster through the crowd, panicked, not knowing where I'm going. I think about just barging through the turnstile doors into the wind and the pouring rain of the car park. Then I see him, standing in his '70s shirt and flares, completely soaked. His curly brown hair flattened out by the rain. It feels like the distance between us has been a lot longer than a few hours.

'Felix!' I yell over all the people, and they look back at me.

He waves at me in that casual manner he effects when everything is going wrong. We both step through the maze of people and suitcases till we're together. I hold him, solid and wet in my arms, the only thing I can relate to at this moment.

'I think I'm going mad.' I grip onto him.

'You're probably not.' He pulls away.

'I saw you get killed.' I lower my voice.

'I saw myself get killed as well.' He looks at me, his eyes wide and honest. 'I'm going to tell you everything I know.'

'Let's go somewhere.' I look at the *Starbucks* crammed with wet people.

He takes my hand and pulls me through the crowd. Like we're heading to a dance floor. We push through to a small table at the back.

'I'm guessing you found the angel,' he says, fiddling with the coffee cup of the last person who was here.

'Yeah.' I have to lean forward to hear him over all the noise.

240

'I shouldn't have hidden that from you,' he says, his eyelids heavy. 'I guess I just wanted to keep things as they were. I worried if we started questioning things, they'd start falling apart.'

'What do you mean?' I try not to be impatient.

'Well, with the first angel, I thought something was up. But I couldn't work out what.' He pops the top off the coffee cup and puts it back on. 'When we found the second one, I knew it wasn't someone following us. The only place they could've been coming from was me.'

'You put them there?'

'No, I mean, it was like stuff was leaking out of my brain into the world. I was scared, so I just pretended it wasn't happening.' He stutters, trying to get out an explanation. 'I found one of those angels in the room in Morocco too and I hid it.'

'But who's leaving them?' I take the coffee cup he's fiddling with away from him.

'I thought you said you remembered – in Egypt.'

'Which bit of it?'

'That thing with the hood. Didn't you see its face?'

It's so strange, when he mentions it, I start to remember, and what I remember is something I wouldn't forget. A white hood and inside it a head with no face, just thick grey veins and a red wound for a mouth. Like something from a horror movie.

'How did I forget?' I worry for a moment that he's planting thoughts in my mind. 'How come I keep forgetting things?'

'This is going to sound crazy.' He pushes wet hair behind his ear. 'But that was the monster from my nightmares.'

'Yeah.' I look into his eyes. 'That does sound crazy.'

'But you saw it too! The only way I can explain it is that this is happening in here –' He gestures towards his head. '– Rather than out there.'

'You're saying we imagined it?' I take my hand off his leg, confused.

'I'm saying, we're imagining all of this.' A flicker of emotion runs across his face. 'All that stuff you told me about my recovery, did that really happen?'

'Yes, I think so.' I glance over at an assistant in an apron bringing a Thai family their drinks.

'You think so!?' He looks at me with disbelief.

'I mean it's blurry.' I feel like he's accusing me now. 'I had problems remembering that as well, but I didn't want to say so because you couldn't remember any of it.'

He purses his lips and doesn't say anything for a while. He just looks at me. 'I don't think I remembered any of it, not really,' He holds my hand across the table. 'I think I just believed what you told me.'

I breathe in the smell of coffee and rain. I remember in the car in San Francisco, telling him that he'd had a heart attack, that he'd been in a coma. In the Little A'le'Inn telling him about the moment that he opened his eyes.

'Is there any way you could've imagined those things?' He asks.

At first, I think this is a ridiculous thing to ask. But when I think about it, everything I told him happened just as I imagined it would. I was so desperate for him to recover that I did that thing he told me about. I tried to imagine it happening so convincingly that it really would happen. Everything from the smell of the room to the nurse to the expression on his face. Now I'm confused over what's real and what's not.

'What do you think happened?' I look at him, just him, the bustle of the airport and the coffee shop fading away.

'I think I'm still in that hospital,' he says, his voice quiet and serious. 'In that coma.'

My urge is to raise my eyebrow like he's mad. But the tone of his voice tells me not to. I'm remembering more. That time on Ayahuasca in Peru when I felt like I opened a second set of eyes. I was back in the hospital room with him, and it seemed so real.

'If you're in a coma, how come I'm here too?' I ask.

'I thought for a moment, maybe I was dreaming you.' He looks me in the eyes. 'But I can tell you're real. I don't need you to believe all this ... just don't not believe it.' He reaches out for my hand.

I hold his hand, solid and real against my hand. I half expect if I fully accept what he's saying that the customers at the other tables, the coffee shop, and the airport will start disintegrating into the darkness, like a spell being broken. I close my eyes and open them, and everything is still there.

'Do you have another explanation?' I ask.

'No.' He takes a deep breath in. 'Just that one.'

'Everything seems so real though.'

'Everything always seems real,' he says.

I press my lips together not wanting to believe what Felix is saying. But I'm weighing it up against my own theories of purgatory and superpowers and time travel.

'You can try and go back home,' he tells me. 'I'll accept it, and I won't blame you.'

'Or?' I notice I'm squeezing his hand.

'Or, we keep travelling, as far as we can, for as long as we can.'

I think of him in that hospital bed and the small chance that he's right, that he never recovered. I think of how hard I wished that I could change things, that I could still travel the world with him. I think of all the places we still haven't been.

'I don't think I can go home.' My lip quivers. 'But even if I could. I'd keep going. I'd keep travelling with you.'

Part 5

Siberia

The click-clack beat of the tracks underneath us. The cold from the window like a winter morning. Gruff male voices, children crying, people shifting things about outside. I look at Felix squashed up next to me on the single pull-out shelf bed, tangled in the woollen blanket.

'What're you looking at?' He says, his face puffy with sleep, his hair messy.

If this was a film the camera would zoom out to show the train from above, a thin line of metal carriages cutting through vast snow and scattered shrubland.

I wait for the bathroom with some beefcake in a tracksuit and a hunched old lady in a cardigan. They seem to be best friends, frowning and laughing with each other. I pull down the window on the door, an icy wind blasts into my face, and they both look around angrily. I have a trickle of a shower in a compact bathroom that looks like it was designed a few decades before I was born. I shave in the mirror and look into my own dilated pupils and wonder if any of this is real. I know what Felix meant when he said he didn't have to try to push the truth to the back of his mind. It actually takes mental effort to hold it there.

We travelled from the airport in a tuk-tuk through half-cleared storm damage. A mess of broken trees and telephone lines being picked at by people in pointy high-vis hats. A shadow hanging over the bright tropical day. Looking at the landscape juddering past, I tried to entertain the thought that all this might not be as real as I had previously thought. I could maybe accept that, but I couldn't accept that Felix might still be in hospital, that he thought this was some kind of joint dream. Felix looked intently out the other side of the tuk-tuk, I think trying to give me space, but that seemed to involve him repeatedly glancing at my face for news.

'If this isn't real,' I asked, 'What would happen if I just jumped out onto the road?'

'I wouldn't.' He gave me a tired smile. 'It felt like it took a lot of energy to come back after Egypt.'

We were the only foreigners on a coach trip through the mountains in China. All the Chinese tourists gossiping and getting out three-course packed lunches. I told Felix about my vision of him in hospital, that I had on Ayahuasca.

'What does that make you think?' He leaned against me.

'It makes it slightly less hard to believe that we're somewhere imagining this.'

'Hmm,' he replied, maybe pleased, maybe disturbed. 'I've taken a lot of hallucinogens. The idea that we're lying somewhere imagining this doesn't seem so farfetched to me.'

I sat there wondering if any of the people around us were listening to what we were saying, or if they were just figments of this joint hallucination.

When we were on our own it was easier to imagine that things weren't real, looking out at towers of rock tipped with green. The kind of landscape a manga character in a computer game would hop across with a giant sword. We walked up worn stone steps, the view disappearing behind trees and undergrowth.

I tore off part of a bush and shouted, 'Nothing's real!'

He copied me, ripping part of a plant up and shouting, 'Nothing's real!' He tore off leaves and threw them in the air, manic and happy, 'Nothing's real!'

I grabbed branches with both hands and hurled them down the steps.

We spooned in a capsule hotel, the inside of the door lined with strips of LEDs. I looked at his hair and the contour of his cheek in the blue-ish light.

'We haven't seen any of those angels in a while,' he said

'– Or had anyone trying to kill us.'

'I worried talking about none of this being real, would make things fall apart,' he stroked my arm. 'When I was on that wall in Nepal, when I was in the hostel in Thailand, I kept meditating, trying to keep things stable. But maybe I didn't need to.'

Then we were walking through tower blocks and castles made from ice, lit from inside in the neon colours of glow sticks. Despite the minus temperature and sleet, Felix ate an ice lolly, his scarves lit in multicoloured neons.

Then we came to the end of the world, trudging around a port filled with massive ocean liners, soviet statues with empty black eyes, and men in tracksuits smoking. Then a night of vodka and sex in a hotel with a musty odour. In the morning we lugged our huge bags onto the *Trans-Siberian* amidst businesspeople, fur coats, and food sellers.

The restaurant cart has a whole range of dated yellowed Formica; worn and chipped at the corners. We're the only people in there, other than two women with really short fringes who look like they could be drug mules.

'– Are you Ginger?' Felix asks.

'Yes!' I pout at him for being too good at this game. Somehow through his zany randomness, he always manages to ask the right question.

'Are you Elizabeth the 1st?'

'No.'

'Boudica.'

'No.'

'Ginger Spice?'

'Yes! How do you do that?' I lift my glass to drink and realise that it's empty

'I'm a bit psychic.' He raises his eyebrow.

'You really think you're psychic.'

'Yes!' He says with a bit of exasperation.

'You didn't know I had leukemia – second time we met.' I unscrew the top of the vodka.

'Things just come to me. Like that time outside *Science Fiction* with your scar.'

'That could've been a guess.' I slosh the vodka into my glass.

'You can believe we're imagining all this, but you can't believe I'm a bit psychic?' He pushes his glass forward, and I give him a Felix sized amount. '– I saw you in a magazine and I knew I had to meet you. We both felt like we'd met before, and you needed a weirdo like me to visit you in hospital when you had Leukemia. That's psychic to me.'

I swill my vodka and think how all of that is true.

Most of the train is a narrow corridor, the rest of the space taken up by rooms. You have to wedge yourself around dumpy Russian mothers and perpetually drunk men dressed in sportswear. Walking down the narrow beige corridor with its little airlock zones is a bit like being on a run-down Soviet space station. I get a brief glimpse of one of the rooms filled with generations of a family. An old lady, an old man, a lot of packages, a large woman with a crew cut looking exhausted at her children bouncing on the bench in front. The corridor windows display a Mobius strip of pylons and ice smattered shrubland. A big guy with a thinning buzzcut talks while holding a beer, to what looks like a slightly shrunken version of himself. I'm very conscious of how gay I am as I squeeze past mumbling gruff apologies in no specific language. I look out the window on the door of the last compartment. Outside, there's a compound of walled-off houses with pointed rooves in red and white. Behind are hills silhouetted by the muted oranges and purples of a sunset. A figure walks across the vast grass and dirt toward some cows.

Felix draws on my arm with a biro: a penis with interlocking swirls around it. We're both wrapped in blankets on our shelf bed, the wheels and tracks juddering away underneath us.

'I feel like we're waiting for something,' I tell him.

'People are always waiting for something,' he says in his way that reminds me of an old New Yorker. '– And then they're dead.'

'If we're imaging this, why aren't we imagining something better.' I pull my arm free a moment to close the curtain on the blue-ish darkness of the landscape.

'I don't think that's how it works.' He maneuvers my arm back into his lap to draw more swirls on it. 'I always wanted to go on the Trans-Siberian express, and I always expected it to be kind of like this.'

'You're imaging it shit on purpose?' I say.

'If I was imagining it, I'd imagine you having a better attitude.' He carries on drawings swirls on my arm. It makes me think how different we are. That he would want to be on a falling apart 80's train hurtling through the Siberian wilderness, and I'd rather be in a hotel bar with celebrities.

'Why do you love me?' I ask.

'I don't know,' he laughs, then looks at me serious. 'You're cute, and you dress funny. You make me laugh, and you're intelligent even though you pretend you're not. Those aren't the reasons though, I think I just love you.'

'I love you too.' I look at his strange, beautiful face with its moles and far apart eyes, more familiar to me than any other face I've known. 'Let me plait your hair. I've never plaited your hair before.'

I sit with my legs around him, wrapping rubber bands around the bottom of the thick 90s rave plaits I'm putting his hair into. I remember how his hair was short and blue and how long it would've taken to grow to this length. How come that never occurred to me before? Still, every split end and follicle looks so real.

We wake up hundreds of miles from where we went to sleep. The bleak sunrise of somewhere a bit more barren and a bit more frozen than the one before. The beefcake and the old lady waiting for the bathroom have been replaced with two broad-shouldered Asian men in short-sleeved shirts. When I come back from washing myself in the sink, Felix is posing naked on the bed, his plaited hair hanging down, ready for sex. He takes off all the clothes I've just put on and sucks my dick. He pushes me against the pull-out bed, the train rattling along, his plaits knocking against my crotch.

The trains stops in Ulan Ude where we quickly bundle ourselves into coats and scarves. Felix strides out into the compacted snow. The buildings, more like an industrial estate than a tourist destination. Names of shops written in big red Cyrillic letters.

'Are you sure this is the way?' I call ahead to Felix, my voice muted by the snow and the traffic.

251

'Yes!' Felix jabs at a printed-off map with his mittened hand, his soviet trapper hat pulled down to his eyebrows.

The path is next to a main road and is mottled with snow and dirt. Felix strides ahead joyfully in his yellow duffel coat. I hang back, my red puffer jacket crinkling as I hug myself. The place is like a walk-in freezer.

There seems to have been a political rally or TV event going on in the main square. There's a row of banners and a large screen with a stage in front.

'I thought it was supposed to be a statue of Lenin,' Felix says.

'Lenin?'

He points towards the huge black statue at the centre of the square. It's as tall as the surrounding buildings, with a thrusting soviet jawbone and huge angular wings held up close to it, like a cape. The rest of the square is taken up by flat regal buildings in pastel yellow. I walk about, kicking at little patches of ice while Felix looks up at the statue. I know what's he's thinking, *it's an angel, it's black, it must be an omen.*

'It reminds me of one my mum had,' he says.

'Except it's about 30ft tall.' I try to usher him away. 'Let's get some food.'

'It's more communist, but I remember the exact one.' He looks up at its face, capped with snow, hands thrust up in prayer. He walks over to it and touches its plinth.

'Let's get some food,' I call out.

We're still talking about it by the time we get to the shop, a dusty cross between an off-licence and a deli.

'— I'm just saying, all the other times it was those little burnt angels,' I tell him.

'And I'm saying, I know this means something.'

The lady behind the counter gives us a wrinkled cross between a smile and a frown.

'What do you think we should do?' I ask him while waving awkwardly to the lady. 'You think that thing in the white cloak is coming to this shop now?'

'I don't know.' He picks up some vodka miniatures.

I pick up an old bottle with a peeling label depicting what looks like a Tsar. I turn the bottle over to look at the Cyrillic writing on the back. 'What would we do if it comes?'

'Run.'

'And leave our stuff on the train?'

'If we're imagining this, I think we can leave our stuff on the train,' he says through gritted teeth.

I look over at the small elderly woman behind the counter watching TV. I don't know quite what I'm annoyed at. Maybe it's our good times being interrupted. Maybe it's being reminded that what we're living in isn't quite reality. I absent-mindedly study bottles and spin the postcard stand. There's a dusty gold bottle titled in Cyrillic encrusted with plastic jewels.

'Look at this,' I say.

Felix comes over with an armful of Vodka miniatures.

'That's –' He looks at the bottle and the price tag. '– Very expensive.'

'If we're imagining this, it doesn't matter, right?' I challenge him.

He's going to say something but then just shrugs. He goes and unloads his vodka miniatures on the counter.

Back on the train, we sit on separate beds. Felix looks out the window at trees in the grey afternoon light. I'm doing a fashion drawing of myself in a diamond-encrusted onesie with triceratops horns, the gold bottle nestled in the bed next to me.

'Are you going to open that?' He barks.

'You want some?' I pose with it.

'Some!' He gets up, his blanket wrapped around him. 'I want all of it.'

'Okay, where's the bottle opener?' I start to pull the plastic jewel and the wax seal off the top.

He searches through the pile of stuff on top of our backpacks and hands me the penknife. I twist out the cork and sniff. Felix takes it off me and pours it into his mouth.

'It's good!' He sticks it in my mouth.

'Yeah!' I say, tasting it. It's kind of like port but stronger. 'We should drink it out of glasses.' I get up to look for our glasses and hear a loud bang. I stop still and look at Felix's face as he sits mouth-open-slightly on my bed.

There are distant screams from somewhere on the train. Then two more loud bangs, muted by the sound of the tracks.

'I think we should go now,' Felix says.

My breath sticks in my throat, and my muscles freeze. I put the gold bottle down on the floor as if I'll come back for it. Felix fiddles with the door handle and pushes it open.

'What about our stuff?' I look at my backpack in the corner of the cabin.

'Kyle!' He calls after me, power walking down the tight corridor.

I follow him, my puffer jacket rustling. I look back through the window on the separating doors and see people filling the train corridor. More shots behind us. Felix is in his yellow duffel coat, forcing the next door open. I just follow him. I don't look back, but I can tell people are coming into the carriage as we leave. There's moving connecting parts of the train then another narrow hallway. Two guys in sports clothes come out of their room. I'm following Felix, pushing the walls away from myself. More gunshots, more screams. I wonder what it feels like to die, even if it's maybe only imaginary. One of the guys shouts something in Russian as we push past them. There's a gunshot and glass shattering. Felix crouches down and runs along the train carriage. I copy him. There's another shot. One of the men twists and falls, blood sprayed over the beige walls. There's another loud crack which leaves an indentation on the door we're heading towards. We scrabble over the body, part of his head missing, scalp and brain scattered, the floor dark red with blood. It makes me start to retch. Felix grabs the handle and rattles open the next door.

We're both crouched in the juddering space between two carriages. Felix yanks open the next door. We're bent over, running down the last carriage of the train. Gunshots ring in our ears.

'What do we do?' My voice calls ahead.

'Jump,' Felix shouts.

We're behind the wall of the last room on the train. I hear the door at the other end of the carriage opening. Felix stands up to pull the safety latch and forces the door open into icy winds, snow-covered landscape whizzing past. Then gunshots, so loud I want to cover my ears. A hole blown through the partition next to us. I look up at the open door, and Felix is gone, just the icy wind blowing into my face and the white below.

I realise the shooting has stopped. I scrabble at the wall of the train to peer around the corner. A man in a suit with a gun hangs back, the figure in white moving toward me, so tall that its head is bent at the ceiling. Under the white hood; grey flesh, thick with veins, a red cut for a mouth. It's meters away from me, as real as everything else on the train, as real as I am. I hold onto the door frame. The wind tugs at my puffa jacket. I see the grey of the sky and the white of the ground, and I launch myself out.

The doctor rolls up his gingham shirt sleeves and shakes our hands. He has thinning blonde hair and a long face. He ushers us toward some chairs in front of an oval table, with a box of tissues on it.

'Felix's situation isn't good,' he begins.

We try to decide where to put our hands. I opt for rolling a ball of gum between my thumb and finger. Felix's grandma folds her hands tightly in her lap.

'It took the team a long time to get his heart beating again yesterday,' the doctor says. 'Generally, the longer it takes to revive a patient the more chances there are of complications. I'm sorry to say that there might be a possibility of brain damage.'

I keep looking up and down, trying not to stare into the doctor's eyes.

He says something about compartment syndrome and reduced blood flow to Felix's leg during the CPR.

I have this image of Felix in a wheelchair with no legs, brain damaged, face twisted.

'I want to assure you we're doing everything we can to help Felix.' The doctor leans forward, and I can smell his aftershave. 'The current situation is, he's in an induced coma, and we've lowered his body temperature to stop his heart being rejected. He's on a heart and lung machine. That's what people usually refer to as life support. If you've got any questions, now or later, I'm here to answer them.'

'Is his leg going to be okay?' I ask, and I'm reminded of how camp my voice sounds.

'His leg should be okay. We might need to do a skin graft.'

'When will he come out of the coma?' Asks his grandma.

'It depends on how well he responds to the dialysis. The situation is still critical. We're waiting for his heart to stabilise, to start beating by itself before we think about pulling him out of the coma.'

'The brain damage, when will we know?' Felix's grandma is able to look the doctor in the eyes, unlike me.

'We're monitoring his brain activity, and we'll keep you informed,' he concludes.

The nurse shows us to the bed where Felix is lying, looking like a failed experiment. Everything is very quiet except for some low electronic beeps and a slow pumping sound. A tube is taped to his nose, one in his mouth, more tubes pump blood, and oxygen, and fluids, in and out of him. There's something so sad about his life being distilled to this. I've been the person in the bed with tubes going in and out of me, but seeing Felix there makes me squeamish. It makes me want to run away.

'Can we sit with him,' croaks Felix's grandma.

'That's why we brought you in here,' says the nurse.

I grab a blue hospital chair and squeak it across the floor for Felix's grandma to sit in. The nurse gets a chair for me, and we look at Felix's face, masked by breathing apparatus.

'Felix,' his grandma whispers, placing her hand lightly between the wires. 'I'm here and Kyle is too. They told us you're in a coma and there's been a lot of problems with your heart.' She lets out a long faltering breath. 'I know you're going to make it – you always

257

do. Just keep fighting.' The skin around her eyes is red and the wrinkles at the side of her mouth are downturned.

'Felix –' I mumble, then turn to his grandma for help. 'I'm sorry. I don't know what to say.' I can't touch him like she did. I'm scared I'd break him.

His grandma starts to talk to him about the weather and her journey here. I look at a grease stain on the almost perfect eggshell wall and feel stupid.

'This isn't your fault Kyle,' she says, on the bench outside the ward, her eyes lined and watery. 'What Felix needs is for us to be there for him. There's no point you feeling guilty. It doesn't help anything. Do you understand?'

'Yeah.' I look ahead at the strip of metal running along the wall.

'I'm sorry.' She touches my shoulder. 'That didn't come out right.'

'I can't talk to him like you can though.'

She spoke to him about a TV show she watched a few nights ago, some verse from the bible, and little plays Felix put on in his mum's living room.

'It doesn't matter what you say,' she tells me. 'He just needs to know that we're here. Do you have family you can go to?'

'Yeah, I have family.' I try to smile for her sake, but it's more of an upturned grimace.

I feel like I've been punched in the stomach. I roll over onto my back and scrape snow out of my eyes and blow it out of my nostrils. Grey sky fills my vision. I roll onto my side and cough a bit of blood onto the snow. I push myself up. My ribs hurt a lot. All I see is rocks and snow.

'Felix!' I call out, spitting blood. 'Felix!'

My voice is absorbed by the snow, stretching all the way to distant hills and forest. I start walking the direction the train came from, my ankle a bit twisted, clutching my ribs. There was at most ten seconds between when he jumped and when I jumped. The images are still playing in my head, Felix crouched by the door, the monster's faceless head. *Could it really be from Felix's nightmare?* I walk further than I should, hunched forward with the hood of my red puffa jacket up, arms crossed. There's not even a footprint in the snow. I don't think he could've walked off without me noticing.

'Felix!! I yell one more time, looking back at my own footprints in the snow, parallel to the railway.

He's gone. I can already see the light turning golden. I know from looking out the train window how far apart the villages and farms can be. I've got no phone, nothing except my coat and the little key-ring torch in my pocket. The air freezes the muscles in my face, but I just keep walking. I don't know what else to do.

Maybe an hour later, the sky starts to turn a purplish-blue. The landscape constricting around me, trapping me. I could keep walking by the railway all night or try and find shelter in the forest. If Felix was here, he'd make the decision. It might be wrong, but at least I wouldn't have to decide. I start walking towards the trees, kicking at the grass and snow. I hear a rumbling and turn around to see the lights of another train winding down the track, opening the landscape with its illumination. I'm a few hundred meters away. I can see the people in the windows. I yelp and jump, trying to get their attention, the cold catching in my throat. I get a brief flicker of someone waving to me. I run and stagger after the train.

'Wait, wait!' I yelp, the lights receding. Then I'm in navy-blue darkness.

I flick my little keyring torch about the tree trunks. If I'm imagining this, how come I'm trapped in this dark frozen wasteland. Maybe I need to imagine myself somewhere else. I remember Felix on the rooftop in Nepal, telling me about how he would close his eyes and recreate the landscape in his mind, the sky, the sand, the sea. I let myself drop down into the dirt and snow against a tree trunk. Hunched up, hands in my sleeves, I try to imagine where he'd go. I close my eyes and try to imagine a hotel room in Moscow. It's not easy with the cold. I create yellow eggshell walls and a worn table with a TV. A maroon cinema-style carpet, a bed with white sheets, and we're on top of the bed. I scrunch up my face, trying to imagine myself there in front of him in the warm room. Then I open my eyes and see the dark shapes of trees.

The forest gets denser, my keyring torch lighting the greyish brown trunks. I see something a few meters away that looks like a pile of logs. I'm desperate enough that I think about arranging them into shelter. I stagger towards them, my laboured breath in my ears. There's tools and logs and buckets, then tarpaulin and a door, a dusty window that reflects the torchlight. I panic a moment about who could be inside and click the torch off. But there are no lights, just the moon through the trees. I kick and yank the door. It's shut, but I find a hand-sized hole where a lock would normally be and reach into it. My heart is beating with the fear that something in the darkness will grab my hand. I find a latch and slide it open.

The first thing I see are rugs on the walls, dark red, ornate and mildewed. Then I see the angel statuette, or maybe it's a statue of Saint George. It's part of a wall of decaying religious pictures and figurines. There's a metal crucifix, melted candles, and jam jars filled with brown liquid. I worry I'm going to find an old shrunken hermit curled up dead under the blankets on the floor. But when I lift them, there's nothing but damp mouldy fabric. I lie under a couple of musty blankets and try to go to sleep. Just one candle on and think maybe I'll be somewhere else when I wake up. If I am, it'll be proof that we're both imagining this.

It's hard to sleep with the noises outside, scratching and creaking and then a sound like footsteps. I lay there hoping it's Felix and not an angry Russian hermit or the creature in the white robe. I worry about it coming to the door and crouching over me as I sleep, breathing on me with that angry red scar of a mouth.

Sometime between sleep and waking I hear my name,

'Kyle, Kyle, Kyle,' a whisper, the same volume as the trees scratching outside.

I open my eyes, but there's no Felix, just the dim shapes of furniture.

'Kyle, Kyle.'

I jolt up and reach in my pocket for the keyring torch and run to the door and fiddle with the bolt. I shine the torch about the tree trunks and call out, 'Felix!?'

But there's just the same scratching and creaking as before.

Morning light fills the room and I look around at all the dusty boxes, mildewed fabrics, and religious paraphernalia. There's a grimy old chair that I sit in, wondering what to do. Go down to the railway and wave about some bit of fabric with the word "*help*" written on it, walk until I find a village, or sit in front of the altar and use all my energy to try and send myself to a hotel room in Moscow. I look up at a gold-framed picture of the Virgin Mary.

'What would you do?' I ask. I remember her doing a lot of travelling in the nativity story, so I decide to head out. I put some rusted cans of sardines and a rusty can opener into a crusty old backpack. I say a prayer to the Virgin Mary that I won't have to eat the sardines. Then I traipse into the hills. I imagine myself in a distant wide shot. A small figure in a red puffa coat amongst this expanse of green and white and grey.

I miss Felix, he'd know what to do or he'd at least pretend he did. The foothills are further than they looked. I find some indentations in the snow that look like they used to be a path and force myself to follow them. My cheeks are red, my breath visible in front of me. Thoughts circulate my head. What if all this is real? Or what if I'm trapped in Felix's mind? Then there's the thought that he's still in that hospital. The one I thought we left a year ago. If that really is the case, what happens next?

'Felix,' I call out.

When I get to the top of the hill, all I can see are more valleys, more vistas of white and grey. The train track is the only thing that breaks up the landscape. Heading down the hill I dig my shoes into the ice and dirt. I wince at a brief icy wind. I let out a whine and almost feel like crying. Then I hear my name whispered in the wind,

'Kyle.'

I look behind me, my arms wrapped around myself. Was it just the wind or could it be Felix trying to contact me? I see the train in the distance, sliding through the landscape with a whispered rumble, this tiny line of colour gliding between the hills.

Back at the hut, I'm pleased to see there's still no hermit. I swear at the Virgin Mary for not saving me from eating food from a rusty can. I find some ancient soap and some fossilised scrubbing pads and trudge out into the light snowfall. I scoop some snow into the pan and use it to scrub the dust off. I don't feel like the same person without all the clubs and the glitter. There are some bits that are the same, and other bits that have changed. And it wasn't almost dying from leukemia that changed me, it was him almost dying. Does that make me a good person, or a bad person? I look at the dusty faded icons, the saints and crucifixes. I decide to give meditating myself back to Felix another go.

The sun is setting, the orange light filtering through the trees drawing shadows around the hut. I light all the candles on the altar and more that I found hidden with religious books in draws. I sit down on a cushion in the middle of the room with a blanket wrapped around me. The smell of must and mould thick in the air. I get the £10 note Felix gave me out of my wallet and try to feel close to him. I try and imagine our hotel room in Moscow, like I'm really there, maroon carpet, yellowish egg-shell walls, a big Formica cupboard, and a TV on a hinge on the wall. I paint the whole room in my mind down to the rubbish bin. I start to feel my body juddering like an engine is starting up inside me. I open my eyes, but I'm still looking at all the little religious icons and candles. I get up and search through the cupboards for some firelighters.

The cabin is gross, but I go through all the draws of rusted cutlery and tools and old postcards. Ancient things from some forgotten life. I'm starting to feel trapped. I go out into the dark to get snow to melt in the oven to make water. While watching the snow melt in the little orange mouth of the oven, I wonder whether I should derail the train. If this is imaginary, then it won't matter leaving logs all over the tracks. Or should I just leave here tomorrow with a bag full of canned food and follow the tracks till the next village.

I leave the oven burning as I lay there trying to sleep. The dark shadows of the room, slightly menacing. All the scratches and whistles and creaks going on outside amplified.

'Kyle, Kyle, Kyle,' something whispers in an almost human voice.

It scares me. I sit up in bed poised, ready to get up. Was it just an illusion of my half-asleep brain?

'Kyle,' it says again, as if coming from everywhere, the trees and the walls of the hut.

A bit more information would be useful, some co-ordinates, a meeting point. Then my mouth opens with a sudden mental jolt. *What if he did give me a meeting point, a long time ago.* The idea shocks me because it was so long ago, but the words seem like they were meant for me now.

'*If I ever go missing, find me here,*' he said, holding the Norwegian postcard, the first time I was at his grandma's house.

I scrabble for the matches and light all the candles, like some religious fanatic who has to pray in the middle of the night. I sit back on the cushion and close my eyes, the faint glow of the candles against my eyelids. I take a deep musty breath in. I think of how Felix talked about putting the sea and the sky and the sand back in place. I try to remember the details of the postcard. the varnished dark wood, and the wall hangings; patterned like Christmas jumpers, reindeer horns, everything neat and properly spaced out. I try to remember it accurately, as if it's the coordinates to where he is, a display cabinet with plates, a chair with an embroidered cushion, a black chimney pipe, a fireplace made of brick, a big animal fur rug. I try not to look at the dark behind my eyelids. I try to really see the room. I'm on the fur rug with Felix sitting in front of me, by the fireplace. I feel my body juddering like before. The fire dancing on Felix's skin. I reach out for his hand. I feel the juddering again, almost like an earthquake. Some of the dark seems to seep out of the picture. I feel his hands gripping mine, and everything looks as if it's actually in front of me. The warmth of the fire, the moles on his face.

I found a list of travel books that he made, while searching through the stuff he left in my beauty table. I went to the library for maybe the first time in a decade to look for them.

'You can search online or on that computer,' the librarian tells me, as I clutch the folded bit of paper with his messy rounded scrawl on it. 'If we don't have it, Tower Hamlets or Whitechapel might.'

They have the one by Bill Bryson about America, and another one about South America, and Greenwich Library has a third one. When I'm holding the two books, a hollow feeling spreads from my heart to my chest and stomach. I could hold it in, but I don't want to. I go to the disabled toilet in the corner of the library and grip onto the handrail. I don't think I've ever sobbed like this before, rasping and groaning, my body shaking, tears bleeding hot from my eyes. The image of my face in the mirror, blurred and red.

'Felix,' my stiff downturned lips whisper, 'Felix.' As if by saying his name I'll somehow reach him across all the miles.

We hold these little three-person conferences in the ward by Felix's bed.

The doctor with his rolled-up shirt sleeves tells us, 'Felix's lungs had started assisting the respirator, and that there was brainwave function.

'– and his heart?' I ask.

'If Felix pulls through, he'll need a mechanical heart while he waits for a new one.'

I imagine Felix having to go around with a battery pack sticking out of his chest. That doesn't compute with almost all the things he likes doing, but I remember that he's done it before.

The bad news comes a couple of days later,

'We've withdrawn all the drugs keeping Felix in a coma and he hasn't woken up. Basically, he's in his own coma now. The brain scans we've done show that there is activity, which is promising, but I don't want to give you false hope.'

A couple of days later he's still lying there, with his eyes closed, brain damage seeming more and more likely.

I bring the travel books into the hospital and try to act like I'm at ease and everything is going to be okay. I add my own comments to what I'm reading. When the author has a gun pulled on him in a hotel room in Chihuahua, I say.

'You were going to make me go to this place!'

His reply is silence, lying there with the ventilator making that synthetic pressing sound. I try to mimic the nurse's chirpy bedside manner. The nurse who shaves him and changes his drip involves him with everything she does like he's a shy pre-school kid. It's not me though. I'm impatient to see his eyes open, so whatever life we're going to have can start again. I imagine us in all the places I've read about. Visiting the forest with the giant trees in California and the rock formations in Arizona. I imagine us crossing the border into Mexico and doing Ayahuasca in the rainforest. But most of all I imagine him waking up. I remember him saying if you imagine something hard enough it will happen. So, while I'm drinking red wine in front of the TV with the volume down, I fill out all the details. The smell of the flowers and the dull autumn light coming from the window. The nurse with the black curly hair and glasses leading us into the room. The feeling of trepidation as I see those alien eyes again, half-open, unmoving. I don't like to be unrealistic. Of course, I have all these fantasies of his full recovery, physical therapy, and him coming home. But mostly, I just focus on the moment that everything changes just a little bit for the better. I don't make my miracle too big or too impossible, as if God and the universe favour the more realistic requests, the ones that take less bending of the laws of physics.

I'm hugging his warm body, his woollen tank top, his polyester shirt. His arms around me and the smell of fire and scented candles.

'I was in a hut in Siberia!' I look around the neat Scandinavian cabin once more, just to triple check I'm actually here.

'How long?' He looks at me wildly.

'Two days, two nights.' I try to remember everything I need to tell him, but it already seems to be fading from my memory. 'I found this abandoned hut. I thought I was stuck there.'

'I woke up here this afternoon,' he tells me, with an expression like he's slightly unsure about this. 'It was harder this time.'

'What was?'

'Coming back –' He pauses. 'There's alcohol in the cupboard. I think we should have some.'

I stand up and look at the kitchen, like a Hobbit house designed by *Muji*. Felix is rooting through a cupboard.

'This changes everything!' I kneel on the sofa, leaning on the fur throw.

'This stuff looks interesting.' He holds up a bottle with a homemade label.

'Felix, stop a moment.'

He holds the bottle and looks at me quizzically.

'Can you believe that just happened?' I ask.

'More than you can,' he laughs.

'How did you know, all that time ago, to tell me where to go?'

'Where did I tell you to go?'

'Here! You said, "*If I ever go missing, look for me here.*"'

'I didn't know.' He rests the bottle on the work surface. 'But like I've been trying to tell you, I'm a little bit psychic.'

We sit on the sofa, face to face, legs intertwined, drinking the strange brown Schnapps. The firelight and the embroidered cushions making this an idyllic Norwegian scene.

'Where did you go?' I lean my head into the sofa, and he copies me.

'I don't really know.' He rubs his head into the side of the sofa.

'I was by the train track for two days.' I emphasise the time difference between our two journeys.

'Okay, I'll try and tell you.' He pauses to sip Schnapps. 'It's like the times when I've been on mushrooms, and I can see all these parts of myself drifting away, and I'm like, "*oh, come back.*" But I don't know who's asking them to come back, and I don't even know if there's a body to come back to. Somehow, I managed to put myself back together, but it took more effort than last time.'

'Do you think you were dying?' I look into my glass.

'I don't know.' He leans back into the sofa, rubbing my calf with his foot.

"Cos if your body really is still in that hospital, maybe I'm here to help bring you back.' I look at his far apart eyes. 'I figure, if I sent myself here, then maybe we can send ourselves back there.'

'To the hospital?' His foot pauses by my ankle.

'It's not any crazier than anything else, and I've memorised what that hospital room looks like better than anywhere. It's almost like this is what we're meant to do.'

'Okay, let's try it.' He grips my leg.

270

'Now?'

'Let's spend a day, half a day here, then –' He makes a gesture, glass in hand.

Why wait? I think. Especially seeing the last time we were together there was a monster trying to kill us. Then I really think about it. If he is still in that hospital bed, then all that recovery is still ahead of us. This could be the last time together for a long while.

'What about the monster?' I ask in a whisper as if it might hear me.

'It took a long time to find us before.'

'Where is it coming from?' I hold onto him, amazed that we're back together.

'Some dark place in here.' He taps the side of his head. 'I started seeing it when I was a kid. I had therapy and took a lot of LSD to try and deal with it.'

'There's always this man in a suit who's with the monster.' I press the Schnapps glass against my chin.

'Yeah,' Felix nods. 'He looks a lot like my P.E. teacher.'

In the morning we have sex, the icy light from between the curtains on our skin. We have sex like we've been apart longer than a few days. Me on my back on the patchwork quilt, he bites his lip while he fucks me. I grab my dick and lean my head back into the quilt as I'm about to cum. Afterwards, Felix cooks breakfast naked except for an apron.

'It's weird.' I kneel on the sofa, watching him. 'I feel like we've been here longer than we have. It feels like the hut in Siberia is some old memory.'

'That's how it was for me after Egypt.' He scrapes the eggs out of the pan with a spatula. '– Like my mind didn't want to remember.'

271

'We need to send ourselves back before we forget.' I grip the reindeer throw on the back of the sofa.

'I don't think we'll forget. But I'll write it on the fridge.' He puts down the spatula and picks up a pen next to a magnetic pad. He acts like he's making a date in his diary. 'What time?'

'Tonight? 6pm?'

We trudge up a path that's been cleared, curbs of snow up to our mid-calves. The Siberian hills have been swapped out for thick forest and snow-covered mountains. Our neighbours are a few silent red houses with grey rooves, that look like they were made from flat packs.

'Do you think there'll be people in town?' The static cold absorbs my voice.

'I mean, there's normally people in a town.' Felix tugs on the straps of the hat he found in our chalet, a red Peruvian one with strips of Scandinavian embroidery.

'It just seems weird,' I say. 'After sending myself here, that there'd be people. Do you think they're real people?'

'When I was taking a lot of LSD, I'd ask that sometimes.' He walks so close that he nudges me. 'I always found it better to assume they were real.'

'If they're real, why are they here?'

'You're talking to someone who doesn't think anything's real. I don't think this world's real – I don't think the one we came from is real – crazy huh?'

'How do you mean it's not real?' I look at him in his Norwegian hat, a lake surrounded by snow behind him. 'You think it's on a giant floating disc?'

'I think, if it's all on a giant floating disc –' He gestures enthusiastically with his mittens. '– What's the giant floating disc made of?'

'You said you thought I was real?' I see my breath in the air.

272

'As real as me.' He swings his arms.

The town looks like something from a Christmas card, with nobody in the streets. We walk a little way, and there are no lights in any of the houses or the tourist shop, with its ugly Norwegian troll figures in the window.

'There's no footprints in the snow,' says Felix. He goes up to a little box house and knocks on the door with his usual rhythmic knock. He does it again, the sound absorbing into the snow. 'Hello?' He calls through the letterbox, then goes to the next house, while I stand at the end of the path, watching.

'Nobody in,' I say, 'That's creepy.'

We crunch through the snow-filled street, knocking on doors until we have to accept that there's no one there. That this is a film set, and we're the only actors. He pauses outside a shop with a dark occult looking display of food in the window.

'We should take a look,' he says.

'You mean break-in?'

'Well, if it's imaginary –' He gives the door a kick, then kicks it hard till it cracks open.

The place smells like old books. I flash my keyring torch around dark wooden shelves of canned food, a display with Christmas trees, ugly troll figures, and a stuffed owl. I spin the torch back to Felix who is already eating something.

'What?' He says with his mouth full. 'They're good.' He offers the pack of liquorice to me, but my attention is on the little door next to the counter. 'There's no one coming.' Felix says, picking up another packet of sweets and giving me an encouraging look.

'How do you know?'

'I don't.' He grabs a bag from the counter. 'But there's no angel statue ... Let's just enjoy this.' He starts stuffing packets of sweets into a bag, packets with short unpronounceable names like *Boika* and *Jolji*. I turn my torch to the dusty alcohol shelves, bottles of brown spirits with pictures of villages and ships on. There's a model of a Viking long boat like the one in Felix's display cabinet. I pick up a white bottle decorated with blue swirls.

'This.' I hold the bottle up.

'Yes!' He stops stuffing his bag for a second. 'That!'

We walk back via a different route, empty red houses with a background of forest. Felix swings his shopping bag, his humming muted by the snow. There's a compact red church with a round spire.

'Oh!' Felix points to the graveyard next to the church.

It's filled with graves topped with age blackened statuettes, mostly angels. We both just stop there and look at them, their heads and wings capped with snow.

'Do you think it means they're coming?' I whisper.

'Hmmm.' He studies the angels with a pensive expression. 'Maybe we should get our stuff from the house and go.'

'Send ourselves back to the hospital?' I dig one foot into the snow.

'Yeah.' He turns to make sure I'm following him. 'Get away from here, then send ourselves back to the hospital.

We're back at the little Norwegian hut, shoving stuff into our backpacks.

'Why would they warn us?' I look over at Felix, bundling candles from on top the fireplace into his bag. 'Why would they give us a sign they're coming?'

Felix looks around for what to put into the bag next. He heads into the bedroom. 'Maybe it's not them warning us. Maybe it's someone ... something trying to help us.'

'Who?' I clip my bag fastened on the kitchen worktop.

He opens the door out of the hut. We power walk toward the forest, the tree trunks like silhouettes against the darkening sky.

'Are those the Northern Lights?' I point to some green lines, almost like clouds against the navy-blue sky.

'Yeah.' He stops, turns around and grabs me and kisses me.

We crunch through the snow, between the dark shapes of trees, the ground uneven with roots. Brambles snag my coat. Despite everything, I have a good feeling about this. This is the end of our journey, it's the right time, the right place, and I know everything I need to know to get us back home. At one point we both stop and look back.

'What is that?' I see what looks like fire somewhere in the distance, disembodied between the tree trunks.

'Something we should be running away from.' Felix turns, adjusting his backpack and walks fast, stumbling on the roots.

'You think it's them?'

'Yeah, I feel it,' he utters.

We finally stop in a clearing, both sweating, bent over and exhausted.

'Here,' he pants.

'Good.' I look around at the dark shapes of trees and smell smoke in the air.

He puts his bag down among the rotting leaves and twigs and starts getting stuff out. I get out my keyring torch and shine it in his direction. He hangs a sheet over a low hanging branch and tries to make a tent, weighing it down messily with fallen branches.

We light a couple of candles and sit opposite each other.

'Close your eyes and I'll describe the hospital room,' I say.

His face is illuminated, the striped sheet billowing slightly.

'You need to imagine it like you're actually really there,' I tell him.

'Like what I used to do in the tent in my bedroom.'

'Yeah. I think this is going to work.' I kiss him one last time, trying not to burn my clothes on the candles. Then I'm describing his hospital room; the thin framed windows, the machines with their LEDs, all the way down to the stains on the walls. I imagine it too, like we're not in a forest clearing, like I'm sitting on that chair in the air-conditioned room, looking at him in bed. The same chair I sat in every day reading those travel books. I start to feel the vibration again, my whole body vibrating. I don't let my concentration go. I fix the image in my mind, as if I'm actually there, the outline of his body, the breathing tubes attached to his face, the smell of sweat and disinfectant. The blurriness starts to seep out of the picture and the vibrating gets more extreme, as if we're crashing through a membrane. Then my eyes are no longer closed. I feel the arm of the chair under my hand.

'You look tired,' Felix's grandma says, as I sit in the plastic chair trying to help her with the crossword.

'I shouldn't look tired.' I lean my head against the wall and look across Felix's bed at her. 'I'm sleeping like nine, ten hours.'

'If you want, you can come back with me.' She adjusts her glasses, her eyes wrinkling with concern. 'I'll cook you something.'

'Thank you.' I say no without saying no. Maybe she's forgotten what happened last time I was there. 'I'll be fine.'

I cancelled all my hosting gigs, all my DJing gigs. The idea of putting on make-up and acting sociable while he's lying in that room seems wrong. So, I get up each day and go to the hospital like it's my job. I sit by his bed, and I read about Nepal and Thailand, and I help his grandma with the crossword. Then I go home, and I eat pizza, and I imagine him recovering. I do see the hypocrisy. I didn't want to be with him, and now my whole life revolves around him, visiting him, thinking about him, trying to be strong for him. I tell myself that this won't go on for months, that he'll start to recover soon. That he'll open his eyes.

Felix's friend Leon messages me to call him. My friends message me saying they're thinking of me. I don't message them back. I try to cut myself off. But James brings people to see me in the flat. Kitten brings a bottle of wine with her. I drink most of it and start ranting about karma.

'When did you become a Hindu?' Says Kitten.

'I just think sometimes, this is what I deserve.' I look in the wine bottle to see if there's any more hiding somewhere inside.

'Babe, I love Felix. But he wasn't exactly looking after himself. I hardly think it's your fault.' She gets out her cigarettes with the coloured tips and pulls one out to offer me. We smoke out the window, looking down at the grass where Felix serenaded me.

'I feel like I don't know who I am anymore,' I say.

'Did you know who you were before.' She takes a long drag.

'Yes, I was Cosmo the carefree club-kid.'

'Before you were ill, you didn't seem very carefree to me.' She taps ash out the window and looks at me with green neon around her eyes.

My parents bring bags of sushi to me and James' apartment. I feel guilty eating it, like I deserve to be eating the low-quality pizzas I buy every night. We pick at a sushi pyramid while James and my sister making polite conversation about politics.

'How is Felix?' Asks my mum after two-thirds of the sushi pyramid has been eaten.

My urge is to be sarcastic, but I know that's not fair on her.

'Not good,' I tut.

'Mrs. Stone next door said she'd pray for him,' my mum comments, which is strange because she neither likes religion nor Mrs. Stone next door.

'You told Mrs. Stone my boyfriend was ill?'

'Yes,' she says with indignation.

'If there's anything we can do –' says my dad.

'If he doesn't get better –' starts my mum.

'He's going to get better!' I tell her. I eat a California roll and decide not to say anymore. I don't want to sound woo-woo or crazy, but I can tell he's still here.

Felix's grandma said she prays for him throughout the day. I remember the angel I saw when I was really ill, and I remember Felix saying something about his mum seeing an angel. So as dumb as it may sound, I pray to the angel before I go to sleep. I don't know if it has a name, and I doubt it really exists, but I ask it to help. Then I sleep, then I wake up, then I get on the tube and go back to the hospital.

I'm on the chair in the hospital room, and Felix is lying on the bed. The only light is a faint blue coming from the window. Felix is pushing himself up.

'Somethings wrong.' I feel my keyring torch in my pocket and click it on.

'We're here.' Felix looks around the room.

'It's not how it's supposed to be.' I walk over to the window with the torch and find the window is not there anymore. It's just shards of glass and branches poking through. I flash my torch around outside and see more branches, more trees. 'It looks like we're still in the forest.'

We walk down the stairwell to the ground floor, no people, no lights. The hospital smells dank and earthy, like it's been abandoned for years. Floor tiles kicked out of place, weeds growing from cracks, and mould on the walls. We both stand in the entrance. The same entrance I imagined him leaving through in his wheelchair. There's no road, just some cracked asphalt and trees towering over us.

'Isn't this how the hospital looked?' He jokes.

'No,' I say, desperate. 'Maybe we need to do it again.'

'We got away from the monster.' Felix tries to be positive.

'Yeah, but where are we?' I feel trapped, and I feel the gravity of my plan not working.

We walk around the hospital, but there are no other buildings, no university, no train station, just the hospital, like some strange research facility in the forest.

The next day, we sit on the entrance steps eating baked beans from an industrial-sized can we found in the cafeteria. There are insects crawling in the faint sunlight and birds flitting about the browning leaves.

'Which direction?' Felix gestures with his fork.

'Are we just going to keep going until the monster finds us?' I ask bleakly.

'Have you got a better plan?'

'I just –' I look out between the trees, trying to see if there are any buildings in the distance. 'I think maybe there's something more we need to do, to get back home. Something we haven't thought of.'

We both wait for the other one to come up with an idea.

'Kill the monster,' I say.

'I'm a pacifist,' he tells me, chewing on his beans. '– That monster has been with me a long time.'

'I'll do it then.' I get up.

'How?' He asks.

'I saw some knives in the cafeteria.'

We set off into the forest again with a couple of bacpacks we found in the hospital, filled with canned food, mildewed blankets, and the biggest knife in the kitchen. It's a long silent walk, through wild branches and thorns. I'm thinking as hard as I can about what to do next. Thinking, with a brain that is normally reserved for pairing eyeshadow colours and wigs.

'What about whoever, whatever's sending these burnt angels?' I stop to make sure he's listening to me. 'Maybe that has something to do with how we get out of here.'

'If the monsters coming from in here.' He taps his head. 'Then probably, the warnings are coming from in here too. The part of me that knows.'

'Is there part of you that knows how to get out of here?' I ask.

He steps back and sits down on a moss-covered rock and looks up at me like he's trying to say something with just his eyes. 'I think –' He pulls up a bit of moss and drops it on the ground. 'There's a possibility I'm not getting out of here.'

'You think you're dying?' The words snag on my throat. 'Is this one of your psychic things?'

'No.' He reaches for my hand and pulls me down onto the rock with him. 'No. It's just this world seems like it's closing in on us. And what I experienced, after I jumped off the train ...' His mouth is open, unable to explain.

I breathe in the thick earthy smell of the forest. He makes that wide-mouthed frog expression at me.

'You're not dying,' I squeeze his hand. 'Remember in hospital when I thought I was dying. This is my turn to tell you.' I look him in the eyes. I realise, if he doesn't believe it, the plan won't work. 'You're not dying.' I try to say it with conviction.

'You don't know that,' he says.

'Yeah, I do.' I push myself up and start walking, hiding my emotions, hiding my doubt.

By what seems like late afternoon we're starting to ask if we could be going around in a circle.

'We can just sleep under a tree,' Felix tries to reassure me.

'On what? Mouldy blankets?' I complain, feeling a patch of sweat under my backpack.

But then there are bits of asphalt, cracked up amidst the dead leaves, and the shape of something big, through the trees. I get the knife out of my bag, trying not to let Felix see it. He jogs up ahead. When I catch up, he's holding onto a crosshatch fence tangled with ivy. Inside is more concrete, cracked, as if by earthquakes, and squat brick buildings, like an overgrown government compound.

'It's my school,' Felix tells me. He puts his backpack on a slab of asphalt and says, 'I never thought I'd want to break in here but give me a leg up.'

I look down at his shoes, covered in dirt, then back at him.

'Okay.' He shrugs and half clambers half hurls himself over the other side, ripping ivy off as he goes. He holds the fence down for me. I sling our backpacks across, then struggle over, gripping the fence like an off-balance cat.

We walk across the shattered concrete, the front steps scattered with weeds and moss.

'It feels haunted,' I say, feeling like we're trespassing.

'I guess it is,' he rattles the front door. 'I didn't exactly have a good time here.' He kicks the door hard. Kicks it again and again, with a lot of anger. So much that his Norwegian hat falls off. The wood splinters, and the door opens.

The air is filled with damp and decay. The light from outside reveals a mould covered mural, a dirty parquet floor, and an assembly hall filled with chairs. I feel a bit like explorers uncovering a lost tomb. Felix shines his torch on some trophy cases at the back of foyer, group photos and big gold cups with marble bases.

'Here's me.' He flashes the torch in my face to get my attention.

I come over and look through the dusty glass at the picture. Rows of teenagers in shirts and ties.

'Second row from the back, third one along,' he says.

'You've got short hair,' I look at the kid version of my boyfriend.

'Some kids jumped on me in the toilet and cut it,' he gives me that look that says he doesn't want sympathy. 'I didn't tell the teachers.'

'That's terrible.' I put my arm around him and squeeze him close.

'It made me who I am.' He shines the torch off down the corridor at a large noticeboard mottled with green. '— And I like who I am.'

'Still, it's terrible,' I repeat.

'Yeah, it's terrible.' He walks off.

I catch up with him, shining his torch around a chemistry classroom.

'I used to have this plan,' he says, 'that I'd take you to all the places where shitty things happened to me and make out with you there. I thought that would somehow make it better.'

'Why didn't you.' I lean on the classroom cupboard.

'I didn't feel like it. I guess, I wanted to keep the past in the past, and keep us in the present.' He wipes some dust off the desk with his finger. 'But I guess the past is always there.'

'Do you still want to make out with me here?'

'I feel more like ripping that pipe off the wall and smashing the place apart.'

'We can do that too,' I laugh.

We both yank at the metal pipe, painted in mint green. We pull until it tears off the classroom wall. Dirty water leaks out of it. Felix takes his hat off and with a massive shattering of glass, he slams the pipe into a glass-doored cupboard filled with vials and Bunsen burners. He pulls open cupboards and throws books and jars of powder onto the floor. He hurls a stool across the room. Then he's attacking the wind-up blackboard. The pipe tears through it. I copy him, throwing a chair across the classroom. I smash the last few test-tubes. He pushes the teacher's desk over and with a mad look says,

284

'Okay next!'

The desks in the biology classroom are set up in an arch shape. He pushes them onto the floor. He smashes shelves with withered plants and discoloured models of the human anatomy. He even smashes a few windows. I feel like the wild youth that I could have been if I hadn't gone to private school, if I hadn't become a society girl. I start smashing things with a chair leg. Felix climbs on top of the pile of chairs and desks. He smashes the pipe into the suspended ceiling, raining down bits of cardboard tile and shouts,

'Fuck you school.'

I drop my chair-leg and clamber onto the pile of desks and chairs and kiss him. His bit of pipe clatters to the floor.

'Next?' I ask.

'Nah, I'm not that angry,' he says.

We go up a staircase, green with moss and mould, past classrooms with grey tables and plastic chairs, and up a ladder and out onto the roof. We look out at the forest extending all the way to the horizon. A few buildings sticking out of the trees like Mayan ruins. In the far distance, the forest builds up into a mountain.

'Do you think maybe you're meant to deal with this before we go back,' I ask.

He stands with his back to me, looking out at the sky, a deep cloudless blue. 'I don't think we're meant to do anything.'

'— But this school ... the monster.' I feel a slight breeze.

He sits down on one of the skylights. 'That lady in the old people's home, the one that taught me Spanish. When her dementia got really bad, she thought she was in the blitz. She thought her son had just killed himself. She kept going back and reliving those memories.'

'But you don't have dementia.'

'But this is that dark place in my mind.' He looks up at me.

I go back to tracing the edge of the roof. I can see the hospital in the distance, sticking out of the patchwork of greens and browns. Behind it are huge billowing clouds that seem to grow out of the trees.

'I guess I can choose to deal with it though,' Felix says.

I think of all the things he's had to deal with. I think of the monster, and my mind goes to the knife in my bag. 'How long do you think we've got?'

'I don't know,' he says, getting up. 'Do you smell smoke?'

'I think I see smoke.' I trace what I thought were clouds down to a distant rift in the trees. It looks almost like a wave, rolling in slow motion toward us.

'We should leave first thing in the morning,' Felix says.

The sunset draws long shadows through the entrance to the assembly hall. Felix kicks open the door of the gym storeroom and flashes the torch about inside. I pick at a bunch of metal javelins and knock over some basketballs. We pull a crash mat into the middle of the hall to make into the bed. Then re-arrange all the rows of chairs into a big mess around it, so if anyone comes during the night, we'll hear them. While he's inspecting behind the stage curtains, I take one of the javelins from the storeroom and put it next to our bed. If the monster is coming from Felix's mind, I think maybe it's better he doesn't know how I'm going to kill it.

We lay under our blankets in the dark and the cold with the rustling of the forest outside.

'If anything goes wrong –' Felix says, his head against mine. '– Where do we meet?'

'Somewhere we both know. Your room, my room?'

'Somewhere neutral. I feel like it should be the squat, Leon's room.' He wriggles his arm around me. 'It always reminds me of my bedroom tent, when I was a kid.'

'Okay,' I say, and with the hand that isn't holding onto him, I feel the cold of the javelin on the floor next to me.

I wake up in the dark, the clatter of chairs, banging against each other. My body tenses, Felix mouths something to me in the almost darkness. There are footsteps. I grab the javelin and peak at the figure standing over the bed. My breath sticks in the back of my throat. As the figure grabs for the blanket, I thrust the javelin at it as hard as I can. There's a loud masculine scream and a gunshot which briefly illuminates the room. I pull myself up, there's a clatter, a scrabbling of limbs, and a gurgling sound. I'm kneeling on the bed looking at the man in the suit contorting and groaning. I reach for Felix to see if he's okay. He's pulling himself up and gesturing to something in the dim light of the open doorway, a figure in a cloak, taller than any person.

'I have to go to it,' whispers Felix.

'No!' I grab his wrist.

'I have to.' He pulls himself free. He's running toward it, the chairs clattering.

I almost trip over the chairs. I see the shape of Felix hurl himself toward the monster, almost like an embrace. Felix grips onto the figure, silhouetted by moonlight. Then it's as if they both crumple in mid-air, their shadows screwed up like paper. Then there's nothing there. I'm just looking at the shapes of the trees through the open door.

There's silence again, even the guttural sounds from the man have stopped. I fumble in my pocket for the little keyring torch. I hope I imagined all that, and Felix will still be in the bed. But it's empty, just the man next to it, contorted and unmoving, his suit stained with blood. I quickly turn the torch back to the spot where the monster was, but there's just motes of dust in the torchlight. I stand there a while, listening to the rustling of the branches and the coo-coo of a bird.

287

I can see that the roots on his blue hair have grown out, that means he's been in here a long time. He has this waxy yellow look, tubed and wired up like he's attached to a prototype virtual reality simulation. I wonder if he's in the room with me and his grandma now, as we try to guess 12-down on the crossword, or if he's off somewhere off in space. His grandma sees me at the hospital vending machine, holding a chocolate bar and eating prawn cocktail crisps.

'Is that your evening meal?' She asks.

'No, I'm going to stop at the pizza place.'

'Come back to my house, I'll cook you something,' she tells me. When I start to make excuses, she says, 'You need a proper meal.'

I'm quiet in the car, looking out at the motorway bridges and roadside estates. I'm thinking about what happened when I was there a month ago.

'I know you had an argument with Felix, last time you were here.' She checks the rear view mirror.

'Yeah, it's not a good memory.'

'That's one reason I asked you here.' She looks at me, then quickly looks back at the road.

'To torture me,' I half-joke.

'No, I want you here. Felix would've wanted you here.'

I wonder if that's true. The Felix I saw all those weeks back didn't want me there. Would he have changed his mind? I know he wasn't vindictive, and I know he probably wouldn't want me to hate myself like I do.

We pull up into this familiar driveway with the gnomes. Most of the flowers are gone, and some kids nearby are screaming in their front garden.

'I can't bring it to you in the car.' His grandma taps the car window.

'You could.' I put on my *Disney* smile, still seat-belted in.

She gives me a weary expression and opens the front door.

'Is hot pot good?' She asks after I've taken off my shoes.

'Anything's good.' I look around the living room.

'You can come in the kitchen while I cook.' She looks at me in my unease.

'Actually, can I go up to Felix's room for a bit?' I ask. I want to be close to him more than I want to avoid the pain.

It hits me when I walk through his door and see all his souvenirs; both the good memories and the bad ones, the first time I came here and the last. The room almost makes me feel like he's here. It's like being inside his brain. His grandma has tidied things up. The wine bottles are gone, and the souvenirs are arranged neater than he ever would've had them. It feels like a museum or a shrine. I go and sit on the bed for a while and just feel him near me. I open his desk drawer and hesitate over whether I should go through his stuff. There are travel plans, psychedelic doodles, and a diary. I sit cross-legged on his carpet and read something he wrote about his ex-boyfriend, some badly rhymed poetry, his funeral plan which is covered in glittery stickers of kittens. There's torn out pages from a porn magazine, some GCSE certificates, a big piece of photo paper that I unfold to find a school photo. It's extensively altered with biro, moustaches, penises, and pentagrams drawn onto it. I try to find Felix. Eventually I spot him on the second row from the back, with short hair. I've never seen a photo of him when he was young, but there's something so familiar about it. I start to get this rogue memory where I'm looking at the photo with him, it's in a dusty display cabinet. I sit there open-mouthed on his bedroom floor with the photo in my lap. There's more; me and Felix smashing up a chemistry classroom, climbing onto the school roof, looking out at forest all around, and Felix asking if I smell smoke. It never happened, but the memory seems so real. It's like when Felix would tell me things that happened during my recovery from the bone marrow transplant. I wouldn't remember, but after he'd tell me something, the memory would come back to me.

There's more; we're lying in bed in the dark and he's telling me, '*Meet me at the squat.*' I stare through the photo, with the feeling that this memory is just a fragment of something much bigger, and if I keep pulling, I'll see all of it. But his grandma is calling me down for dinner.

'Are you okay?' She asks when we're sitting at the table with the hot pot and chutneys.

'Yeah, just lots of memories,' I say.

I sit on the central line with two other passengers. I put my face in my hands and try and take another glimpse of this other world. It seems too strange, too real, too 3D to be one of the futures I imagined for us. Maybe, this is what I've been waiting for, a message, a sign. It's not what I expected, but I'll take it. As we get closer to central London the train fills up with people. A girl slouched next to me in a short black dress talks very loudly and drunkenly with her friends. My house is at the end of the central line, but I surprise myself by instead getting off at Oxford Circus and walking with the crowds to the Victoria Line. Is it crazy to go to the squat now, like he said? What would I find there other than Leon smoking weed? I hold onto the pole near the door of the tube. It is crazy, but any chance of it being something, a message or a coincidence – I should take it.

I walk from the over-ground station, under streetlights in the Autumn breeze. For the first time in a long time, I feel a strange hope. The guy who played the guitar with five strings last time I was here answers the door.

'Is Leon here?' I ask.

He stumbles off wordlessly. A couple of minutes later Leon comes down the stairs in a stripy jumper covered in holes, a joint hanging from his hand.

'Kyle,' he says, stoned and confused. 'What's up? Is Felix okay?'

'Something weird happened,' I say. 'Can I come in?'

I tell him about what I saw, and what Felix said, '*Meet me at the squat.*' While I'm telling him, new stuff is coming to me. Images of me and Felix having sex in a hut in the snow, me and Felix walking through the forest.

Leon tokes on his joint, his body splayed across his side of the sofa. 'I don't know what to tell you, man. He's definitely not in my room.'

'I wasn't expecting him to be in your room. Maybe something to do with him.'

'Uh ...' Leon spaces out for a moment '... I've got a couple photos of him.'

'Can I see?' It's not what I was hoping for, but actually I don't know what I was hoping for.

Leon hands me a creased up, badly taken photo of Felix outside his beach hut in Brighton. It's the dingy hippy mess I would expect it to be, a picture of Shiva on the wall and some blankets on the floor. Then there's Felix standing in the sea with a brightly coloured scarf billowing in the breeze. The photo looks worn enough that with Felix's clothes it could've been taken in the '70s.

'I always thought he was a time traveller,' I say, as much to myself as Leon.

'He didn't always dress like that.' Leon leans against his cupboard. 'When I met him, he just wore orange.'

'How long have you known him?' I ask.

'Maybe three years.' He breathes out smoke while he talks. 'I met him in Brighton. Slept with him on his ex-boyfriend's sofa.'

'Did you go out?'

'No, I love Felix but he's kind of self-destructive.' I must give him a disparaging look because he says, 'I know I'm destructive! But Felix is destructive, and he doesn't know it.' Leon accidentally drops cigarette ash on the floor. '— I messaged you about coming to visit him some time.'

'Sorry I didn't reply, my phone is basically off at the moment.' I turn the photos over in my hand. "*Sea, Brighton*" and "*Felix's beach house*" are scrawled on the back in biro.

'I had this dream about him a couple of weeks back. You were in it, and we were in some car chase in the desert.' Leon laughs and coughs.

'Yeah?' I say with a feeling a bit like my brain is turning inside out.

'In Morocco, in my Dad's car.'

'I was in the back,' I say, 'The white car crashed into us!'

'Fuck, that's weird.' Leon scratches his neck.

'He's contacting us,' I say. It feels like the moment when a scientist throws all his papers in the air. If he's contacting us, then he's still in there. He can still wake up. I hug Leon, the smell of stale marijuana smoke in his dreadlocks.

'Do you remember any more?' I step back. 'Did you see him again?'

'No.' He squints, 'Did you?'

'Yeah, I think so,' I stutter, the memories starting to come back from some leaky sealed off place in my brain.

I try to go to sleep on the worn-out sofa in the big downstairs room of the squat, a musty sleeping bag on top of me. In the darkness, my mind is filling with all these memories. Me and Felix drunk dancing by the sea. Me and Felix hiking in the mountains. Me and Felix walking through ruins in Egypt. Me and Felix on a bus in South America. Me and Felix on the beach in San Francisco.

I walk down Old Compton Street where I used to flyer in Soho. It's now just a narrow path through trees and undergrowth. The collapsing brick walls of a few bars and sex shops, still partially intact. The sign for *Burger Bar* is perched among some branches. I shine my torch inside. There are the same red velvet curtains, decayed to the degree that parts of them have fallen off. Plants and moss are growing from the furniture. A tree has taken over one side of the club with fallen masonry all around it.

After Old Compton Street, the road disappears, just a few pieces of cement amidst roots and bracken. The statue of Eros in Piccadilly Circus glints gold and unnatural through the trees against the blue twilight sky. Then the National Portrait Gallery and Trafalgar Square start to become visible through the greenery. They're like partially excavated Mayan ruins. I walk across concrete tiles, the cracks in them sprouting with ferns and weeds. Nelson's column has fallen over, the pillar shattered across the square. Nelson's head is lying there in the undergrowth covered in moss. I stop still, seeing movement in the trees. A deer scarpers across the remains of the square, its hooves making a sharp clatter on the stone.

Despite where I am, my mind is filled with the real world. The world where he's lying in that hospital bed, waiting for part of him to return. I'm here to find him. To bring him back. I'm trying to work out what went wrong last time we tried to send ourselves back. Maybe he had to confront the monster? Maybe he had to go wherever he's gone? Maybe I had to remember the other side?

I spend the night in the remains of a furniture shop in a suburb of London, the suspended ceiling collapsing. I sit on a bed and light some candles and listen for his voice. I close my eyes and let the shapes of the candle flames float around my retina. As the afterimage fades, I bring Leon's room into focus, the wall hangings, the signs from protest marches, the fabric strewn mattress on the floor. I imagine Felix sitting on the bed in front of me, smiling as I reach out for his hand. But there's no juddering sensation, just the big dark empty room.

The next night I'm in a family home, baby toys everywhere, and plants growing from the floor. I stand in the kitchen and open the back door. I thought for a moment I could hear him calling, but it's just the trees and the breeze. I sit down on their discoloured cream sofa, candles flickering on the carpet. I close my eyes and imagine myself back on Leon's bed at the squat again. Still no vibrations, no hands holding mine. I don't let myself get desperate. If I can't send myself there, I'll walk there, through the forest and ruins to Gatwick.

The next morning, I smell fire. It reminds me of bonfires in the Surrey countryside when I was little. Then I remember the last time we smelt burning, from the roof of the school. I don't know how long I've been walking. what's left of the road disappears for long stretches, then there are big open spaces of shattered concrete. Amongst the undergrowth and trees, there's an airplane, stained green with moss, lichen hanging from it. It takes a couple of hours more to find the squat. The area around it has been totally eaten up by the forest. It's like a bunker, hidden by vines, branches, and brambles. Almost as if the plants are protecting its secret. I kick the door till it opens, all the vines that have grown onto it trying to pull it closed again. Amidst the snapping and crashing, I think I hear my name.

'Felix,' I say into the darkness. My voice cracks as I call louder, 'Felix!' I click the torch on, but there's no one there, just the posters and the net hanging from the ceiling, sunken with dirt and damp. The room breaths out a damp rotted breath as I flash the torch around. The stairs creak under my foot, and I hear his voice,

'Kyle.' This time it's definitely not my imagination.

'Felix.' I clamber up the dark aching steps. I push open the door to Leon's room and flash my torch around the wall hangings. I don't see him.

'Kyle.' I hear his voice, a loud whisper coming from all around me.

'Where are you?' I ask. I realise that after this place there's nowhere we arranged to meet. 'Where are you?'

There's no reply, I just hear him whisper my name again, quieter than before.

I get on the bed, the same bed we slept in all that time ago. I close my eyes and try to block out the mouldy smell of the room and try to just imagine myself with him. The feeling of his body, the warmth of his skin, his spine pressed against me. His arm on top of mine, his hair in my face, and the whistling of his breath. I grasp at the picture of him in my mind as if I'm reaching for him across space. But there's no destination to hook ourselves to. I open my eyes, and I'm still in this dank dark room. I squash my fists into the bed. I can smell the smoke outside. Maybe this world is shutting down. Maybe when he asked me to meet him at the squat, he really did just mean the one in the real world. He just wanted me to remember this other world that we created together. But I hear his voice, calling me again. Then suddenly I see it in my mind scrawled in biro on the back of the photo, "*Felix's Beach hut*". I get back on the bed, legs crossed, I scrunch my eyes shut. I do it like he told me on the roof in India. I imagine all the contents of his hut, and then I put the sky and the sea and all the pebbles back into place. I feel the vibration running through the room, running through my body like everything is accelerating. The mattress drops away from underneath me and is replaced with lots of little things, clattering. I'm landing on them, and they're landing on me.

I scrabble upright and open my eyes. There are pebbles everywhere flooding the hut and ahead, the dark line of the horizon. I feel him next to me, pushing himself up out of the pebbles. He takes short sharp breaths, like he can't quite work out how to breath. I grab him and squash him into me, feel the solidity and the warmth of his body.

'You weren't at the squat,' I say, tasting the salty air.

'I was ...' He breaths hard, looking down at his hands and up at me. '... gone ... really gone.'

'How do you mean?'

'I ...' He starts, then shakes his head. 'I don't know ... Some bits of me were very far away. It seemed like they'd been gone for a long time ... and some bits, no time at all ... and I had to put them all back together.'

I grip him tight and feel the laboured movements of his ribcage. I squash him into me, amidst all the mess of the beach hut, as if letting go of him might mean he'll disappear again

We go and sit on a ridge of pebbles and look out at the dark restless sea. Felix wraps his arms around his legs.

'The monster?' I ask, looking at his face in the dusky light.

'I think it's gone,' he says.

'What happened?'

'You said it was something I had to deal with.' He contemplates the dusky blue sky a while. The waves sloshing and breaking below us. 'When I saw it the last time, it was like this imaginary friend that had been there all my life. I just ran up and hugged it. Then I was in all these memories; memories from when I was a kid. I couldn't stay in any of them. I was drifting apart. Then I heard you calling.'

'I saw it!' I remember what I've been aching to tell him. 'The other side. I was there! You were in a coma. I went to the squat, and Leon showed me a photo of you in your beach hut. How did you know I'd see that?'

'I didn't.' He looks bemused.

'But you knew to come here?'

'This was just the place I'd memorised best, from all those mornings meditating on the beach. I guess that's how this psychic thing works. You just have to follow it.'

I put my tongue in the side of my mouth, mesmerised by these strange trails of events that keeps leading me back to him.

'Like when I saw the picture of you in the magazine.' He moves his hand to cover mine. 'And I knew had to meet you.'

I look up at loose whisps of cloud, almost purple in colour. I imagine all these strange, interconnected moments like constellations of stars.

'Why do you think you had to meet me that first time?' I ask.

'I don't know.' He pulls his mouth into a half-smile and shrugs. 'Because of everything that was going to happen maybe. I've found the universe never gives many good reasons or conclusions.'

We spend a while on the pebble beach together, just looking out across all those miles of water. I wonder if he needed to meet me because I'm the one who saves him.

'I want to try it again,' I say, 'Sending ourselves back.'

He takes a deep breath in through his nose and leans into me.

'That doesn't sound enthusiastic,' I respond.

'I don't want to waste this time with you.' He squeezes my hand. Then looks from the sea to my face, his far apart eyes traverse from deep to shallow. 'I'll try it – for you.'

'I'm worried it won't work if you don't believe in it.' I keep looking into his eyes so he can see I'm serious.

He leans backwards, dislodging pebbles which roll down the ridge. He lays there looking up at the clouds, still holding my hand.

'You think you're going to die,' I say.

'We're all going to die,' he tells me.

I press my lips together in irritation at his answer but lay down next to him.

He leans towards me. 'When you were really ill in hospital, you thought you were going to die, and I didn't.'

'What're you try to say? That you're always right.'

'No.' He whacks my arm with his hand. 'I'm saying ...' He pauses to think what he's saying. Then he stands up and I hear the pebbles shifting under his feet as he walks around. '... We should walk in that direction.'

I'm still looking up at the sky, I can't see where he's pointing.

'What if we built a raft and just started sailing,' I suggest, unsure if I'm joking.

'A few months ago, you didn't even want to go on a chicken bus,' he calls back to me.

I push myself up and walk over to him. I see what he's looking at. It's the mountain that we saw from the school roof, not far away, a green shadow on a skyline of trees and rubble.

We collect up some stuff from the beach hut and put it in a gym bag. Felix scoops candles and a sleeping bags out of the pebbles. Then we clamber up over the crust of earth and roots behind the beach. There are pieces of limestone bricks, like something from ancient Greece, only with pipes and furniture sticking out of the mess. Then we're back in the forest following a faint path. We duck under branches, and Felix pulls his yellow duffle coat free from thorns. There's the shape of the Brighton Pavilion, partially collapsed, tree branches bursting out of its

Indianesque rooves. The mountain disappears from view as we enter a canopy of leaves.

'I don't remember there being a mountain at the back of Brighton,' I say.

'No.' He tries to walk next to me on the narrow path. 'There's somewhere called Burgess hill.'

'It's a big hill!'

'It's where I used to live with my mum.' His voice is quiet.

I nod, I guess if we're heading into the dark part of Felix's mind, that would be the centre. I wonder if that's where we send ourselves back from.

'This place really wants you to deal with something.' I step over a root.

'This place is my brain,' he says.

We soon reach the crazy paving remains of what was probably a main road.

'We're always walking,' I remark, kicking my way through a mess of brambles and bricks.

'I like walking.' Felix balances himself against me. 'It makes you feel like you're going somewhere.'

After that, the jagged red brick remains of suburbia peter out into forest. It gets so dense we have to crouch, pushing through the trees. There's an uneven patch of grassland, from which you can see the foot of the mountain. Some crows flap, synchronised from the grass into the deep unfading blue of the sky.

'You saw the other side,' Felix says, lifting a stray bramble branch to walk under.

'Yeah, it feels like days ago.' I lift the brambles for myself.

'How was nan?'

'Your grandma?' I breathe in the earthiness of this new patch of forest. 'I had dinner at her house. She visits you every day in hospital ... She's a strong person.'

'She acts like she's okay, you mean.' He pulls a few curled up brown leaves from a low hanging branch and scrunches them in his hand. 'I remember after the fire, waking up and her being there by my bed. I asked her if my mum was okay and she said, "*I'm going to look after you now.*"' He drops broken bits of leaf on the ground. 'We planted a tree for her in the arboretum and put some of her ashes and jewellery under it.'

'You never told me that.' I look at his face in profile against the tree trunks.

'I guess it still hurts.' He looks at me a moment then gives a bleak smile. 'I know my mum was crazy. I know it wasn't about me. But I guess part of me still feels abandoned.'

'I haven't abandoned you though.' I hold the sleeve of his yellow duffle coat, so he stops and looks at me. 'I've given up all my night clubs. I visit you every day. I didn't stop searching this place till I found you.'

He holds my hand and looks at me, his eyes bleary.

'Your grandma too,' I tell him.

He nods, squeezes my hand then keeps walking. '... I wrote my nan this postcard when I was on acid. With all the things I wanted to thank her for.' He bends under some branches. 'One of those moments when drugs make you regret everything.'

'I know about that,' I laugh. 'What did she say?'

'I ended up coming back to stay with her before I could send it.' He shrugs.

The ground starts to slope up. Bits of root cling to rifts in the earth like tentacles. There's something that might've once been a road, the concrete now cracked up, almost like steps.

'If things don't work out –' Felix grips onto a branch and pulls himself up the steps.

'Things are going to work out.' I shake my foot free of some climbing plant.

'I don't want you to regret stuff.' He says.

'I know what you're going to say.' I heave myself up the steps. 'You don't regret anything.'

'Well, I try not to. I regretted throwing that glass of wine in Milo's face.'

'Really?'

'He was always talking about that Illamasqua makeup. So, I bought him a couple of Illamasqua lipsticks to apologise.'

'Really?'

'Yeah!' He pouts. 'I gave them to him at your birthday. That stuff is expensive!'

There are steep areas where trees cling to the mountainside their trunks bent at strange angles. There's a house, torn apart, the floors and bricks hanging from the incline. The path disappears at one point, and we're climbing over rocks and bits of concrete, the light finally starting to fade. We turn a bend and there's part of a village church wedged onto a precipice. The roof caved in, the spire collapsed into the undergrowth.

'Maybe this is where we live tonight,' Felix says.

We walk through the archway, around a pile of fallen masonry. I shine my keyring torch across the shattered stained-glass windows as we walk down the aisle. There are centuries-old memorial stones cluttered with debris. The altar sheet is so discoloured it could be green, plants and moss starting to grow out of it. I flash the torch over figurines in alcoves at the back of the church.

'Angels.' I fix the light on one, rosy cheeks, painted in whites and golds. 'You think somethings coming?'

'No.' He doesn't seem concerned. He inspects the candles and the cross on the altar, and peeks underneath the cover. 'I thought I could smell fire a while back though.'

'Yeah, I smelt it too.' I shine the torch at him. 'I smelt it when I was walking to the squat as well.'

'It makes sense with where we're going.' He kicks aside a mess of broken roof tiles.

'We should've built that raft,' I tell him.

I watch him from behind, sitting on a little cliff of grass outside the church. He watches the dark shapes of trees and buildings, an ocean of stars filling the sky. I wonder what he's thinking; that he might die, that he might survive. I walk over and sit next to him in silence and let out a long breath. I think about the peak of the mountain like a diagram of a wormhole I saw in a science fiction film. It reaches this funnel point and then widens out at another point in the universe. Would it feel the same travelling back to the real world as it felt when I sent myself from Siberia to Norway?

We make a bed out of all the musty prayer cushions and roll out the sleeping bag from the beach hut. Felix lights a few candles around the bed, like it's a little shrine to us. We lay there looking up at the darkness of the ceiling.

I wake up holding onto him, coughing. The smell of burning, stronger than before. Sleepy, I push myself up onto my elbows and blink at the ruins and debris. I traipse to the door, my bare feet on the cold stone. I inch across rock and grass and weeds. Between the trees, I can see moats of ash rising up, and to the left; thick smoke dispersing into a shadowy sky. When I get back into the church, Felix already has his shoes on.

'Fire?' He asks.

I nod, seeing that our mission now has a time limit.

The path is steep, and with the dim blue light, it seems like an early morning trip to a temple in Peru or Thailand. The smoke wafts up through the trees almost like mist. At times the path disappears, and we have to cling to trees and outcrops of earth. We step over bricks that have tumbled down the hill and been swallowed by ferns. Looking down the slope I see glints of bright orange flame amongst the thick clouds of smoke.

'I used to ask myself every time I left the house.' Felix coughs. 'If I died today, would I be okay with it?'

'And?' I hold onto a branch and stumble toward some fragments of concrete.

'I don't know.' He waits for me to catch up with him. 'It's weird, sometimes I think it's the bad stuff that makes us hold on.'

'When I got really sick, just before my bone marrow transplant.' I cough into my hand, stepping over some brambles. 'I think it was you that kept me holding on.'

He squeezes my arm in response.

We don't stop.

The smoke fills the sky, and the glimpses of flames tell us we don't have much time left. We stumble up a pile of bricks, moss slipping off under our feet, then follow a narrow trough that might've once been a path. I pull my jumper up over my nose to stop myself wheezing.

'Before my bone marrow transplant –' I mumble '– I went out in the cold and I promised myself I was going to get better, that I was going to live.'

'I had a moment like that, after my transplant.' Felix pulls his jumper over his face. The view below disappearing into the smoke. 'I was like, I'm going to live, I don't know how long, but I'm going to live the best and the hardest that I can.'

Felix goes ahead of me and tries to find a footing in the rocks and dirt. He offers his hand, but I manage to haul myself up. My eyes are stinging from the smoke, the sky misted out of view. I turn around, trying to work out if we're at the top of the mountain.

'It's there.' He points through the trees.

There's the vague shape of a building, but I can't see the ground for all the smoke. He grabs my hand and pulls me down a steep rocky path. The smokescreen parts and I see the scrub and rubble of the ridge Felix is leading me along. I look to the side and see flames and black silhouettes of trees. I cough and wipe my eyes and try to look straight ahead. We walk quickly, knowing now it's a race to get there; to this place where we might be able to open up a portal back home. Felix pulls me onwards, the sleeve of my puffer jacket twisted in his grip. The shape of the house emerges out of the smoke, its red brick walls fully intact. There are broken paving slabs amidst the grass and weeds. Then a red front door. Felix rattles the door, then gives it a kick with his Doc Martens, then another more violent flailing kick. It swings open.

Walking into the house, I feel a vibration running through my whole body, like an earthquake. I look up at the Artex ceiling, worried it's about to fall on top of us.

'Did you feel that?' I ask.

'Yeah.' Felix slams the door shut.

We're in a dim living room with purple walls, the light being filtered through the net curtains. There are woolen throws on the sofa and angel ornaments everywhere.

'So, this is my house,' he says.

It seems so unreal, after all the rocky outcrops and burning trees to be standing in this cosy domestic environment.

'What do you think?' I stand in the middle of the living room carpet.

'I think –' He looks around and sighs softly, doesn't answer. He goes and picks up a large ornament of an angel with its hands pressed together in prayer. 'I think my mum tried to make a nice little home for me and her.' He weighs the angel in his hands, acting like there isn't a fire outside.

'Do you think we should do it here?' I ask.

'What?' He puts the angel back on its shelf.

'Send ourselves back.'

'No.' His coat rustles, and I think I hear the fire crackle outside. 'I know the place.'

We walk upstairs, amateur paintings of angels in ethereal pastel colours on the landing walls. Then we're in this kid's bedroom with outer-space wallpaper, the same satellites and ringed planets repeating themselves all around the room. A yellow tent pitched in the middle of the carpet.

'In here.' He pulls me into the tent.

It's filled with blankets and cushions.

'I think we have to lie down,' I say.

There's just enough space to stretch out next to each other if we lie diagonally.

'Okay,' I squeeze his hand, and we look at each other, hearts beating.

We close our eyes, and I start to describe the hospital. The walls, the machines, the bed, the window with the half-fresh carnations. It's like I'm weaving some kind of spell. I feel the vibration running through my body and I know it's working. After I've described the hospital, I keep my eyes shut tight and grip the blanket in my hands, painting the downstairs of the squat in my head. The stale smoke of the sofa, the net with all the cuddly toys inside it. I imagine it as if I'm looking up, lying on the sofa. I feel the vibration again, like the whole house is shaking. I hear a massive crash, things pinging off the side of the tent.

'What happened?' I ask him, still lying next to me in the tent. He gets up and unzips the exit and pokes his head out. I smell smoke.

'Part of the wall is missing,' he says.

'What!?' I poke my head out of the tent with him. We're looking at the smoke outside, the treetops visible through the jagged broken wall in the corner of the room. I pull my head back into the tent.

'I think I know what we did wrong.' I'm kneeling, looking at him, his eyes wide. 'We need to do it together, no description. We have to really believe it.'

'Okay.' He lays back down, looking across at me, the faint yellow glow of the tent on his face. 'One more time.'

306

I close my eyes and start to paint the squat, vivid and real in my mind. The sofa, the net of toys, the messed-up carpet tiles, the bar, all the detritus around it, the posters and the damaged light fittings. I feel the vibration again. Another massive crash outside, things hitting the tent. I don't stop, I hold the image in my mind like I'm actually there. I reach out to touch the sofa, but I feel Felix next to me and smell the smoke.

'One more time,' I say.

'No.' He looks at me with those far-apart alien eyes. 'Just be here with me now.'

I let out a frustrated snort. I can't look at him. I want to punch the wall, I want to kick the tent down, but I just squash my face into the cushion.

'I fucked up,' I whine, my throat feeling blocked. 'This isn't fair. I want to live with you. I want to have that apartment in Bethnal Green.'

'Live with me now.' He looks me in the eyes, the vibrations getting stronger, our faces shaking. He pulls my body into his and wraps his arms around me. 'If you could see it like I do, you'd see that it's okay. We wouldn't be us if we hadn't done the things we did, and I liked being us.'

'I liked being us too.' I push my face into his hair and hold tight onto his torso. Everything is shaking so hard, all I can do is hold onto him. I hear cracking, the tent being pelted with rubble. Then we're falling, everything juddering like a rocket leaving the atmosphere. I'm not just holding onto him in this moment now, I'm holding onto him in all these memories. In the hospital; kissing for the first time, on my kitchen floor; making up after he sang outside. In science fiction rolling on the dance floor. In his bed at his grandma's house, with the traffic outside. Somehow, I'm in all these memories at once. The first-time outside Science Fiction, when he told me I got a cut from falling out of a tree, and the last time, arguing in his bedroom. And I'm thinking, it's so strange, the world is so sad and so beautiful.

The blank screen of the TV, James' art books under the glass table, the beigeness of the sofa either side of me. I remember sitting here with Felix, watching Thelma and Louise, painting each other's toenails, trying to stop him from throwing wine at Milo. It used to seem like a home. Now I'm sitting in the middle of the sofa in this slim-fit suit, waiting for James to get dressed. I know Felix would've wanted me to wear something crazy, but I don't want to stand out. I don't want to be the widow covered in black net, crying big mascara tears. I just want to get through this. James comes out dressed like he's going to the prom. I give his ribbon-striped black flares a look of disdain.

'This is the kind of thing Felix would've worn,' he argues.

'You're right,' I tut.

'Come on.' James looks at me, sitting rigid on the sofa.

The weather is grey, starting to get cold. I stand there in the field by the crematorium with all these people he knew. Some of my friends, some people from the squat, lots of people that I don't know. I recognise his ex-boyfriend from a photo Felix showed me. I wonder if any of them know who I am. I wonder if any of them blame me.

The guitar riff at the start of *Octopus's Garden* by *The Beatles* plays distorted from the speaker. People in mascot costumes lift his coffin unsteadily from the hearse. There's a rabbit, a Dalmatian, a raccoon, and a chicken, all carrying his coffin. They almost look like they're dancing to the music. Some people start to laugh, some people cry. I want to slap my hand into my face because it's so stupid. They put the coffin in front of a bouncy castle, yellow turrets illustrated with cartoons of a dancing wizard and a princess. We file into rows of plastic chairs, the chair legs sinking into the ground. Helium balloons tied at the end of each row, flapping about in the autumn breeze.

I remember during one of those early visits when I was in hospital, he told me his favourite bar in Brighton was *The Poison Ivy*. In his funeral plan, it said he wanted a drag queen rather than a priest. So, I called up the leathery female impersonator normally found manning the karaoke machine at *The Poison Ivy*. She's standing awkwardly in front of the bouncy castle in her big black ruffle boa, heels sticking into the grass.

'You're all looking in a much better mood than my usual crowd,' she starts, one wonky eyelash twitching.

Felix's grandma stands up there in a bobbly over-washed black dress and cardigan fumbling with the microphone. She reads off a piece of paper about Felix's creativity and his medical problems and finishes with a bible verse.

"... What are the angels, then? They are spirits who serve God and are sent by him to help those who are to receive salvation." She seems strong and frail at the same time, the breeze blowing strands of her hair.

We all sing *I'm Going Home* from *The Rocky Horror Show*. My lips press together hard, and my mouth pulls down at the sides, and I try not to cry. I've cried more in the last week than I think I have in my whole life. It's like something inside me that's been holding tight all this time, just snapped. I was just these raw emotions, the grief, the guilt, the anger, and these strange brief moments of ecstasy.

The morning after that last dream, I woke up feeling like I was falling. I got straight up off the sofa at the squat and walked to the train station. I was still holding onto the hope that when I got to the hospital everything would be like I imagined it. The nurse with the black curly hair and glasses was there, but she told me Felix was in the MRI. I sat down and waited till they wheeled him through those mint-green double doors, on his bed with all his life support apparatus. The doctor looked down at me and in that moment, I knew something was wrong. In the room with the oval table and the tissues, the doctor told me and Felix's grandma that there was no brain function. That we'd need to start thinking about taking Felix's breathing tube out. I held it together till I got back to me and James' apartment. I slammed the door and screamed, pulled wig heads off of shelves and kicked them across the floor, the polystyrene breaking into pieces. James grabbed me from behind and stopped me, the tears hot and sore in my eyes.

Behind the podium, Leon seems less stoned than usual, his dreadlocks tied back, wearing an ill-fitting suit. He talks about meeting Felix in a pub in Brighton, Felix writing on the toilet wall in marker pen. He talks about Felix's beach house and how hard he found it to fit into society. Then he finishes with a brief rant about capitalism. I shiver and take some deep breaths. James is nudging me, and I hear the drag queen repeating my name into the microphone. I didn't want to give a speech, but I feel like I owe it to Felix. I walk past all the people in their funery fancy dress. I don't really look at them, the moment is a blur. I'm in front of the bouncy castle holding the microphone feeling the cold of the breeze, feeling like something is caught in my throat. I notice my mum and dad sitting at the back, their expressions pained.

I had all these plans of what I was going to say. How he saved my life, how he changed me, how he made me make out with him

311

in the bed in IKEA. That I never realised how fragile what we had was. How he sang a song for me once and I never got the chance to sing it back to him. I'm too choked up to say any of this, so I just unfold the piece of paper with the lyrics on and read it into the microphone like its poetry,

'*Nobody does it better, makes me feel sad for the rest, nobody does it half as good as you, baby you're the best –*'

The wake is at Felix's grandma's house. She's replaced the card table with a trestle table decorated with potato salad, coleslaw, and prosecco. The association of potato salad and death seems strange to me, so I just drink prosecco. I tell myself, today it's okay to drink as much as I want. I talk to Kitten, who thinks black PVC is acceptable funeral-wear.

'Maybe you should start organising funerals as well as parties,' she says.

'Or maybe I'll never organise either ever again.' I give her a doleful smile.

'Any more dreams?' Leon asks me in a lowered voice.

'Not since they took him off life support.'

'Hmm.' He tries to think of something else to say.

'I'm not going to tell anyone,' I murmur.

'Why?'

'They won't believe it,' I shrug, not even sure if I fully believe what happened. 'It means too much to me, to go around telling people.'

People compliment me on my speech, and I try to hang onto some sort of sobriety while listening to their stories.

'I didn't know him well,' says a lady with a neat brown bob clutching her pearls. 'But he looked after my mother when she was in a home and she thought the world of him. They'd always be speaking Spanish together.'

312

'Ahh!' I wag my finger at her. 'He told me about her.'

I go off to Felix's room when I've got too drunk, and I need some space. I sit on his bed, the same as I have a few times this week, and I try to feel like he's all around me. Like this is a shrine to him with all its statues and souvenirs. The little snow dome with the golden gate bridge, the glittery Las Vegas postcard, the Aztec pyramid. My eyes eventually focus on the cut-out pictures on his noticeboard. There are some receipts, a shiny picture of a Hindu God, a postcard of the Brighton Pavilion. I un-pin the postcard and on the back, it's filled in but not stamped. It's what I hoped it would be, "*Dear Nan*," it says in Felix's italic scrawl. "*I find it hard to talk about these things, so I thought I'd write you a postcard. Thank you, for always being there for me and ...*" I leave it on the desk where she'll find it. Then, I open the cabinet and reach behind the NASA spaceship and the alien figurine. I pull out a dusty wooden box that probably hasn't been touched since last time I saw it. I open it and take out Felix's little bit of Mars meteorite. I wrap it up in cotton wool and put it in my pocket.

Felix's grandma gives me half the buffet to take home in Tupperware boxes. James has to carry them to the tube because I'm too drunk. He puts them in the fridge, and I throw my jacket on the sofa and start to unbutton my shirt. I let out a series of increasingly more exhausted sighs.

'You wanna do something?' James shuts the fridge.

'Maybe finish packing.' I support myself on the sofa arm.

'You look like you need to relax.' He comes up and kneads my shoulders.

'I'm a proactive drunk,' I tell him. 'I need some time on my own.'

He pats my back, unsure how to help.

My room is a plain bed and a beauty table, surrounded by cardboard boxes and suitcases. My beauty table is going to my parents, and the rest is going into storage. I pick a cotton pad and some cleanser up and wipe the make-up off from under my eyes. Coming back here today, I'm glad I'm leaving. I couldn't stay here and pretend nothing's changed. Pretend that the funeral is like a full stop, and then we just carry on with the next paragraph. James said he thinks I'm trying to run from it. It hurts bad enough that I think I should be allowed to run. But there's nowhere I can run, because everywhere will remind me of him. I need to go somewhere, where I can find a way to forgive myself, where I can try to be the good person that he thought I was. I've got a flight to San Francisco that my boyfriend bought me, and after that I'll just keep going, as far as I can for as long as I can.

Note From the Author

The Space Between Galaxies, took me about a decade to finish. I learned how to write while writing it. During that process, I have re-written it multiple times, visited about half the countries featured, and had three boyfriends who deeply influenced the way I portrayed Kyle and Felix's relationship. The idea for the book came to me in a series of dreams I had when I was 18, about a Christian guy I had a crush on. It was important to me to write a gay novel where the point of interest was the plot rather than just the characters' sexuality, and to write non-mainstream gay characters, rather than simply men who have sex with men.

My first major writing project was a one-off zine called '*My life as a Goth*' which I distributed drunk around London night clubs. I also wrote a novella during the pandemic called '*Two Million*,' about a chaotic drunk who takes his one-night stand on a two week-long journey across East Asia.

If you loved the book, please leave a review on Amazon or Goodreads. Publishing this novel is a one-person mission and positive reviews help me so much. Thank you, Alex Fear x